Blood Creek

DOMINIC MILES

The Book Guild Ltd

First published in Great Britain in 2024 by
The Book Guild Ltd
Unit E2 Airfield Business Park,
Harrison Road, Market Harborough,
Leicestershire. LE16 7UL
Tel: 0116 2792299
www.bookguild.co.uk
Email: info@bookguild.co.uk
X: @bookguild

Typeset in 11pt Minion Pro

Printed on FSC accredited paper
Printed and bound in Great Britain by 4edge Limited

ISBN 978 1835740 972

British Library Cataloguing in Publication Data.
A catalogue record for this book is available from the British Library.

To Alison

CHAPTER ONE

Cassie's legs were tired by the time she reached the bridge. She had only just got back into running after her period of despondency and despair – which her mother, Eve, insisted on calling her 'illness'. In fact, Eve, in her usual categorical manner, had strongly suggested that she should try some gentler exercise to ease herself into physical activity, perhaps going to the gym instead. But Cassie couldn't face the gym. However familiar this place seemed at times, she was still in a foreign country – with all the possibilities of cultural and social confusion and misunderstanding that entailed – and going to the gym would mean meeting people and talking to them. And then, inevitably, the questions would come and the explanations. Or she might just lie about herself, which meant she would run the risk of being eventually found out.

The gym would also involve driving to get there and, though she wouldn't admit this to anyone else, she was still a little nervous about the roads here and actually finding her way around. They drove on the left, which was a good thing as far as she was concerned, and they drove everywhere, just like Americans, but the car was an automatic – theoretically easier than a car with gears, but it depended on what you were used to. The car seemed enormous to her, much bigger than the little Kia she used to drive in her former life, which seemed so long ago now.

Anyway, Cassie didn't want aerobics classes or HIT training – or whatever they called it. Cassie liked – you could actually say *loved* – running. She liked to push her body, feel it make the effort, get into the rhythm of breathing and moving. And there was that mental aspect to it; you could think and work things out in the bubble of solitude you created around yourself. She ran 'naked'. She had only just discovered it was described as this and it didn't mean she ran without clothes. Of course not – perish the thought. Instead, it meant being without a phone, headphones, a smart watch or the like. She just had her old, beat-up Casio on her wrist to give some sense of time and distance. Cassie preferred it this way. After all, what was the point of running in the countryside if you were too absorbed in music or a podcast to really see where you were going.

As soon as they had moved in, Cassie had started thinking about running routes. *Started* thinking about them, but not doing much about it, because of the sheer unfamiliarity of the place. The house was one of a number of dwellings, all quite different, strung along a random pattern of roads, most of them dead ends, south of a lake that you couldn't actually seem to get to unless you plunged into the bush, as her neighbours called it, which seemed to her a reckless thing to do. She didn't want to be *that* tourist; the one that's found – if they do find her – stumbling around, delirious and dehydrated from days in the bush and then plastered on every daily newspaper as a cautionary tale.

She had wondered, at first, if people actually ran around here. Would she, by doing so, attract attention, funny looks or the like, or even be apprehended by the police? Her worries, however, proved to be without any foundation as when she tentatively tried a jog to the end of the road, she saw her first runner, who gave her a wave, even though he was absorbed in some private world of his own. And there was the other one: the ever-so-serious walker, as she thought of him, who strode the same road at a brisk, no-nonsense pace every morning, giving her a friendly nod whenever he saw her.

After these encounters, she started doing more than thinking about routes and actively planned them instead. She didn't have a map, but she did have a map app on her phone. She thought she would aim for a five-kilometre run to start with and build herself up. That was when she first saw the bridge and the creek it spanned on the digital map: Blood Creek. She didn't do more than think briefly, in passing, about the name. It seemed just the right sort of distance to run to and back. It was all along a road, but not a main route. The road appeared to end at the bridge, but when she switched to satellite view, she could see that it turned into a track – you could actually discern the difference between tarmac and dirt – running onwards to the coast a few kilometres away.

She had set out that morning as early as she could, just before 7am, but it was already hot. She'd put a baseball hat on to protect her from the sun – *Be sure to be sun-safe*, as they said out here – but by the time she got to the end of the road, she was soaked with sweat. It felt good, though – the whole physical work-out. She knew that she would be tired later, but it would be a good sort of fatigue – a wholesome one.

She ran on the right side of the road, facing the traffic like a good citizen; not that there was much of it and what cars there were made a point of giving her plenty of room and more than often a nod or wave of acknowledgement. After all, many of them were probably from that small tribe of neighbours she had acquired by moving here.

There were a number of dead toads on the road – her neighbour, Linda, had told her they were cane toads – lying there, pancaked by tyres or dead from some other mysterious cause and flattened post-mortem. And then there were the kangaroos. Creatures that the locals took in their stride, but which had worried Cassie at first. Some people here fenced off their plots – and the plots were big, much bigger than was normal in Britain, where people lived crammed together – but many of the houses had left their gardens open, so the kangaroos could graze and pass through. *Do they graze?* Cassie asked herself, not knowing the answer. One morning, when Cassie had been running on one of the nearby roads – one of her short trial runs – she had seen a whole herd of them. Was herd the right word? They were on the lawn in front of two holiday bungalows – a dozen of them, at least, comprising females and joeys all under the eyes of a big male. The big male roo had looked at her as she went past, as if it was staring her out. When she had told Linda about it later, the old woman had said: "Yes, well, you do have to watch those big males. They're big boys and you should give them a wide berth."

This seemed to completely contradict her earlier assertion that the roos were basically harmless.

"They've been known to kill dogs. Well, you know what dogs are like. They won't leave well alone."

Cassie did not, in fact, know anything about dogs as there'd never been any family pets. Her parents had had strict views on the subject: pets were unhygienic and a waste of money.

"They get their arms around them and then bring their hind legs up..." Linda left it there, to Cassie's imagination, but she made a mental note to never let a kangaroo cuddle her.

She didn't see any kangaroos on the way to the bridge. The only animals she saw were human ones: three cyclists, a couple and a lone rider, who all gave her some sort of friendly acknowledgment. It did seem a long way to her, a bit of a stretch, and it was the furthest she'd been. As she turned at the junction from the more familiar network of roads and headed towards the bridge, the metalled road gave way in places to dirt track and, after a gentle downhill stretch, beneath the welcome shade of a clump of trees, she saw a gate in front of her with a sign that said she was entering a national park with a list of things that she could and couldn't do – none of which she had intended on doing anyway. Beside the gate was a gap allowing pedestrians through and beyond it was the start of the dirt track proper, an old road of some sort, which led into a landscape of low trees and shrubs, with a wetland to the south side of it. Directly in front of her was the bridge.

As bridges go, it wasn't one of the most prepossessing. It was a basic affair, heavy, sturdy-looking planks strung across two wide beams, which crossed the few metres width of Blood Creek. No guard rails or any other embellishments. There was an old redundant sign telling drivers that it was a weak bridge not suitable for heavy vehicles, though it looked stout enough to Cassie. Blood Creek disappeared on either side into tree-covered darkness, flowing so silently you were hardly aware of it.

The track went on, wide enough for the cars that once went that way and overgrown in the middle. *Like farm tracks back home*, Cassie thought. Still, it was generally clear, which suggested that some park employee kept the growth down. She ventured a little way up the track and found a sun-whitened bench positioned thoughtfully about half a kilometre further on for weary hikers. This was as far as she went; the bush on one side of the track and the swampy land on the other were just too unfamiliar to her and she was unsure of what might slither, crawl or run out of the trees or the water.

She retraced her steps to the bridge and it was then, standing on the planks, that she heard the sound. It was a regular splashing sound, too regular to be a fish or any other aquatic creature. It was rhythmic, too: the splashing noise was followed by a thud or a slap, then the pattern was repeated. Intrigued, she peered into the trees that shaded the banks and leaned over the water, but could see no one. She thought that the sound must be coming from further up, somewhere along the course of the creek as it flowed to the lake north of there. Suddenly, she understood. It was the sound of someone washing something, clothes probably, in the creek; that age-old cycle of pounding wet clothes against the rocks and then rinsing them in the water, repeated until they looked clean. Just as she figured this out, she heard another sound – a high, keening cry on the air. Someone was singing, but in a language she couldn't understand. A song to accompany the work: a shanty.

Then, abruptly, the spell was broken. There was a swish of tyres as a mountain bike came down the track towards her, followed by a hurried "Good day" as the rider swerved past the gate and then… silence. Whoever was doing their laundry and singing had stopped.

CHAPTER TWO

"Probably some hippie camped out in the woods," Linda said.

The old woman inhabited a world stuck somewhere in the sixties, when there were such creatures as hippies, and Cassie suspected that she had probably been one of them, decamping eventually to Queensland, where, though now in her seventies, she lived in a cloud of joss sticks and billows of Indian cotton.

"But the song, it sounded… Aboriginal, I suppose," Cassie said.

"Well, there wouldn't be any indigenous Australians living on the land around here anymore," Linda said, using the correct term – sensitive to such usage, as any child of the sixties would be. "There are still people with Kabiri heritage in the local area, but they are all living in houses as far as I know."

Linda Arkwright was their closest neighbour, though they didn't exactly encroach on each other. She was a small, wiry, grey-haired lady, who looked bleached and withered by the sun, but was as fit and lean as one of those kangaroos that bounded over her property. She'd introduced herself soon after they'd moved in – "Call me Linda," she'd said, though Cassie had some difficulty doing so, as it seemed a little too chummy. She'd then told them that she lived on her own – a widow, she confided, more than once over – and was, or so she said, an alternative medical practitioner. Cassie wasn't exactly sure what that was. Linda was delighted to find out that they came from the UK, as she'd been a 'Ten Pound Pom' – Cassie's mother had had to explain this reference to her – emigrating in the sixties or seventies. Cassie was vague about the details as the woman talked so quickly.

Cassie hadn't intended to become friendly with Linda – as she must remember to call her, not Mrs Arkwright – but with her mother often out at work in the day and nobody else near enough to ask those mundane, crucial questions like when did the rubbish go out, what was recycled and what wasn't, and how the hell did the cooker or the ride-on mower work – not that Cassie had actually used the ride-on yet – Linda was the only source she could consult. And Linda, it had to be said, was easy-going, if a bit eccentric. One of her eccentricities was feeding the kookaburras with mince bought from the supermarket and the result was that these birds, with their raucous, laughing cries, were regular visitors to the property.

Linda was also a fount of information about the various forms of dangerous wildlife, especially those that most concerned Cassie. Linda had told her that she didn't have to worry about snakes, as the birds would put up a fuss if there was one around; that spiders weren't such a problem as everyone imagined; and that you were more likely to drown in the rips off the local beach than be taken by a shark, which wasn't exactly reassuring as both options involved death.

It was therefore unsurprising that, after returning from her run, Cassie had told Linda about what she had heard at Blood Creek.

"But would anybody really camp in the bush?" she asked.

"Probably not," Linda said, "unless they were hiding from someone or something. And wild camping is not allowed in a national park, so they would be moved on pretty quickly if they were found."

It was the sort of topic that could have furnished a morning's conversation, but Cassie heard the crunch of gravel, which signified that her mother was back from the university. And she knew that Eve had their afternoon planned out. It was time to go home.

Cassie came through the back door and saw Eve at the front door in a tangle of handbag, briefcase and laptop. *She carries so much cargo*, Cassie thought, *as if her baggage signifies her worth in life.*

"Oh, there you are, Jocasta," she said. "Been out?"

"I went for a run and then popped in to see Linda."

Her mother gave a tight little smile. Cassie knew that she didn't approve of her running on these lonely roads. Or of Linda, for that matter.

"Well, I'm glad you're finding things to do."

She doesn't look all that glad, Cassie thought.

"I didn't want you to feel stranded out here," she continued, "and I am trying to sort out with Dev whether my visa status allows you, as my dependent, to work. He thinks it does, but he's checking for me."

That, Cassie knew, was the game plan: she'd find a job – somewhere like MacDonalds, or Macca's as they called it here – or perhaps something on campus, in the library or canteen, so her mother could keep a close eye on her. It didn't actually bother Cassie if she didn't work; she was quite happy lazing about the house, sleeping, reading or watching Netflix. But she knew her mother didn't approve. The idea of her coming with Eve to Australia had been to get her out of that introspective little cocoon she had built around herself and to get her away from the environment that, as far as Eve was concerned, had made her ill.

"Anyway, we have to be at Dev and Annie's at 5.30pm," Eve said. "I'll have a quick shower and then we'll go."

꙳

Dev and Annie lived on a road near the university. The university was relatively new, especially compared to some of the British universities Cassie was more familiar with, and a sort of town had grown up around it, with pubs, restaurants and shopping centres to service the academic community. To Cassie, it still felt pretty rural and the grounds of the university – swards of grass interspersed with groves of shelter trees – accommodated at the same time groups of students, between classes, and kangaroos, between eating, sleeping and whatever else they did, and sometimes it was easy to confuse each group for the other at a distance, with both sets having something of the same expectant air about them.

Dev and Annie's house predated the university and was what they called a 'Queenslander' – a traditional, single-storey house with a veranda enveloping it. Eve had told her that Dev and Annie had painstakingly restored it, though what she really meant was that Dev and Annie had paid workmen to restore it. Whichever way you put it, it was quite a house and Cassie found herself sitting on the veranda at the back of the building, recovering from an exhausting afternoon. Her mother had had a hair appointment, shopping to do and various errands to run all in the full glare of the late day's heat, when Cassie should have been sitting in the shade with a book and a cool drink.

Looking out from the veranda, Cassie could see Dev busy at the barbecue – well, everyone knew that Australians loved barbecuing nearly everything – while her mother and Annie stood nearby nursing glasses of wine. Every so often, her mother would give her a nervous glance. Cassie knew why; she wanted her to enjoy herself and to be seen doing so.

Annie, following these nervous glances, said: "Why don't you come down, Cassie, and join us? I'll pour you a glass of wine."

"Oh, that's kind of you, Annie," her mother replied for her, "but Jocasta can't drink because of her medication."

Her mother was technically right; she was still on her meds, but on a lower dosage. And they were gradually tapering off. She had ten days left.

"Oh, that's a bit of bad luck," Annie said and smiled at Cassie. The smile seemed to say that she would slip her a glass of wine when her mother wasn't looking – or perhaps Cassie was imagining it. She had taken to Annie, for the sole reason that she called her Cassie, rather than Jocasta.

It had happened the first time they had met in the uni,

when she had been left with Annie in the office she shared with her mother, while she waited for Eve to finish a lecture.

"Do you want a coffee or a tea, Jocasta?" Annie had asked.

"Coffee, please," Cassie had said.

"Do you abbreviate?" Annie had enquired and, for one moment of blind panic, Cassie had not quite understood what she was saying. In her head, misguided as it was, it sounded like she was asking her if she masturbated. She knew that Australians were more direct than the British, but still. Finally, what Annie had actually meant managed to get through to Cassie's foggy brain.

"My name?"

"Yes, dear. What did you think I meant?"

That was just it, it didn't bear thinking about.

"I like to be called Cassie," she said.

"Cassie it is then. Milk and sugar?"

Now, Annie waved her over and handed her a lemon squash – a drink in a can that was particularly Australian.

"You finding your way around, Cassie?" Annie asked.

Her mother had that tight smile on her face again. She definitely preferred Jocasta. Abbreviating names was something she and Cassie's father shared an abhorrence of, but if they were going to choose Jocasta as their baby's name, what did they expect?

"Yes, thanks," Cassie said, though she wasn't really.

"Well, that's good and perhaps we can help you find a job. Or what about doing a course to fill up your time?"

There was something about Annie that was so open and funny and helpful that Cassie couldn't help warming to her.

"Or what about volunteering or an internship, Evie?" Annie directed the question to Cassie's mother, who hated been called Evie, preferring Eve, but, as Cassie noted, didn't correct Annie. The woman was, after all, her mother's head of department.

"Well, that would be a start," Eve answered, her tone much lighter and breezier than usual.

"Have you had any thoughts about what you'd like to do in the future?" Annie asked. "Any ideas about a career?"

The question stumped Cassie, as she had no answer to it, and her mother just looked embarrassed. Luckily, Dev interrupted them by saying the food was ready.

The best word to describe Dev was avuncular: he was big, warm and friendly, just like your favourite uncle. Or perhaps your favourite bear, as he was large and hairy and given to hugging people. Like Annie, you couldn't help but like him. On first sight, though, Cassie had had her reservations about him. You had to be careful about bears, even tame ones. And uncles, of course – you had to be careful about them, too.

Part of the reason that Dev was so affable was that he was a good degree less serious than Eve and Annie. Dev worked in the anthropology department – Cassie thought that he might actually run it as he was a professor – and anthropology seemed to be a more fun subject, judging from the department's generally relaxed atmosphere. Especially compared to the department that Annie and Eve worked in: gender and women's studies. There were few laughs in gender and women's studies, or so it appeared.

There were quantities of food: steak, fish – barramundi, apparently – and a variety of salads. Eve and Annie were of that liberal persuasion that is clumsily described as 'woke', but this didn't extend to vegetarianism, or veganism, so they had no ethical difficulty in consuming the meat. Dev ate for two people, as if there was a smaller Dev inside him, alien-like, which needed to feed as much as the outer Dev. Annie and Eve also swilled the wine enthusiastically, and the beer, in Dev's case, though he drank moderately compared to the others. Cassie was left with the lemon squash and picked at her food. She couldn't help it; her body didn't seem to crave nourishment as it once had. It burnt enough energy, but didn't seem to want to replenish what it used, consuming itself instead. The result was that she was so thin that she used to get embarrassed when she went to the beach. It wasn't an anorexic thing – she had enough problems without that; it was just that eating too much and forcing food sickened her. Ever since… but she wouldn't let herself think about it.

"Not hungry?" Dev asked.

Eve and Annie were deep in conversation about something. Probably transsexualism, if that was a word, because that was the issue obsessing feminist thinkers at that time.

Cassie just smiled; she didn't want to answer, didn't want to explain. Instead, she just said: "The food's lovely… absolutely gorgeous… but I had a big lunch."

It wasn't true, but it would do.

Dev, like a lot of men his age – he was in his forties, she guessed – didn't really know how to talk to nineteen-year-old girls, unless they were his students or daughters. He did his best, though.

"So, you started a history degree, Eve told me."

He smiled encouragingly – a sign that he expected her to wax lyrical about the subject – but she just confirmed the fact.

"We have that in common, then," he said. "Anthropology and history aren't that far apart, you know. Both involve the study of cultures and societies."

Cassie racked her brains for something to say – she was as awkward with older men as they were with her – and then found something, remembering her conversation with Linda.

"Do you do any work on the indigenous people of this area? The Kabiri, are they called?" She had blurted it out, not setting it in any context, but he took to it like a duck to water. It was a subject he could happily converse with her on.

"Well, it's not my specialty. I tend to focus on New Guinea and the Torres Straits, but I do know the bare facts."

It was her turn to nod encouragingly.

"Of course, even the name itself, like many other things, is in dispute; particularly how you pronounce it. But, from what I know, their story is quite typical. They lived in harmony with nature, mainly on the coast. It was quite a rich environment, in terms of food sources, so European settlers noted that they were fairly well-nourished compared to other Aboriginal peoples they encountered—"

Dev would probably have gone on – most academics don't know when to stop when it comes to their pet subjects – but Annie interrupted him.

"Time for dessert, dear," she said.

As if we need it, Cassie thought, *after all that food*.

But Dev did say one last thing to her, before he followed

Annie into the kitchen, "If you are interested in the Kabiri, you must meet Kate... Kate Mackinnon... she's our specialist in local indigenous tribes. And she is of Kabiri heritage."

～

In the car on the way home, Eve and Cassie were silent, as they often were with each other. It was, in fact, their usual way of coexisting; how they got by. It was as if they had run out of things to say to each other since the day it was all settled. The day when her mother and father had decided what was best for her.

A grey morning in Oxford – but weren't they all at that time of the year; her parents, two personable, capable and successful people in their forties, who just couldn't understand what had gone wrong with their daughter. Surely, she could be fixed. After all, if the washing machine broke down, you called someone, didn't you?

"It can't go on like this, Jocasta," her mother had said. There had been shouting and tears, recriminations and excuses.

You should have been there for her, Malcolm or Eve – delete the name as appropriate. Each blamed the other and, in turn, forgave them.

"You aren't doing anything with your life, love," her father had said. "Giving up uni. In and out of hospital. On meds. You're in a cycle, a downward spiral."

Like a washing machine, Cassie had thought, *stuck on spin.*

"Grieving is healthy, darling. I'm not saying it isn't," Eve returned to a usual theme, "but it can become obsessional, all-consuming. Carys is gone, dear... She's dead. Nothing will change that."

They had to say her name, didn't they? Cassie had thought. *Neither of them was fit to carry it on their tongues.*

"It will a be a new start," her father, Malcolm, had said. "A new opportunity. God, I'd give my eye teeth to move to Australia."

He's delighted, Cassie had thought, *to get rid of a defective daughter and palm her off on the mother who, as far as he is concerned, was never there enough.*

"And it will be good for us, darling," Eve this time, speaking as if she really believed it. "Good for our relationship."

Did they have a relationship? Cassie had asked herself. Apart from the fact that she'd birthed her – and Eve never let Cassie forget what an ordeal that had been; a fourteen-hour labour, or so she said – Cassie was hard-pressed to find anything they had in common.

They had wanted her agreement, or so they said, but they didn't really mean it and, *Frankly, my dears*, she had told them, but only in her head, *I just don't give a fuck.* If Carys was no longer in the world – and Carys had been her world – she might as well be dead, blotted out. She could be equally dead in a plane on an endless flight and then dead at the end of the world in Australia. Geography no longer concerned her. And you could be dead in a living body, a fact that never ceased to surprise her – though she was trying, as hard as she could, to be alive again. To get her head above the water of that seductive sea, the lure of non-existence.

Her mother was driving too fast, as if she was angry. Angry with Cassie, as always.

"Mum," Cassie said, "slow down. Think of the kangaroos."

There were signs with kangaroos on, saying, 'We live here too'. Linda had told her that people ran into them all the time.

Her mother glanced at her, not sure if she was being sarcastic, but she heeded Cassie's words and slowed down.

CHAPTER THREE

She wasn't left on her own for the next two days. Eve was – and it was quite obvious – trying to fill her time up, robbing her of time to think, to brood. Her mother would work at home in the mornings and then take Cassie out in the afternoons; a frantic series of cafes, restaurants, shops and beaches. But Cassie could only drink so much coffee and never wanted a cake to go with it. She ate only a sparse lunch, whatever was offered, and, as for the shops, Cassie didn't want anything, however much her mother tried to urge clothes on her. As far as Cassie was concerned, cut-off jeans and a charity shop T-shirt were clothes enough. And when it came to the beach, it was always too hot and too glaring, and the sea never calm enough to swim.

Eve did her best and kept her composure with her recalcitrant daughter, only once voicing a complaint: "There's no pleasing you, is there, Jocasta?" she said, when they were on their way home.

Cassie, for some reason, found the observation to be hilarious and laughed.

"What's so funny, Jocasta?" her mother asked, irritated, on the verge of anger.

"Nothing, it's just that you're right. There *is* no pleasing me. That's the point, Mum."

"Well, it's not exactly easy for me, you know," Eve said, a catch in her voice.

Don't cry on me, for fuck's sake, Cassie thought, but they descended into their usual silence after that.

On the third day, Eve had to go into the university to give a lecture, so Cassie was free at last. But though she had intended to get up early and go for a run, back to the bridge, she got up too late. She'd woken up just after dawn and heard her mother in the kitchen, but, for some reason, her eyes wouldn't open and she drifted back into a sleep that was hardly dreamless. Instead, it was filled with Carys and so real that when she eventually woke up again afterwards, she thought she felt her just departed presence in the bed, a vagrant warmth, a familiar smell, as if Carys had just got up for a pee or gone to put the kettle on for a cup of tea and wasn't really buried in the cold earth of an Oxfordshire churchyard.

Heart-breaking as it was, and despite the fact that she couldn't get out of bed for ages, couldn't stop sobbing even for the next hour, the dream, vivid as it had been, was welcome. She would take the pain, just to have some more time with Carys, however illusionary that time was. If she had believed in an after-life, if she had thought they would be together in it, she would have had no hesitation about leaving her own life – Goodbye, cruel world. But she didn't believe. She knew that what was gone would not come back again, and she was left with pain and a modicum of regret. *I'm too fucking young to deal with this*, she thought to herself, in a selfish moment. And that thought helped her get up and make herself a coffee. She tried to force down some breakfast, but couldn't do it: the spoonful of cereal made her feel sick. *Life goes on*, she told herself. This was one of her mantras, which she hardly believed.

For want of anything better to do, and to get Carys out of her mind, however guilty she felt about doing so, she decided to walk to the bridge. It was too warm for running. It was late, getting towards noon by the time she decided on it, and blisteringly hot, but she figured it was only five kilometres or so, there and back. If she carried water, wore a hat and took it easy, she should be alright.

She filled a bottle, found a wide-brimmed hat of her mother's – an olive drab bush hat of some sort, purchased on a whim – and was just about to set off, when she saw Linda watching her from her own front garden.

"It's none of my business, love," she asked, "but where are you off? On safari?"

"Out for a walk," Cassie replied, feeling like she'd been caught doing something questionable.

"Bit hot for a stroll," Linda said. "Want to borrow my bike?"

※

The bridge was shimmering in the baking heat and the shadows that the trees cast seemed all that much darker in the white glare of the sun. Cassie didn't really feel comfortable on the bike, but she'd been too polite to refuse Linda's offer. As she wobbled off down the road, not feeling particularly safe, Cassie told herself that being overly polite was one of her major faults. It was a vestige of her English middle-class upbringing and it stopped her from telling people what she really wanted, what she really felt. The bike helmet felt heavy and cumbersome in the heat, but Linda had insisted she wear it – "It's the law," she'd said, and Linda could be very persuasive about those sorts of things. Her shorts and T-shirt felt like the wrong clothes to have on: where was Lycra when you needed it? But she had to admit you could cover a hot and dusty five kilometres relatively quickly on two wheels, so she was glad she had accepted the offer.

Now, as she balanced the bike against the gate and took the helmet off, she wondered why she had come. Her mum and dad, when dealing with what they regarded as her whimsical nature, would often fall back on the same tired few words to describe her: "You're oversensitive, love. Highly strung." She always found that latter term particularly apposite – as if she was balancing on a tightrope, which it felt like most of the time.

She knew what her mum and dad would have said, if she'd told them what she had experienced: that she had overreacted to a random noise, heard something she had misinterpreted and let her imagination invent a phantom laundress. Or the male equivalent, though in her experience it was usually women who got stuck with the laundry.

So, was that all there was to it? Another one of Cassie's fancies or fantasies, whatever you wanted to call them. With the helmet off, the sun beat down on her head and was already making her feel giddy. *How long does it take to get sunstroke?* she asked herself, not sure of the answer. She was a little afraid of the shadows that ran along the bed of the creek, her usual fear of snakes and other unknown, alien creatures, but it would be cooler there, and she could hear the soft, whispering of the creek water – terribly faint though the sound was – which also promised relief from the heat. She left the bike and the helmet, figuring they would be safe enough. Seeing a narrow path leading off the track along the bank of the creek, she followed it.

As she had foreseen, it was much cooler among the trees. She followed the path, which wasn't much of one – *Probably just a trail that fishermen use*, she thought. Not exactly well-trodden. She didn't intend to go far and she was wary about where she put her feet, but soon her initial fear, although it didn't completely disappear, lessened somewhat. Following that trace, she came to a stretch of riverbank where the trees thinned and gave her an unobstructed view up the creek. Suddenly, she felt weary, emotionally drained after that dream of Carys. She wanted to sit, but still didn't trust the ground. However, there was an outcrop of rock, extending out into the creek, that looked more inviting. Before settling down on it, she made sure nothing was basking or sheltering in its lee. The rock was warm, as if the sun had heated it up, but not too much, just enough to be pleasant. She settled down, gingerly at first, but then more confidently. She looked downstream, the soft susurrus of the water lulling her. She could feel her eyelids closing and fought sleep, but then she thought, *Why not surrender to it?* She might even see Carys again.

She woke abruptly to a strange noise, but a familiar one: that song. Looking up the creek, her eyes confused by the play of sun and shadow, she tried to discern what she could see. Shadows? No, figures. Dark and silhouetted like black-and-white cartoons. No, not cartoons, that wasn't right; more like stick figures drawn on a cave wall by some Palaeolithic artist. But then the figures filled out and took on a life of their own, far enough away not to alarm her unduly, but close enough for her to see detail. Men in the shallows of the creek with spears and nets, some in a hotchpotch of clothing, but some naked, their wet skin looking as if it was oiled in the sun. Indigenous Australians – the word sprung into her head. But what were they up to? And what was it with the whole nudity thing?

Cassie felt mildly feverish, but also embarrassed, as if she was witness to something she shouldn't be seeing. Then, she spotted the other figures under the trees along the creek: women and children. The women were chatting or working. Cassie couldn't see exactly what they were doing, but there was a languid air about them, as if the noonday heat had put paid to any attempt at industry and they had all surrendered to sloth. One old girl, who was as wrinkled and shrivelled as a century-old prune, with dried-up tits like two deflated bags, was alternately puffing a pipe and cackling. The kids were splashing about in the shadows of the creek, as if they were the only ones who had any energy left.

The sun had moved around since Cassie had settled in the shadows of the rocks and now it beat down on her head, making her feel confused, her thinking sluggish. What was she seeing? Were these the Kabiri people she had heard of? But Linda had said that they all lived in houses now and drove pickups – utes, as she called them – so why would they be out here doing what they were doing?

There was that sound again, that high-pitched ululating song that seemed to emanate from the air around her. She realised that it was, in fact, the women who were making it – a conversation in song – but it seemed to be more than just sound. It got into her head, clouding her thinking even more. She shook her head and closed her eyes, and when she opened them again, they were all gone, all those shadows, all those people. *Fuck*, she thought, *I'm seeing things.* Perhaps a side effect of the meds she was in the process of getting off – anti-depressants, and quite a hefty dose of them – or had it just been a vivid daydream, just like that dream of Carys this morning? Whatever they were, these visions or hallucinations, whatever you wanted to call them, they completely threw her off kilter. She felt giddy and was starting to feel nauseous. She hadn't really eaten that morning or had more than half a cup of coffee, which was probably a mistake, she decided.

She got up and turned her back on the creek, retracing her steps. She was itching to look back, but she remembered what had happened to Lot's wife – those brief interludes at Sunday school hadn't, as it turned out, been completely useless – so she didn't dare. It would have been something, though, to see the look on her mother's face when the Queensland police turned up to tell her: "It's about your daughter, Mrs Williams. I'm afraid she's been turned into a pillar of salt."

Eve wouldn't have missed a beat, Cassie was sure, but would just nod resignedly and then quickly correct them – told them it was 'Ms' not 'Mrs'.

It helped to laugh, to chuckle to herself, and it made her feel somewhat better. As she walked, she was still looking down at the path in front of her, just in case, but then she heard a noise just off to her right, just before the trail came out back at the bridge. She looked up and there was a girl standing a few feet away from her. Cassie couldn't figure out where she had come from – that slight rustle of undergrowth was the only noise she had made and that had been barely perceptible. She was looking straight at Cassie and Cassie, in turn, stared back at her.

Cassie couldn't, in fact, stop herself from staring, as the girl looked so outlandish; she was dressed in a loose cotton dress or shift, so sun-bleached and faded that you couldn't make out its original pattern, or if, indeed, it had ever had a pattern. She was slightly shorter than Cassie, but looked somehow sturdy. She wasn't fat or anything, just well-rounded and compact. Her dress was hitched up at the waist and thus only reached down to mid-thigh, showing off her well-muscled legs. *Runners' or walkers' legs*, Cassie thought. Her bare feet splayed on the path, white with dust. She had a mess of dark curly hair over a pretty, pert face – Cassie noticed such things, had an eye for them – and was obviously indigenous or of mixed ethnicity. The latter made sense, as her skin was a light honey colour. The girl glared at her and didn't say anything.

"Hi," Cassie said, at last, "you startled me."

Cassie could smell the girl – which seemed an impolite thing to think or say, but it was accurate – even from a few feet away: sweat, woodsmoke, dust, salt and a sweetish musk that must have been her very own scent.

The girl kept glaring at Cassie and then suddenly clicked her tongue and hissed, as if she was a snake. The sound was startling, as if it shouldn't have come from a human mouth. Then she ran straight at Cassie, brushing past her at the last minute. Just a touch of dress and flesh, like the gossamer of a passing butterfly wing, and then she was gone.

CHAPTER FOUR

"Quite a view," Eve said. "Well worth the walk, Annie."

They were standing on a lookout point, part of the boardwalk they had followed up from the beach in the heat of the late afternoon. The cooling winds as they climbed had been a welcome relief.

Cassie had noticed that Eve always seemed to gush with enthusiasm when she talked to Annie, as if her mother's usual cynicism was quite washed away by the change of continent and she had become a much more positive person. To Cassie, it sounded rather simpering and she wondered if it was all an act. Was Eve, in fact, sucking up to Annie? Cassie wouldn't have put it past her.

"It's called 'the boiling point', for obvious reasons," Annie said, as the waves below churned against the rocks, bubbling up as if on cue. "Though it used to be called 'the witches' cauldron'. I don't know why they renamed it, probably because of negative connotations. Should be right up your street, Evie."

Eve smiled, obviously flattered. Cassie was vaguely aware that her mother had published various articles about witches and feminism. How all those so-called witches, who were put on trial for dealing with Satan, were, in reality, just ordinary women who threatened society because of their refusal to conform to gender stereotypes. Fair enough, Eve deserved some credit for her work, but she hoped Annie's remark didn't open the verbal floodgates, because her mother had a tendency to whitter on for hours when somebody brought up her pet subject.

They retraced their steps down the boardwalk, as their table was booked for seven-thirty and time was getting on. Cassie was conscious that she was just tagging along. This was really dinner for two, a head of department taking a new colleague out, and she was just there because Eve didn't want to leave her to her own devices. Just the other day, her mother had said that she needed to get out more, to socialise. "Join a group," she'd said. This latter suggestion had made Cassie laugh.

"What sort of group do you mean, Mum?" she'd asked, not willing to let Eve get away with such a throwaway remark.

"What about an evening class or volunteering? There must be plenty of things you could get involved in."

Cassie doubted it somehow, but she hadn't argued.

Her mother was avid for Cassie to fill her time up and, when she showed no inclination to do so, would take her along to wherever she was going and involve her in whatever she was doing, including this evening out with Annie.

With idyllic beaches and ocean vistas, eucalyptus forest, high-end shops and swanky restaurants, the town – perhaps call it a resort – had everything anybody could want. Anybody, that is, but Cassie, who found that whatever she did, whatever external factors she was exposed to, only managed to emphasise how trapped she was in her own head, her own thinking. The nicer the place, the more it underlined her feeling of being imprisoned in herself. She might as well be back home, she thought, lying down in a darkened room. England had suited her; everybody there felt locked in over winter, trapped by the vagaries of the climate, so she was no exception. Ultimately, the weather stymied all your plans there. Here, it was different. For a start, there was just so much of here, and all this good weather, all these wide-open spaces just made matters worse for her. As if she was some sort of hibernating creature forced suddenly out of its den, feeling weak and defenceless in the open air and glaring sunlight.

Annie and Eve were dressed up – sort of. Not too smart, but not too casual, in cool, colourful dresses. Eve had baulked at Cassie's wardrobe choice – cut-offs and a T-shirt, as usual – and persuaded her to wear a pair of linen trousers and a blouse from her own wardrobe. They were supposed to be loose-fitting, so the fact that they hung off Cassie's spare frame didn't matter that much; she was meant to have that sort of billowy silhouette.

As they passed the runners and walkers on the boardwalk – it was that sort of town – Cassie felt light-headed, unsteady on her feet, but she tried not to show it. When she'd got back from Blood Creek, she had been pleased, at first, that Linda was out. She had left the bike and the helmet on Linda's front terrace. She was going to write a thank you note, but couldn't find paper or a pen, and you couldn't really go into someone's house and rifle about, even if the door was unlocked.

She had drunk most of the contents of her water bottle on the way back. She had wondered if dehydration had played a part in what had happened – what she had seen, whatever it was – or the fact that she hadn't eaten, but she found, as usual, that she had no appetite when she got home. She didn't think she could stomach food and couldn't even think about what she could eat. And it wasn't the people that she had seen – or perhaps dreamed or imagined – that disturbed her, so much as the girl. The girl had been a real physical presence, not a vague figure like the others. A play of light and shadow, but a tangible presence. She had not only felt her, as she had brushed past her – however light that touch had been – but, to put it bluntly, she'd smelled her. Ghosts, visions and hallucinations didn't smell of woodsmoke and sweat, did they? But she had no answer to the question, as she wasn't sure of much anymore.

It was then, when she thought about the girl, that she regretted that Linda wasn't home. The woman seemed a bit batty, a bit away with the fairies, but Cassie got the impression that she could have told her what had happened without the same sort of judgement she'd get from her mother. Eve would have blamed it on the meds or perhaps incipient paranoia, then got her seen by the appropriate professional, but Linda would have listened and put it all down to the conjunction of the planets, freak weather conditions or alien intervention, but not to Cassie being wired differently – not to it somehow being her fault.

Cassie ate some chocolate, just to get some calories into her body, but almost immediately felt nauseous, as if the sugar, the rush of it, was too much for her thin blood. She curled up on the settee and put the TV on, but whatever programmes she scrolled through – and they had all the streaming channels – however many descriptions she read, she couldn't seem to raise any interest in them. Instead, she kept seeing that face: the girl with the honey-coloured skin, the dark hair with barely visible streaks of blonde lit up by the sun, full lips in a permanent pout, and those ever-so-inquisitive, angry eyes looking at her from under those full eyebrows. She recalled the girl's face as if it was from a photograph she had taken, set in her memory, like a negative fixed on paper.

And Cassie found that the girl, though she had stared at her with such hostility and hissed at her like a snake, didn't scare her at all, not in the slightest. Instead, and it wasn't something she would have admitted to everybody, she had been intrigued by her and she had been attracted to her. A feeling that she hadn't felt for a long time and which took her by surprise. But her thoughts were disturbed before she could pursue them further. Her phone pinged; her mother had texted her, reminding her that they were going out that evening, telling her to get in the shower and to smarten herself up.

The restaurant was one of those stylish, trendy places that you saw all along the seafront. It specialised, like a lot of the local restaurants, in seafood. It was packed like all the establishments along the strip and Cassie felt a sense of incipient panic, which she tried to suppress. Being in a restaurant, it was difficult to avoid eating – usually Cassie had enough strategies to get away with not eating, but none of them would work in this environment – so

Cassie ordered an avocado salad to start and a fish curry to follow. She surprised herself by managing most of the two dishes and felt better afterwards, though her stomach felt uncomfortably full. Annie and Eve were both consuming copious quantities of shellfish and white wine. Annie wasn't drinking much as she was driving, but Eve was drinking for the two of them. Cassie was driving home, apparently, though she wasn't exactly pleased by the prospect; all those dark, unfamiliar roads and Eve was getting more voluble as the night went on. *Parents are embarrassing enough, anyway,* Cassie thought, *without them getting drunk.* But generally, Cassie was just a spectator, listening to the conversation of the two women, occasionally smiling or nodding agreement, but saying little.

All that changed when Eve went to the rest room, as she called it, somewhat over-politely. Cassie was left alone with Annie and she realised, all of a sudden, that the woman was looking enquiringly, if not concernedly, at her.

"So, how are you settling in, Cassie?"

Cassie gave the usual non-committal answer: "Okay, I'm doing okay." But Annie still looked concerned and, to make matters worse, she reached out her hand to where Cassie's was lying on the tablecloth and patted it.

"Eve told me that you'd suffered a bereavement. A friend, was it?"

Annie must have sensed the look on Cassie's face, as if it was about to crumple up, folding like a paper fist.

"Or more than a friend, I think," she added.

What do you say to that? Cassie thought. The warmth of Annie's hand on hers was more oppressive than it should

34

have been. Cassie wanted to move her own hand away, but thought it would be impolite to do so.

"You know, Cassie, you can tell me to mind my own business, if you like, but I just want to say that if you ever feel the need to talk to anyone – and sometimes, it's more difficult to talk to close family members than to anyone else – I'm here. If you just want a chat about nothing, over a cup of tea, that's fine. Whatever. Just bear it in mind."

The hand that was weighing Cassie down was finally taken away. Cassie could breathe again. Eve came back and the look she gave Cassie and then Annie said it all. This little chat had been arranged between the two of them.

"Oh, and I don't know if you're interested," Annie said, "but if you are at a loose end, we are always looking for volunteers in the department and in the college library. No money, of course, but something to do and it could lead onto other things. Come in and have a chat with me sometime and we'll see what's available."

Driving home in the dark, her mother dozing beside her, Cassie was too focused on the road and not losing her way to think of what had happened, but when she got home and went to bed, after saying a terse goodnight to Eve, she decided that she had been well and truly ambushed by the two women. She knew that she couldn't turn down the work offer, unpaid though it was, as it would cause too much trouble: her mother would be annoyed; Annie would be disappointed; her father would be dragooned in by video call to persuade her to change her mind. And she felt that she had no energy left to fight what other people were deciding for her, no will of her own, so best to go with it, to go with the current, as if you were caught in one of Linda's rips.

Then there was that offer of being there for a chat – or whatever Annie had called it. When they had first arrived, Eve had told Cassie that Annie, apart from all her academic credentials, was also a qualified counsellor and therapist, so it looked like she was being set up to be one of the woman's unofficial clients. It was all a bit overwhelming and she couldn't help thinking that, all of a sudden, there was just too much Annie. The woman was all-encompassing. Not only did her mother work with her – for her? – she was also becoming the mainstay of her social life. *That's just like Eve*, Cassie thought. She always did this with people she liked; dived in with all guns blazing, full on, almost as if courting a potential lover. And now Cassie would also be working with Annie – for Annie? One more encroachment in their lives.

She switched the light off and tried to sleep, hoping against hope that she would dream of Carys. And sometime in the night, she found herself walking down a long road, in winter, between the skeletons of bare trees, and there was a figure walking in front of her, getting further and further away. She knew it was Carys; she called out, but the girl didn't hear her. She ran, but she couldn't catch up – it was a recurring dream, or should that be nightmare? – but eventually, after running until her whole body ached, she did catch her up. Putting her hand on her shoulder, she stopped her. But when the figure turned, it wasn't Carys at all. Instead, it was the girl from the creek with the same hostile, but interested, face.

CHAPTER FIVE

It was days before Cassie got to Blood Creek again. She had kept putting it off, making excuses to herself, but, in truth, she knew that part of her was scared at the prospect, though another bigger part was intrigued and attracted, like a moth to a flame. She hadn't dreamt any more of the girl – or of Carys, for that matter – and had entered one of those sterile periods, as she thought of them, in which you didn't seem to dream or, at least, remember your dreams. It made for more restful nights, but also led to an abiding sense of loss, of yearning, which permeated her days.

She had arranged to go into the university on the Friday morning with her mother, to have that chat about volunteering with Annie. So, after almost a week of slothful inactivity, as Eve called it – she said it jokingly, but Cassie knew she meant it critically – she steeled herself early on Thursday morning to run down to the creek. For once it was raining, but it was just a light drizzle and it did nothing to dissipate the heat. It just made her wet, not cold.

Looking back later, she did not know what she had expected. Perhaps to be instantly transported to that other place, the girl's place, which was also somehow this place and also her place? But when she got to the gate, before the bridge, there was a pickup truck – or a ute, as she should get used to calling them – and she could hear the sound of power tools in the woods by the creek. She panicked when she first heard the noise; a sudden feeling of fear coming over her that someone was cutting down the trees. And if the trees went, she was sure that she would never see the girl again. She instinctively knew that the trees, the creek and the girl were inextricably linked. Then she reread the sign by the gate and remembered what Linda had told her: this was a national park, so it seemed unlikely anyone would be clear-felling timber. At the same time, she saw the two men in hi-vis jackets along the trail ahead of her, cutting back the bush. *Path maintenance*, she thought, with some relief.

But whether it was the presence of the men, the weather or some circumstance she couldn't fathom, there were no visions that day. Instead, all she saw was an old bridge, the brown waters of the creek sluggishly flowing and the wet umbrella of the trees around her. There was no life, no sound. At least, there was no sound that she could hear above the noise of the chainsaws and the brush cutters.

She was lingering by the bridge, ready to start running again, but hesitating just in case, when she heard a noise from among the trees. As she turned to see what it was, it felt like her heart gave a little flutter, as if she was pleased but also a little fearful, but she didn't see what she had expected. Instead of the honey-coloured girl, there was a man in a hi-vis jacket coming towards her, kitted out in overalls, high boots and a wide-brimmed hat. He was carrying an armful of debris: old canvas, metal poles and a rusted billycan.

It was obvious that she had startled him, standing there motionless as she was, but, after the initial moment of confusion, he laughed.

"Didn't see you there, love," he said. "You gave me a shock."

He saw her eyeing his load and as he boosted it into the back of the ute, he answered the question she hadn't actually asked.

"Old camping gear, left up the creek," he said. "They know they shouldn't do it, but there's not much to stop them."

"Who?" she asked.

He looked at her quizzically, as if he was wondering about her.

"Sorry?" he said.

"I meant who are 'they'. Who would camp out here?"

Seemingly reassured that she wasn't some random crazy woman, he said, "Well, you do get people who want to go wild camping, rather than go to organised sites, but you also get some homeless people, who are just travelling about looking for work or somewhere to live. Who knows?"

He smiled at her, but it was obvious to Cassie that he wanted to get back to work without any more interruptions, so she checked her watch and started the run back.

Near the house, Linda was feeding the kookaburras again. Cassie would have kept away – she was a little wary of the creatures – but Linda saw her.

"Fancy a cuppa, love?" she said. "You look all in."

⁂

"So, the noise I heard was probably someone camping," Cassie said, when they were sitting on the terrace with a pot of tea – mint tea, as Linda only did caffeine occasionally – and biscuits – shop-bought, as Linda didn't bake – on the table in front of them. The rain had stopped and the sun was coming out. There was a tang in the air, almost metallic, as the land dried in the heat. Cassie had already told Linda about what the man at the bridge had said and the debris he had been carrying.

She hadn't realised how disappointed she was until she got home. At first, the man's words had been something of a relief. She hadn't been hearing things; there had been someone washing clothes – or themselves – in the creek. A wild camper. But the shadow people she had seen, well, that must surely have been a daydream or the disorientation of waking from sleep with the sun beating down on her.

Then there was the girl. She was something of a separate consideration, as she had seemed so real. It was still possible that Cassie had imagined her, too, in the same way that she had imagined the others. However, her meeting with the man had suggested a more attractive possibility, one that demonstrated that Cassie wasn't going bonkers. She *had* been real – some homeless girl living rough, who Cassie had disturbed. She was the wild camper; the phantom laundress. No wonder the girl had been frightened; she wasn't supposed to be there. *And you would smell like that if you were living rough*, Cassie thought.

These explanations, logical as they were, should have been convincing, should have reassured her that she wasn't losing that fine balance of sanity that she was trying to maintain, that the meds were meant to have bolstered, but instead she just felt forlorn. As if she had been robbed of something.

"Looks like you've solved that mystery, then, Cassie," Linda said. "But that creek is an eerie place and I've been told that there are various old stories about it. Like the name, for instance."

"What about the name?" Cassie asked.

"I was told when I first moved here – I don't know if it's true or just a story – that at certain times of the year, during the rains, the creek runs red, as if flowing with blood."

Cassie gave an involuntary shudder. "Someone just walked over your grave," her Nan would have said.

"God that sounds weird."

"Somebody told me that it's down to minerals in the creek bed being washed down," said Linda, "but you can imagine what the local Aboriginals made of it."

CHAPTER SIX

No dreams that night, though Cassie longed for them, and an earlier morning than usual, as she was going into the college with Eve. People got up early in this part of the country because of the heat, so there were a lot of people and cars about, even though it was only around seven-thirty when they left the house.

"You're looking nice," Eve said. The praise pleased, rather than irritated, Cassie, as she had made something of an effort. She was wearing a loose white shirt and grey jeans. She'd aimed for smart casual. And she had figured that the college would be air-conditioned, so she wouldn't feel too hot.

But when they got to the college and Eve parked the car, Cassie started to feel panicky. There were just too many people around.

"Come on then, Jocasta," Eve said. She got out of the car; bur Cassie sat in there as if glued to the seat.

"Just give me a minute, Mum," she said.

Eve looked at her watch, impatient. "Okay now?" she asked, after a few moments.

Cassie still sat there.

"No," she said, "I'm not. My anxiety levels are through the roof."

But where she thought her mother would be unsympathetic and tell her not to be so silly, Eve instead bent down and put her arms around her.

"Take your time, darling. Take a deep breath…"

※

"Well Cassie, I'm glad you came in," Annie said, as if she had dropped in uninvited, rather than being all but summoned.

"Let's have a coffee and then I'll take you over to the library and we can get you sorted."

Cassie wanted coffee. She knew it would probably spike her anxiety even more, but she needed the caffeine. This was an early morning for her.

Annie was breezy and chatty, as she led her through the corridors to the vast central hub of glass and steel that was the library. Cassie didn't say much; indeed, she felt as if her tongue had swollen up in her throat. She was all too familiar with the feeling. However, everybody they met was friendly and welcoming and soon Cassie was starting to feel a bit more relaxed, as if those taut nerves of hers were being loosened a notch.

"This is Elaine, Cassie, who you'll be working with," Annie said, when they got to a cubby-hole of an office in the deep, dark interior of the place. Elaine, who liked to be called Lainey, was only a little bit older than Cassie, with short hair

43

dyed a light shade of blue, eye make-up to match and an all-black outfit. She also had the same sort of complexion as Cassie – dead white – which you didn't often encounter among all the local gilded youth. Cassie thought it probably spoke of late nights and a life lived in darkened rooms, but that was just a guess.

"The library is catalogued as you would expect," Annie continued, "using the Dewey Decimal System… but each section is linked to a department and has its own departmental reading room, where the students, mainly the PhDs, can study and spread out. Elaine is our own tame librarian. And there is always plenty of work to do: shelving, cataloguing, book repairs, ordering, etc. The catalogue is computerised, but there are some books that aren't on the system… mainly old ones in the basement storage… so we do have a back-up card catalogue." Annie looked at her, smiling. "Any questions, Cassie?" she asked.

Yes, Cassie thought, *I've got one. Why the fuck did I let myself in for this?*

"Well, if you don't have any, I'll leave you in Elaine's capable hands."

Please don't, Cassie thought. *It means I'll have to talk to her, ask her things, tell her things I'd rather not.* But Annie was gone and she was left with this stranger.

"She's quite something, isn't she?" Lainey said. "Professor Johnson. Like a force of nature."

Cassie smiled and nodded her agreement, but she got it. She'd seen the way Lainey looked at Annie. The girl had a crush on her; she was obviously quite smitten. And this became more obvious as the day went on. But the hero-worship aside, Lainey was surprisingly easy to get on with. She was a PhD student who worked part-time in the library to support her studies. She told Cassie that she'd majored in women's studies and English literature and was now researching 'queer perspectives in the works of Jane Austen'. Cassie wasn't sure what queer perspectives were or why they were particularly queer, and what little Austen she had read had seemed singularly heterosexual, but she was willing to take Lainey's words on trust.

Lainey was upfront about her sexuality – she was wearing a double Venus necklace, which was pretty conclusive – but that didn't bother Cassie, as most people had *her* down as a lesbian. And Lainey didn't make a big thing about it. As far as she was concerned, it just was. Cassie spent a pleasant enough morning shelving books and flicking through some of them, and soon it was lunchtime.

Just when she had got used to Lainey and thought she could probably bear to spend the lunch hour with her, she found herself on her own. Lainey had a meeting with her supervisor – Annie – which she wasn't going to miss. Apart from academic matters, there was also the fact that she was besotted with the woman. Cassie found herself having to do what she had dreaded; buying a sandwich – half of which she later chucked away – and a drink from the canteen, and then sitting on her own in the shade of one of the trees in the university's grounds. It wasn't that bad, after all, and she had taken a book with her, *Pride and Prejudice,* attempting to crack its secret sapphic code.

She thought, at first, that people were looking at her, but then realised that they weren't. Not particularly, anyway.

And the one thing about universities is that they always have their share of odd and eccentric people, so Cassie didn't particularly stand out.

By the end of her lunch break, when she was back in the library, Cassie had constructed a new narrative for herself. She and Lainey would become firm friends. Lainey would say, "There's some people I'd like you to meet." And she would be caught up in a social whirl of bright young things. There'd be laughter, evenings out in pubs and clubs – surely not as dire as they were in the UK – and nights where they stayed up talking until dawn. There'd be heartbreak, of course, and tears, yes, but it would all be part of her new life.

But Lainey was less effusive when she came back from her meeting. *It can't have gone well*, Cassie thought. After an hour more of working quietly together, Lainey grabbed her bag and said, "Thanks for your help, Cassie. See you... Tuesday, isn't it?" And with that, she breezed out, unwittingly taking Cassie's dreams along in her wake.

Who was I kidding, anyway? Cassie asked herself. After Carys, there was no such relief. For her, mourning was a lifelong sentence.

Cassie spent another hour flicking through books, looking for the more risqué passages, but most of them were dry academic works and not at all sexually stimulating.

Mid-afternoon, Annie turned up.

"I'll drop you home, if you like, Cassie. Evie is still tied up."

Cassie sat in Annie's car conjuring up a picture of her mother tied to a radiator in her office. She had always been too literal as a child.

"I've just got to do some shopping in Coles, if you don't mind, lovie," Annie said, full, as always, of endearments. "You can stay in the car if you like."

But there was no way that she was going to miss the opportunity. Cassie loved supermarkets in other countries, seeing what other people bought. She could see that Annie was quite taken aback by this new-found animation.

"You are actually enjoying this, aren't you?" Annie said, smiling.

And Cassie was. *Simple things please simple minds*, she thought. *And why not?* Why not enjoy herself? Even for a few brief moments until that leaden cloud descended again.

And when Annie suggested getting a drink on the way home, Cassie agreed. Annie drove to the little town on the beach near her house and they found a bar. A pub, Annie called it, though it was smarter and nicer than most of the pubs Cassie was used to in Oxfordshire.

"What do you want, Cassie?" Annie asked. "And don't feel you have to have a soft drink; you'll be fine on just one glass of something."

They both had glasses of white wine. Unused to alcohol, Cassie felt that warmth, that elation that came after the initial quenching of thirst, all the more keenly. It felt good, but a little frightening, as if she was losing control. And the one glass was a big one.

"You had a good day, Cassie?" Annie asked and Cassie said she had, that it had been a good day, one of the better ones. "So, you'll be back in on Tuesday?"

Cassie nodded and smiled. She knew this was going somewhere; somewhere she didn't really want to go.

"It's good to see you getting stuck into something, enjoying yourself," Annie said.

Is it, though? Cassie thought. *And what's it to you?* But she carried on smiling at the woman. Perhaps Annie was just being nice.

"Evie told me about your friend…" Annie paused, as if to gauge Cassie's reaction. "Carys, wasn't it?"

"She died," Cassie said. It was a simple statement, which said it all, but also said nothing at all.

"It must have been hard for you, love," Annie said. "From what Evie told me, she was more than a friend…"

What was the Auden line? 'She was my North, my South, my East and my West, my working week and my Sunday rest.' But that didn't even begin to cover it. Carys and Cassie, like Lainey's two Venuses intertwined, interlocked, then torn apart. One heart in two.

Fuck, Cassie thought. She didn't want to talk about it and, strangely enough, Annie, who had started it all, and was usually so loquacious, was also lost for words.

"Look," Annie said, "I think I know how hard it is for you… Well, I don't actually know, how could I? But I can guess. As I said before, if you ever need to talk…"

Cassie shook her head, looked down at her glass.

"One day you might want to, but it's up to you. No pressure at all, dear." Annie smiled. "Well, let's get you back."

⁂

"You sure you want to walk from here?" Annie asked, looking concerned.

"Yes, I'd like to get some fresh air," Cassie said, "and it's only down the road."

It was still light, though it wouldn't be for long.

"Okay, if you're sure," Annie said, reluctantly. "See you Tuesday."

It felt good to be out of the car, away from Annie and her questions. And Cassie had suspected, perhaps unfairly, that if Annie had dropped her home, she would have to invite her in for coffee. Then Eve would have come home and they would have turned it into one of those interminable sessions, rehashing conversations they'd already had earlier in the day.

As Cassie walked, she tried to breathe deeply, to gulp in the air, but it was moist and promised thunder. It was close, humid and clouds were rolling in, darkening the late afternoon. She saw a roo in the distance on the road. It looked like one of those big males and she wondered what she would do if it didn't shift, but then a car came along and the roo bounded off.

The lowering cloud, the leaching of the daylight, was starting to bother her. She wished she hadn't insisted on walking and ran all the events of the day over and over in her head, in that obsessional way that she had. *Fuck, did I say that? Did I do that?* She hated it, reviewing events like this, but she couldn't stop herself, couldn't help it.

She was deep in her thoughts when she heard the steps behind her. A runner, she thought, stepping back to give way, but then a familiar shape barrelled into her. It was the girl, the honey-skinned girl. She knocked her onto the verge and threw her whole weight on top of her, knees on Cassie's thighs, pinning her down. Her small hands, surprisingly strong, gripped Cassie's hands, holding them tight, and she pressed her hips and pelvis into Cassie's stomach, robbing her of breath.

"I got you, ghost woman," the girl said, with glee in her voice.

CHAPTER SEVEN

Eliza had seen the ghost girl on a number of occasions before the evening she caught her. There was that first time at the creek, when she had come face to face with her, but that was only the first sighting of many others. She had seen her on the edge of her vision, in the corner of her eye, several times over the last few days. She was there in her dreams most nights. It was clear to Eliza that the girl was haunting her.

Eliza called her a ghost because Mrs Cleary had read the mission girls a story at Christmas about such spirit creatures. The ghosts were not the only strange things in Mrs Cleary's story; there was also the weather. She described a world, England, where people shivered and strived hard to keep warm. A place of bleakness and harshness: mists, frosts and snow. Eliza could only imagine those things or look at pictures of them – in which the people were always shrouded in coats and hats – while staring out of the schoolroom window at the sun beating down on the land.

The story took place in London, a place she could hardly conceive of. Everybody knew, of course, that it was the heart of the white man's empire and was ruled over by that little woman, who, for all her supposed majesty, looked rather dumpy and pasty-faced to Eliza, though she wouldn't dare say this in Mrs Cleary's hearing. It was Mrs Cleary who had the pictures of London that Eliza had seen, taken with a machine that trapped the light, capturing it and keeping it captive. They were black and white, washed of colour, and Eliza had asked Mrs Cleary if there was no sun in England. Mrs Cleary had laughed, as she often did when the girls asked such questions – or any questions, in fact, but how were they to learn if they didn't ask? – saying that, of course there was a sun, though it was weak in winter. Eliza thought that a world without colour was a poor one.

In the story, an old man, who was mean to everyone and wouldn't share his money (that stuff the white men made such a fuss over) was visited by three ghosts – haunted by them, Mrs Cleary had said, because ghosts haunt – and had to fix his ways. Or so Eliza thought the story went, because she had dozed off in the heat of the classroom as many of the girls had. Those who weren't asleep were scratching themselves or picking their noses to keep awake. It must have been a sad story, because Mrs Cleary had tears in her eyes at the end of it, but it didn't particularly touch Eliza. *Why*, she asked herself, *didn't the Scratchits* – she thought that was their name – *just up and move to a better place, somewhere they could hunt and fish and feed up Tiny Tim in the sunshine and the sea air?*

"But perhaps there was nowhere like that in England," her friend, Vicky, had said. "And you know that white men can't feed themselves. They need money to buy food."

It was true what Vicky had said. The white men cut down trees or ran sheep and cattle, making life hard for themselves, all because they loved their money. If they could have eaten money, they would have.

Vicky was a bright girl, everyone said so, but being bright didn't do you much good in the end. Better to be stupid. Vicky's mother had called her after the Queen of England – whatever her people thought of it – but that wouldn't, Eliza knew, do her any favours. She was a full-blood and the whites preferred brown-skinned girls, like Eliza, for their servants. A girl like Vicky wasn't going far, Eliza knew. Better if her mama had kept her out of the school and gone bush, Eliza's granny had said.

Eliza's granny didn't believe in ghosts; she said that there were no such things. People passed out of the world into the dreaming and became spirits, waiting to be reborn. Ghosts were just something white men had made up – lies, like most of the things that the white men said.

Eliza's granny didn't live with Eliza and her mother, but with her people along the creek and the lake shore and anywhere else where they fetched up: in the mountains looking for honey, on the seashore searching out mussels and oysters, or in the forest getting her medicines. She would sometimes stay at the station, sleeping outside their shack on the creek – she would not sleep with a white-man roof over her head, saying it was too hot and, besides, it might fall on top of her – arriving and leaving without any warning or prior notice. A gnarled, wizened figure, skin like old leather, with just her waist apron and a kangaroo skin cape. Her dugs were as flat as punctured water skins, while Eliza's mother's were ripe and full, and the contrast made Eliza laugh behind their backs. Her own breasts were filling out and she had seen how men looked at her because of it, both black fellows and white fellows. If she had been living with her mother's people, it would have been the time when they looked to betrothing her, hooking her up with some man to keep her in line.

Mrs Cleary was clearly offended by her granny's lack of clothes. She had told Eliza that godly people clothed themselves. Everyone in the Bible was clad, she said, so Eliza had an abiding vision of Noah and his sons in frockcoats and top hats, and his wife in bombazine and a corset. Mrs Cleary frowned on the brazen way that black women and girls flaunted themselves, as she put it, and was reduced to dumb shock by the sight of black men, young and old, walking along with just a small piece of possum hide hardly concealing what she called their 'private parts'.

Eliza and her mother, being on the edge of the white man's world, wore white women's clothes and these were mainly cast-offs: cotton dresses or shifts, sun-bleached and patched. Her mother, while willing to accept this necessity, would not wear drawers, seeing them as an irritant and an inconvenience, though she made Eliza don a pair when she went to school. Sundays were also an exception: drawers had to be worn to church for propriety's sake. Fortunately, Mrs Cleary had no strong beliefs about shoes, so all the girls went barefoot to school. And, anyway, their splay feet, wide with constant walking, would never have fitted into boots. Eliza often thought that Mrs Cleary must have been hot, in all her layers of cloth, her corset and stockings, and those fettering

54

black boots of hers. Indeed, the teacher did seem to suffer from the climate, being constantly flushed and fanning herself.

Mrs Cleary, or so it seemed to Eliza, was particularly harsh on herself when it came to bathing. Eliza and the other girls, when they were hot or dusty – as they often were – would go down to the creek to the place where the women bathed – where they could avoid the prying eyes of men – and strip off before diving into the water. There was a series of pools that the creek water collected in, which were perfect for the bathers, shaded and private. But poor Mrs Cleary confined herself to a secret weekly ritual. She got her servant, Betty, to fill up a tin bath with tepid water from the fire and then hid herself in the outhouse, taking her clothes off in secret, as if she was ashamed of her body or had some deformity.

"She never even lets her husband see her in the buff," Betty had said, laughing. "And they sleep in clothes, both of them."

Her mother and Betty had laughed about this and about Betty's more cruder comments: "How did her husband get through all those layers of clothes to fuck her?"

Eliza couldn't quite picture Mrs Cleary fucking – Eliza was old enough to know what fucking was – but she didn't doubt Betty's words. She knew that Mrs Cleary thought nakedness sinful; why else try to cover it up all the time? But as much as she admired Mrs Cleary in many ways, Eliza would never share that belief. She never felt better than when she was bathing in the creek or lying on the rock ledge to dry herself off in the sun. She felt vibrant, alive, her body flushed with her youth.

One of the reasons why her granny often visited was that they were never short of food. Eliza's mother, Grace, was the cook at the station house and she always brought back plenty of food. One of the only perks of the job, according to Grace. Grace often talked like a white woman, because she spent so much time with the stockmen – or so Eliza's granny said, adding that she was catching their whiteness and would fade if she wasn't careful. Granny complained about the white man's food – even the meat. She preferred bush meat to beef, but she liked the tea Grace brought back with her and the sugar, though not so much the coffee. And, of course, the tobacco and rum. Granny particularly liked the rum and would spend days in a half-stupor of drunkenness, sitting on their front porch.

It was on the front porch that Eliza had asked her about ghosts and she couldn't help telling her granny about her own particular ghost: the white girl.

"You better catch her and see what she wants," her granny said, laughing loudly and filling the air with rummy fumes.

CHAPTER EIGHT

But Eliza had other things to worry about than ghosts. And one of these was Cal Armstrong. He had taken a shine to her, as Grace put it. Eliza knew that she was more fortunate than most of her sisters among the people. She had some small degree of protection from white men and their appetites. The fact she was a mission girl and the formidable presence of Mrs Cleary were both factors in this, as was her mother's position as a station employee. In short, she wasn't just an ordinary gin, who could be hunted out of the bush, rounded up, chained to a tree and tamed, beaten and raped into docility. This was a common enough occurrence to be unremarkable, especially on remoter stations, and when the black fellows fought back, it was usually guns against spears, so the result was predictable. And if the black fellows did, by chance or guile, get the upper hand, the black police would be called in to disperse them – and dispersing them really meant slaughtering them – as these black fellows working for the white men had no fellow feeling for others of their kind.

So, while Eliza was pretty sure that Cal Armstrong wouldn't just grab her and chain her to a tree like a whipped dog, as Mrs Cleary and the other church folk might have something to say about such a blatant act, Eliza knew that she had to be careful with him, not anger or belittle him, and to make sure that he didn't catch her alone in a dark or lonely place. Eliza knew what white men were like; she knew they said you couldn't rape a black woman, that they were always 'up for it', as they put it. She'd seen the way that some of the stockmen looked at the mission girls when Mrs Cleary wasn't about and heard them joke about the girls – some of them much younger than Eliza – being 'birds ripe for the plucking', so she had no illusions about how precarious her position was in respect of Cal Armstrong.

It was obvious that Grace thought it would be better for Eliza to become Armstrong's mistress, so that other white men would, hopefully, leave her alone. It was, after all, what Grace had done when she was a young girl and this was where Eliza had come from, fathered by some white man who had moved on long ago, perhaps back to England, where, hopefully, Eliza thought, he was freezing his balls off.

It was obvious because Grace was all but encouraging Armstrong to come around, which he did with alarming frequency. He would usually bring some sort of gift – sugar, flour or a length of cotton – and would always act as if he was just passing, as if he had no real interest in Eliza, but was there by circumstance. He often brought a bottle or a keg of rum, too, which pleased Grace, who was as much a slave to the grog as her mother was.

Armstrong would sit on their porch – Grace called it a porch, although it was just a piece of stamped earth shaded by the protruding iron sheet of the roof – trying to make conversation with Grace, who wasn't the most talkative of women, and gazing at Eliza with a bovine look, as lumbering and awkward, in Eliza's eyes, as the animals he tended to. He always smelled of horses and leather, along with a sharp tang of sweat and tobacco; a contrast to the smell of her mother – the woodsmoke in her clothes, the salt of her own sweat – who was that much sweeter.

Eliza had to admit, though, that Cal wasn't as crude as the other stockmen. He was a Scotsman, dispatched to the country by his family to make his fortune. Some favour had procured him the job of foreman on the station – the owners were Scottish, Cal had told them one evening when he was in his cups, and distantly related – and he thought himself to be a cut above his men, as he was educated and had some pretentions to being a gentleman. The pretensions, of course, would not stop him from seducing a half-caste girl. While he might want a wife who was chaste and virginal and white – it went without saying – a vaguely willing, brown-skinned girl would do him for now.

Mrs Cleary had told the girls about a show she had seen in Sydney once. She had called it a circus and there were acrobats – people who could do the most death-defying feats, like swinging across the void above them, clinging on with their hands to ropes and bars. And she had talked about a man, a Frenchman, who had walked on a cable above the crowd in that big tent, a tightrope she called it, while the audience held their breath waiting for the inevitable fall, which never came. Eliza felt that she was like that Frenchman, walking on a tightrope where Cal Armstrong was concerned, having to make sure she didn't let her guard down, get too friendly with him. But when Jimmy came home, she could relax for a while, because Cal, like most white men, was wary of Jimmy.

Eliza's brother, Jimmy – same mother, different father, though both white men – had brushed the dust of district off himself a while ago. He had worked as a stockman – sheep, rather than cattle – but never really took to it, being too black for the company of white men. Then he'd gone bush for a while, but never really fitted in, being too white for the company of black men. He had eventually gone to the goldfields over Gympie way and was still there, apparently, working at something or other. Eliza didn't know much about what he did, as Jimmy wasn't exactly forthcoming with the details of his life.

Jimmy dressed like a white man – a stockman, to be precise – with his wide hat, high boots, canvas trousers and loose shirt. He had a stock whip and a dustcoat, but, unlike most stockmen, he also carried a pistol. And not any pistol; one that shot a quantity of bullets without reloading. Jimmy kept it in his saddlebag when he was visiting, but he had showed it to Eliza, boasting to his little sister.

"But why do you have it, Jimmy?" she asked, fascinated, almost mesmerised by the angular, metal weapon.

He had just smiled and shaken his head. "Don't tell the old girl about it," he added, meaning their mother, so Eliza knew that Jimmy was up to no good in Gympie. It stood to reason. You didn't use a gun like that for shooting roos.

Cal and Jimmy made a point of avoiding each other. If Jimmy was there, Cal would stay away. And if Jimmy came back from his wandering to find Cal on the porch, he would make an excuse, go visit some other relative, allowing time for Cal to slip away. Eliza did wonder at the history between them, whether there was something in their past, but she knew that neither of them would tell her what it was. *So why dwell on it?* she thought.

It wasn't that they were hostile to each other. They were civil enough, but reserved, limiting themselves to nods of acknowledgment rather than greetings. But then Cal was reserved with everybody; he was shy, Grace said, as if it was a good thing. As foreman, he had to stay somewhat aloof from the stockmen under him and he seemed to have a certain delicate distaste for their crude ways. Grace often said good things about Cal, praiseworthy things, and Eliza did wonder if this was to get her keen on him or if, indeed, Grace herself had a hankering to take Cal to her own bed. Grace wasn't that old, and though she was a little frayed around the edges from the hardships of her life, she was still pretty enough in a sort of washed-out way. *Well*, Eliza thought, *she can have him if she wants him and then he'll leave me alone.* But whatever she thought, she could see that Cal had eyes for her, not Grace.

CHAPTER NINE

When she was younger, before she had bled and become a woman, Grace would allow Eliza, on occasion, to go off with granny to see the people – her people. Though you could never predict where they would be on any particular day, the lake and the creek were places they kept coming back to. The men would spend mornings fishing in the lake from their boats; mostly dug-outs, but some white-men boats of timber and canvas. From these, they would spear or net the fish or the wildfowl. The lake was a shallow pan of water that almost dried up in the summer, but was teeming with life in the rainy season. While the men fished, the women would gather along the course of the creek, going off on brief foraging expeditions, weaving and mending or just laughing and playing in the cool, sparkling waters. In the afternoons, they would lie in the shade watching the children play in the waters, their bodies gleaming and jumping like some new exotic species of fish.

As Eliza got older, Grace was more reluctant about letting her wander off with the old woman. This, Eliza learned, was due to one particular abiding fear of hers:

"Don't you come back, girl, with some black fellow's baby swelling your belly."

This amused Eliza, though she couldn't let Grace see that it did: her mother would slap her if she saw a smirk on her face or even take a switch to her arse. Eliza wasn't stupid and she knew that it took a while for a baby to show; you didn't go off and fuck someone and then start swelling up. She did wonder if Grace knew this or was just generally confused about such matters. But Eliza also knew that it wasn't just about that – repeating history, but in Grace's case with a white fellow – it was also due to the fact that Grace was all but shunned now by her own people because of her defection, as they saw it, to the white men at the station.

It was obvious to the people that the white men wanted to clear more of the trees, to open up space for their beasts to range, and that they regarded the black fellows as a rather irritating obstacle to this. While the scrub around the creek bed and along the shores of the lake was too hilly and broken to make for good cattle country, those cows were 'terrible thirsty', as Granny put it, and the white men wanted to water their beasts where the people's sacred spirits and guardians held sway in the rocks and the trees and in that very liquid that those alien animals were drinking in copious quantities.

The people were far from pleased with this, but they didn't quite know what to do about it. They knew of old what the white men would do if they tried to stop them. The white men had guns; the people had spears, knives they had traded, but no guns, apart from a number of rusty, old fowling pieces that a few of the men who'd worked for the white men had acquired. They'd never really got the hang of firearms and, besides, a spear and a spear-thrower were just as effective as a ball and shot for hunting and much quieter. They didn't scare off game.

Despite these worries, the people still congregated along the banks of the creek, sheltering from the heat of the afternoons, half-slumbering in the shadows, and Eliza would slip away when she could and renew old acquaintances with cousins, uncles and aunties – people she'd known all her life, off and on, finding some peace and respite from her other life among them.

Because apart from Cal Armstrong, there was also Mrs Cleary. The woman, she knew, would not have approved of Eliza swimming in the creek and basking on the rocks like a goanna, or lazing about in the shade laughing with the women. Mrs Cleary had one purpose in life and that was to turn her girls into upright, industrious Christian girls, who could make their contribution to colonial society.

"She wants to turn you white, girl," her granny would say, laughing, and there was much truth in the old woman's words, because to Mrs Cleary, the natives, as she called them, were feckless, lazy and immoral. Her girls would be assimilated into white society, becoming loyal subjects of the queen, rather than the ignorant savages their ancestors had been. Of course, it went without saying that they couldn't be totally assimilated into white society, couldn't become actual Britons, because they weren't actually white. They would have a place somewhere at the bottom of the social pile, in the most menial jobs, but they wouldn't be ignorant, godless and amoral anymore, and no longer savage.

But Eliza quite liked being savage, wandering around in the buff, or nearly so, eating what the land provided and doing what she wanted, not what someone else was telling her to do. At the mission, Mrs Cleary always kept the girls busy, whether at schoolwork or at sewing and mending, often by candlelight where you strained your eyes, and there was the laundry to be done, boiled in coppers using soap and starch, as all the Clearys' smalls had to be as white as chalk, along with the reverend's shirts. Out in the bush, if Eliza wanted to wash her dress, she would just rinse it in the stream and then pummel it against a rock, rather than getting steamy and sweaty in an outhouse.

Mrs Cleary, Eliza knew, had ambitions for the mission. She wanted the tin-roofed church to grow like some great tree into a high-vaulted airy space, where the sound of bells would be heard every Sunday and angels hovered and soared over the heads of the crowds of worshippers. And she wanted – Eliza knew, because she had told her so – the miserable little clutch of shacks and outbuildings around her equally miserable house to grow into dormitories and workshops, where the girls would sleep and work and exist in a new Eden. An Eden that had more denizens than the pathetically small group of girls that she ministered to now, most of whom came because of the free food and the second-hand clothes.

"That white woman won't last," Eliza's granny had said. "They never do, you know. She'll be back on a boat to England in no time and she'll blame us black fellows for her failure."

Eliza had first seen the ghost girl down by the creek on one of the days that she spent there with the people. In fact, she'd almost bumped straight into her. She'd just been bathing, had lain down afterwards on a slab of rock to dry herself, as she usually did, and had fallen asleep. She'd woken up abruptly to the sound of horses, men shouting and cattle lowing further down the creek. Eliza knew that the stockmen used a shallow fording place, where a track cut across the creek, as a watering place and, hearing the noises, though the white men were a distance away, she quickly dressed and set off back towards her people, where, at least, there was some safety in numbers. She wouldn't want to be caught out there alone by some stray stockman.

She was still sleepy, hardly awake, when she blundered back onto the trail and almost straight into that strange, bleached-out person. The girl – because it was a girl, though the creature was thin, her hip bones sticking out and no paps to speak of – stared at her, as if she was as surprised as Eliza, and said something in a voice that sounded like Mrs Cleary's. The girl had strange clothes on. It looked like she was wearing underwear and nothing else. And not women's underwear, more like those of a man. Eliza had never seen a white woman before with so few clothes on. And the girl's head was shorn like a convict. *Surely a girl wouldn't willingly have her hair cut like that*, Eliza thought. But then a chill came over her as she realised the truth: this was not a flesh and blood girl. It was a ghost and it had come to haunt her and perhaps to do unspeakable things to her. So, she did what her granny would have told her to do. She hissed like a snake and ran past the ghost. It was a stupid trick really, but Granny swore by it.

"You make that noise and they are too busy trying to spot the snake to think about you," said Granny.

The trick worked this time, because the ghost girl looked astounded as Eliza ran past. Eliza turned once to see her standing there, forlorn, before she was back among her people and the girl was out of sight.

Normally, Eliza would have felt safe enough there by the creek, with her people around her and the sounds of the white men and their beasts receding into the distance, but the sudden sight of the girl – the ghost – had disturbed her and she wasn't sure she could feel safe again with that creature in her world, crossed over from wherever it had come.

CHAPTER TEN

Eliza had no idea how you caught ghosts; it wasn't an area of study that they covered in the mission school. In fact, Eliza had got the impression that, though Mrs Cleary loved the Christmas story she had read to them, she didn't believe in or really approve of ghosts. It didn't go with her particular set of Christian beliefs. Eliza had tried to broach the subject a few times when they were on their own – Mrs Cleary liked Eliza to brush her hair out at the end of the day, as she said she found it soothing – but Mrs Cleary, surprisingly, was of a similar view to her granny.

"Ghosts don't exist, Eliza. They are made up. They are just in stories, my dear. Nothing for you to be frightened of." As she said it, she put her hand up to Eliza's cheek and smiled.

Eliza wasn't the only one who'd noticed Mrs Cleary's particular fondness for her. Her granny, who was quite a sharp old bird when she wasn't drunk, had noticed, too.

"That woman is going to steal your girl away, Grace, if you're not careful," she would say. "Those white women have a fondness for brown-skinned girls."

Grace would tell Granny that she was a silly old bat – that Mrs Cleary was just being nice and kind, but Eliza knew different. Mrs Cleary was always on at her to come and live with her as her maid.

"Why don't you, Eliza dear? You wouldn't just be a servant, but a trusted companion."

As she said it, Eliza could see the longing in her eyes. She was a lonely one, that was clear. Her husband was away a lot and there were no other white women around to keep her company.

Eliza would make an excuse and say that her mother wouldn't allow it, but she was, to be truthful, rather afraid that Mrs Cleary would ask Grace directly, because Eliza wasn't sure what the answer would be. Grace might think it was a step up in the world, as well as one less mouth to feed.

Granny was no use either when it came to ghosts. They were white man's things, she said, and should be left alone, if they even existed and weren't a lie. It was no use reminding Granny that it was she who had told Eliza to catch the ghost. The old woman denied all knowledge of saying it. "You do get some strange notions in your head, Eliza," was all that she would say. "It's spending all that time with white people."

Eliza might have tried to forget the ghost girl – though she still saw glimpses of her – if that strange thing hadn't happened.

She had gone with some of the girls to pick bush plums. Because of the white men cutting timber and clearing the land for their cattle, the plums were getting more difficult to find, so when Granny told them of a tract of bush west of the creek where they grew in abundance, she gathered Vicky and some of the other girls – mission girls and creek girls, both – and mounted an expedition. They were careful not to be seen setting off in the late afternoon as they didn't want any trouble from white fellows or black fellows. This was a female affair, not for men, even ones you could trust.

When they got well past the creek and could see that there was no one about, they started to enjoy themselves, singing, dancing and laughing. Out here, they could tell each other things about men and talk about women's secrets, they could make fun of their elders and, especially, of Mrs Cleary with her long nose and the little spectacles she wore perched at the end of it. Eliza felt a little disloyal, talking in this way about the white woman, but she told herself that it was just a bit of fun. Anyway, they would never dare say such things in Mrs Cleary's hearing.

They spent the afternoon out in the bush picking plums and putting them in the baskets they had brought with them. The plums were good eaten fresh, but could also be dried. Mixed up into a paste, they made a medicine that could be rubbed on your body to ease pain – even monthly cramps, Vicky told them – or used to ward off white fellow sicknesses, like colds.

They were all but finished, sitting down together, eating handfuls of the plums to give them nourishment for the journey home, when Eliza saw the white ghost, walking quickly along in the bush, as if she was heading somewhere and knew exactly where she was going. "Bold as brass", as Grace would have said.

"Hey," Eliza called and got to her feet.

"What you doing, Eliza?" Vicky asked.

"Can't you see her?" Eliza replied.

"See who?" Vicky said, but Eliza was already up and running, the girls looking worriedly after her.

Eliza ran as swiftly as she could, but the dusk was coming down the way it did, fast and abrupt, darkening the land around. And there was something else; apart from the dusk, the light seemed to be fragmenting, as if it was being blown away like threads of mist. She could still see the girl in front of her, but she was less distinct now. Eliza kept running, pulling the skirts of her dress up, so they wouldn't hinder her. Suddenly, her feet thumped off soil and grass and onto something hard, black, almost metallic. She almost stopped, but she could see the girl in front of her, quite close now.

She ran straight at her, a last burst of speed, catching her hip with one arm and forcing her over, onto her back. Eliza was on her in a flash, pressing her down, holding her arms tight.

"I got you, ghost woman," she said. In fact, she almost crowed, she was so triumphant.

"Fuck off, you stupid bitch," the ghost said, struggling under her. Though Eliza was small, she was strong and she wouldn't let go, but she was little shocked by the ghost's words. She'd never heard white women curse like that – white men, yes, but white women, no. That is, if this was a white woman, which was by no means clear. It was in the form of a white girl, but who knew what it really was?

The girl struggled some more. "What is this? A mugging? Or are you just fucking insane?" She struggled a bit more, then gave up. "You're amazingly strong for such a small girl."

Eliza felt complimented.

"Look, I've got hardly any money on me and my phone is a piece of shit," the ghost added, "so if this is a robbery, it's not a very successful one."

"What do you want from me?" Eliza asked suddenly.

The ghost girl looked at her and smiled. "Shouldn't I be the one asking that question?"

When the ghost girl promised not to run – *Could you really trust a ghost?* Eliza asked herself – she let her up. She was reluctant, at first, because she quite enjoyed having the girl in her power. She had a sudden, perverse vision of Mrs Cleary in the girl's position, pinned by Eliza's body. Despite shocking herself with this mental picture, she was pleased by it, almost excited. Eliza was, if truth be told, a little confused, because the girl felt like any other human girl. She was warm to the touch and smelled human: of sweat and skin and hair. Her clothes were different tonight: she had trousers on – a girl in trousers was a new one for Eliza – and a shirt that looked like something a man would wear. All in all, the girl was puzzling.

When Eliza stood up, she finally looked around her, seeing the dark shapes of houses that shouldn't have been there, the strange roadway, the lamps on poles along the highway. She suddenly realised that she didn't know where she was.

"Where am I?" she asked, looking at the girl. It was her turn to be scared.

CHAPTER ELEVEN

The girl was reluctant to come into the house, so, at first, they sat on the terrace. The offer of a cup of tea got through to her – she understood that.

She had been almost mute after she had let Cassie get up, disorientated. She'd looked around with those big, beautiful eyes of hers – well, Cassie couldn't help noticing them – and seemed distraught.

"Where am I?" she asked again.

Cassie parroted out the address – her address – but it made no sense to the girl. So, instead, she reached out for the girl's hand.

"It's okay," she said. "You're safe. You're not in any danger."

The girl had initially pulled her hand away, but then she let Cassie take it. It was warm and the girl's grip was firm, but the skin was rough. *Working hands*, Cassie thought. The girl looked at Cassie, examining her.

"You're a girl," she said.

Cassie laughed. "What did you think I was?"

"A ghost," the girl said. "Are you a ghost?"

"No," Cassie said, smiling, "I don't think so." Seeing the alarm that suddenly filled the girl's face at this flippant reply, she added, "No, I'm definitely not a ghost."

"But how can this all be?" the girl asked, looking around.

Cassie was almost as confused as the girl. She was still a bit shaky after being knocked off her feet and she'd gone down hard on one of her elbows. She wondered if it was cut and bleeding and then worried that she'd ruined her mother's blouse. After the initial shock, after she had realised who it was that was on top of her – not some leary guy trying to rape her – some of the initial fear had dissipated. It was the girl. The one she had seen at the creek and, however savagely she looked at her, Cassie didn't think she wanted to harm her.

Cassie's pride was a little bruised. She'd never have thought that someone could have come up on her like that and rendered her completely helpless in a few seconds. She'd always felt that she could handle herself or, at least, put up some sort of fight, but she was amazed at how deftly the girl had done it. Her approach had been almost soundless. There was just the impact and the sudden sickening realisation of another presence. She now knew what one of those antelopes felt like when a lioness pounced on them in a BBC documentary.

"Look," Cassie said, "I live just around the corner. Why don't you come home with me and we can talk."

The girl dropped Cassie's hand abruptly, but, suspicious though she obviously was, she followed her. They went on in silence, there not being much to say – or perhaps, there being too much to say – and small talk didn't seem quite apt in their situation.

"Here it is," Cassie said. "By the way, my name is Cassie."

"This your house?" the girl asked. "It's like a… mansion."

The house was small by local standards: a three-bedroom bungalow.

"I suppose it depends on what you are used to," Cassie said and the girl gave her another suspicious look.

While Cassie made the tea, she kept her eyes on the girl through the kitchen window. She was afraid that the girl would run away or walk away, as there was nothing to keep her there, after all – though a little voice in her head kept telling her that perhaps that would be for the best as why had she invited a stranger – one who had just assaulted her – back to her house anyway? *That's how people get murdered*, the voice said. *The girl is probably insane, absconded from some institution.*

Cassie made the tea, leaving the tea bag in one of the cups because she didn't know how strong the girl liked it. She brought the milk and sugar in with her on a tray, along with a packet of biscuits.

The girl looked suspiciously at the two mugs. "What's that?" she asked.

"Tea," Cassie said, wondering if the girl was perhaps learning-impaired – as people said, trying to be polite.

"Where's your pot?" the girl asked. "And what is that twist of paper about?"

Cassie had to explain the tea bag, though the girl looked unconvinced. She put three teaspoons of sugar in her tea and milk. She sniffed at the milk and looked suspiciously at the carton before pouring it, then she grabbed a handful of biscuits.

"Well, it is tea," the girl said. "I'll give you that."

Suddenly, she smiled at Cassie, showing a mouthful of perfect white teeth.

She won't have those for long, Cassie thought, *if she goes on eating that quantity of sugar.*

"I got you good, didn't I?" said the girl.

Cassie bristled a bit, but the girl said it so mischievously, with what could only be described as a twinkle in her eye, that Cassie couldn't take offence.

"Yes, you did," Cassie replied, "though you did have the element of surprise."

"Still, I got you good," the girl said.

Cassie wasn't going to argue the point.

The girl kept on smiling. "You sure you're not a ghost?" she asked.

"Sure."

"Okay then," she said. "I'll tell you my name. It's Eliza."

"Pleased to meet you, Eliza," Cassie said, shaking her hand formally and they both laughed.

"What's up with your arm?" Eliza asked.

Cassie had been rubbing her elbow. It wasn't bleeding, but it was sore. Thankfully, the blouse hadn't torn.

"I banged it," Cassie said, "when you…"

"Yeah," Eliza said, looking slightly shamefaced, "sorry about that. Let me see."

She didn't wait for an invitation, but crossed to the couch where Cassie was sitting and undid the cuff of the blouse. She rolled the sleeve up quickly and deftly, until she got to the elbow.

"It's nothing," she said. "Just a little knock. It will be right soon enough."

And then she started rubbing and kneading the joint with those hands of hers, firmly but gently.

The sheer physicality of Eliza next to her was a shock to Cassie: people didn't often get that close to her. And Eliza was looking straight into Cassie's eyes without the slightest trace of embarrassment, just concern. Cassie was conscious – too conscious – of the salt tang of her own sweat, but that was overpowered by Eliza's own smell: the girl's perspiration, woodsmoke in the folds of her dress, an open-air smell like freshly laundered clothes that hung in her hair, and that underlying sweetness – the musk that was the girl's own and was more than pleasant. Cassie felt like she was drowning in the sea of Eliza or as if she was falling under some enchantment.

Eliza massaged the whole arm from shoulder to wrist.

"God, you're good at this," Cassie said. "You could be a masseuse."

Eliza laughed and the spell was suddenly broken. "I don't know what that is, but I hope it's a good thing."

≫

Eliza had kept saying that she must get back, but it was obvious to Cassie that she didn't know exactly where she was trying to get back to. She only had a vague idea of where she was.

"Look," Cassie said, feeling surprised by her boldness, or perhaps her recklessness, "why don't you sleep here? And then we can figure it out in the morning."

"Doss in your crib?" the girl asked, seeming unsure about the whole thing.

Cassie didn't know what she meant by a 'crib' – Eliza was now sounding a bit like a character from a Dickens novel – but 'doss' was a vaguely familiar word, so she nodded.

"Yes. The spare room is still full of our stuff, I'm afraid – we just moved here – but you can take the couch. Or sleep in my room."

Eliza looked around the house and seemed thoughtful. "Your room is fine," she said.

※

Cassie was thankful that Eve wasn't home yet. She was teaching an evening class that night and often went out for a drink with the students afterwards, so she didn't have to explain why she was letting a stranger – strange in all senses of the word – sleep in her bedroom.

Cassie felt awkward about it, but she didn't know what else to do. It was obvious that Eliza wasn't going to let her out of her sight. She was the only familiar thing in an alien world. She showed Eliza where the bathroom was.

Eliza looked at the toilet and said, "They have these in Sydney, Mrs Cleary says. Rich folk do, not like a dunny in an outhouse."

She got the gist of its use, hoicking her dress up and pissing in front of Cassie without any embarrassment, but she was more perplexed by the washbasin taps.

"You don't have to pump water?" she asked.

She watched Cassie clean her teeth – she definitely didn't want to let her out of her sight – and was very amused by the whole process. Cassie was getting tired, especially of explaining, so she didn't. She closed the door on Eliza when she was having a pee, though.

In the bedroom, Eliza surveyed Cassie's double bed with some amusement.

"That's a big bed for a thin little girl," she said and Cassie couldn't help laughing.

"Plenty of room for the two of us, anyway," Eliza added.

Cassie had vaguely thought of one of them sleeping on the floor, but, of course, this made more sense. The bed was wide enough for the two of them. Cassie took her clothes off, conscious all the time that Eliza was watching her. She stripped to her pants and then shucked on a T-shirt, embarrassed to sleep in the nude next to this girl she hardly knew. She turned down the covers and slipped into the bed.

"Come on, then," she said to Eliza. "What are you waiting for?"

Eliza laughed and then stripped her dress off. It was the same dress, Cassie suddenly realised, that she had seen her in down at the creek. Did she only have one of them? Beneath the dress, Eliza was naked and... quite stunning.

"Budge up," Eliza said, and Cassie did as she asked.

The girl was asleep almost immediately, but Cassie lay there for a while, unable to drift off, too conscious of the body next to her. She hadn't shared a bed with anyone since Carys and it felt both strange – and perhaps not right – and pleasant. She'd have liked to cuddle up to Eliza. She wasn't being particularly sexual; she just wanted her animal warmth, but instead she turned her back on her and drifted off. At some point in the night, she was conscious of Eve coming back, hearing the car on the gravel of the drive, and then, later, of Eliza waking up, complaining of the softness of the bed, before falling back to sleep again.

≫

In the morning, when the early light woke Cassie, Eliza was gone. Cassie did wonder whether it had all been a dream, but she could still see the ghost form of Eliza in the sheets and coverlet of the bed, still smell her particular scent on the pillow. The girl's absence hit her with a jolt of regret and of grief. At the same time, she couldn't help thinking about Carys. It was as if she was eliding the two women together, a symptom – or was it a phenomenon? – of her troubled mind.

She knew she wouldn't sleep any longer, so she padded out to the kitchen to make coffee. Eve was there at the table, eating her breakfast and looking over her papers.

"Morning, darling," she said. "Are you okay?"

"I'm fine," Cassie said, almost snapping at her mother for no reason except that she was there, intruding on her morning thoughts.

Eve nodded and went back to her papers. Cassie got her more coffee to make amends for her snappiness.

"Friend of yours?" Eve asked.

"What?" Cassie said, taken by surprise.

"I bumped into a young person this morning… almost literally… she gave me a shock. I think I gave her one, too. She was coming out of your bedroom."

Fuck, Cassie thought. She had explaining to do and no energy to do it with.

"Yes… just somebody I met."

Eve looked at her quizzically. The look said it all. *Do you think it's wise to invite strangers back to your bedroom, to your bed, in fact, because there's nowhere else to sleep in your room? What do you know about the girl? She could be anybody. She could be a thief or a murderer.*

It was amazing how much one of her mother's looks could communicate. "She's just a friend … Eliza…" stumbled Cassie.

Eve nodded.

"Well, at least you learnt her name," Eve said, unable to avoid being just a little sarcastic. "She's a very pretty girl, but a little… how can I put it… alternative…"

Cassie sipped her coffee in silence.

"I mean, bare feet, charity shop dress…" Eve said.

"They call them op shops out here, Mum," Cassie replied.

"Well, you know what I mean."

They went back to drinking their coffee in the increasingly ominous silence.

"It's your business, love, but do you think you're quite ready yet?" Eve said at last.

"It's not like that, Mum," Cassie said. "She's just a friend."

But Cassie wasn't sure if that was really true.

CHAPTER TWELVE

It was her granny who woke Eliza up. Well, not her actual, physical granny, shaking her with her bony, gnarly fingers and asking her what she was doing sleeping in a white girl's bed. It was in a dream. Snuggled down in that white expanse of bed, which was too soft and yet not soft enough, next to that scrawny girl, who was breathing so quietly in her sleep she could have been a doll rather than a living creature, Eliza had a series of dreams. In one of them, the last one, her granny had appeared from out of a vast expanse of colourless plain, like a snowscape – or what she thought of as a snowscape, having never seen one, except in pictures – and said: "Time to come home, Eliza girl. You get your fat arse home, now."

Dream Granny was as rude as real Granny.

"But how, Granny? I don't know the way," dream Eliza replied.

"You do, girl. Your feet and your legs do," dream Granny said. "Just get walking."

She got out of bed and put her dress on. She needed a piss, but decided it could wait – the dunny was too noisy. She looked down at the girl – at Cassie – and had an urge to touch her hair, her face, to caress her. The girl had been kind to her, surprisingly so, because, in her experience, young white women weren't always kind to girls like her. But she didn't want to wake Cassie; she was sleeping so peacefully, though she was drooling a bit. She opened the door, stepped into the hall and came face to face with a woman, who was as startled as she was.

"Oh," the woman said, taking the situation in, "you must be a friend of Cassie."

"That's right, missus," she said, "but now I've got to go."

"Well, you're welcome to stay for breakfast," the woman said, but Eliza was already out of the screen door and onto the porch.

She realised, as she made her way down the short drive to the road, that the woman did look a little like Cassie – an older version of her – so she was probably her ma. She didn't think much about it after that; in fact, she didn't think at all, but just let her legs and her feet do the walking as granny had said.

There was a mist on the land; it had been raining overnight and the sun hadn't yet broken through. Her feet led her through the wet grass into the bush, the light fragmenting about her in woolly clouds that snagged on bushes and shrubs. She walked for some time – she couldn't measure it, but didn't need to – and then, suddenly, realised where she was. The stand of bush plums was close by. She rested there for a while and ate the rest of the biscuits the girl had given her, which she had stowed in the pocket she wore around her waist under her dress. Then she just kept walking, until she cut the track and then the creek, threading her way up that familiar path, overjoyed to be back in her own world. *Perhaps*, she thought, *Cassie was a ghost here, as she was a ghost in Cassie's world.* She didn't understand it, but she thought that Granny would. She could tell her what had happened.

Grace wasn't exactly pleased to see her.

"Where you been, girl?" she said. "You been off with some boy, popping your cherry?"

She looked at Eliza with disappointment. Grace had ambitions for Eliza – that's why she'd sent her to the mission school – and keeping her legs closed was an integral part of them. Eliza suspected that these ambitions would never be realised. Grace had more faith in the white man's world than she had.

"Nobody's going to want used goods, girl," she said.

"I got lost in the bush, Ma," Eliza said. "Had to sleep out and then found my way home this morning."

Eliza wasn't sure that Grace believed her, but she accepted her explanation for now. Anyway, she was off to work.

"Mouths to feed," she said. "White men want their tucker on time."

Eliza was left with Granny and they sat on the porch in silence for a while, as Granny puffed her pipe.

"Good girl, Eliza," Granny eventually said, when the pipe had run out, "finding your way home. You didn't forget everything I taught you."

"But it was you, Granny, who called me home. Don't you remember? You were in my dreams."

Granny shrugged. "That's as may be, girl, but I don't recall it." She laughed. "I had a bellyful of rum last night."

Then, she turned serious and said, "You should hearken to your mother, though... what she says about men. She's not right about much, but that might just be one of the things she knows something about."

"I haven't been with a man, Granny," Eliza replied. "I was just lost."

"Then, where you been, girl?" Granny said. "I don't believe you could have got that lost. Not you."

"Oh, but I was," Eliza said and she told her about the ghost girl, about Cassie and that strange place.

Granny watched her closely as she talked. As Eliza had suspected, the old woman wasn't surprised by anything she said. Granny's everyday existence was, after all, full of supernatural entities; spirits of time and place existing in the world all around her. At the end of the story, the old woman just nodded, acknowledging the truth of it.

"I thought she was a ghost, Granny," Eliza said, "and that I was in a ghost world, but now I'm not so sure. She seemed real, smelled real, felt warm to the touch."

"And she took nothing from you, girl? Not even a hair on your head?"

Granny leant over and took her face in two hands, which were rough as bark. She stared into Eliza's eyes, looking into them as if into her very being – that soul that Mrs Cleary said that she had. "She did you no harm?" she asked.

It was a question, but it seemed that she had received her answer, because she let Eliza go and sat back on her haunches.

"I don't know nothing about white girl's magic," Granny added, as if she had said all that needed to be said on the matter. "But if the ghost girl meant you no harm..."

"She didn't, Granny. She tried to help me."

The old woman looked thoughtful. "Then there must be some reason why she came to you. Perhaps she's meant to help you."

"Help me in what way?" Eliza asked.

Granny chuckled. "Doubt if she knows herself, girl."

CHAPTER THIRTEEN

If Eve hadn't seen Eliza, Cassie might well have thought that she had dreamt her. Her elbow still hurt, that was true, but she could have easily fallen over on the way home – rather than being rugby tackled – and her unquiet mind might have invented the rest. But Eve *had* seen Eliza, so the girl was real – no figment of Cassie's longing, her own loneliness. And the fact that Eve had seen Eliza added another layer of complexity to something that was in no way simple or straightforward.

If Cassie hadn't dreamed Eliza or conjured her up from some rogue part of her thinking, then who was she? Was she just some waif and stray – some sort of homeless drifter – who had, for some reason, attached herself to Cassie? How else to explain the fact that Cassie had encountered her twice in different places? Had Eliza followed her, stalked her?

Cassie remembered what the girl had said, calling her 'ghost girl', asking her later if she was a ghost, how loath she had been to enter the house, how timid she had been of her at first. Cassie wasn't used to people treating her that way, as if Cassie could or would do them harm. There was one obvious explanation: that Eliza had psychiatric problems. In other less polite words, she was a nutter. Cassie had known her share of such people – after all, according to her GP back in Oxfordshire, she was one of them – but Eliza, once you got past her ghost girl suspicions, seemed eminently sane.

The 'Who is Eliza?' question was inextricably linked with another one: 'What is she?' Because Eliza wasn't like anyone else Cassie had met in Australia – or anywhere else, for that matter. There was something almost feral about Eliza; she could easily be taken for someone who was homeless and lived rough. Her clothes and hair smelled of woodsmoke and she didn't look like she got quite enough to eat. She didn't appear to be unhealthily thin– the way that Cassie was – but she had hardly any spare flesh on her body. She was lithe and compact – Cassie couldn't help remembering that glimpse of her naked body – and she'd set about the biscuits Cassie had offered her as if she hadn't eaten for a month. When Cassie had told her to help herself, to take as many as she liked, the girl had scooped up a handful and secreted them somewhere under the folds of her dress – surely the behaviour of someone who wasn't sure where their next mouthful was coming from.

And that dress itself – or would you call it a shift? Cassie wasn't quite sure what a shift was – was enigmatic. It was strangely old-fashioned, with a scooped neck tied with a lace and short sleeves, falling almost straight from the girl's bust down to just below her knees. It looked like something you might sleep in, rather than wear out. It was sun-bleached, mended in places, and didn't look like anything you'd buy in a shop – more like some retro craft item you'd find on Etsy.

The girl was obviously of mixed ethnicity: she was part-Aboriginal – or should that be indigenous Australian?

– but that couldn't account for her mode of dress or all-round strangeness. Or so Cassie thought. She didn't really know much about it. Linda had told her that there were no indigenous people following traditional ways of life out in the countryside – at least not in this part of Queensland – but she might be wrong. Or was Eliza perhaps a member of some strange back-to-nature cult living out there in the bush?

But if Cassie had questions, so did Eve. Eve's questions didn't come all at once; there was no barrage, but instead a constant drip of enquiry, ambushing Cassie when she least expected it and clouding her thinking, making it harder to figure out the mystery of Eliza. The questions started at breakfast and went on through the day. It was a Saturday; Eve wasn't in work, so Cassie had no respite.

Eve had hurried Cassie out of the house, because they were going to a market in a nearby town – though 'nearby' in Australia was often a long way away – and within an hour of waking up, Cassie was sitting in the passenger seat of the car as they set off.

Cassie had forgotten about going to the market – the market was apparently a big thing: a major tourist attraction – and would rather have spent the morning thinking about Eliza, but the arrangements had been made and Eve wasn't going to break them, especially since Annie and Dev would be meeting them there.

"I don't feel too good, Mum," Cassie had said as Eve all but pushed her into the shower.

"All self-inflicted," Eve said, "so expect no sympathy."

Cassie couldn't help smiling to herself in the shower. Eve obviously thought that Cassie had just passed a night of drunken debauchery. She was probably jealous, Cassie told herself.

All in all, Eve wasn't in a good mood by the time they arrived at the market. She had wanted Cassie to drive, but Cassie had refused.

"My blood alcohol levels could still be high," she had said, making use of her mother's assumptions as an excuse.

As they drove along, Eve had tried to gently probe her.

"Where did you meet your friend, Cassie?"

"Oh, you know, around."

"At the university?"

"No, Mum."

Cassie almost laughed at that question: Eliza didn't look at all like a student. She could possibly be taken for an art student – with all that grungy fashion of theirs – but the university didn't have such a department.

"At a bar?" Eve looked concerned when she asked this. She didn't like the idea of Cassie trawling bars.

"No, Mum," Cassie said, then realised she'd have to say something more or face an ongoing interrogation from Eve for the duration of the journey. "I met her while I was out running, if you really want to know."

"Well, she doesn't look like much of a runner."

"What do runners look like, Mum?" Cassie asked.

Eve realised she'd said something stupid and clammed up for a while.

They had to queue for the car park. The market was a vast place and seemed to fold around most of the little town, taking up what would have been parklands or playing fields with God-knows-how-many stalls. Cassie, looking over the number of cars and the crowds of people, felt quite intimidated at first. But she put on her hat and dark glasses – it was a hot, sunny day – and these props helped her to feel somewhat anonymous.

You could buy anything there, from a local seascape to a thirty-minute reiki session, from a kangaroo leather handbag to a jackfruit burger. As they passed the first set of stalls, Eve – looking slim and elegant in a mid-length cotton dress and a Panama hat – took a long, measured look at Cassie in her ragged cut-off jeans, old T-shirt, faded baseball cap and cheap sunglasses – and seemed to come to a decision.

"I think we need to get you a new wardrobe," she said.

Cassie shook her head. "I haven't got any money, Mum."

She didn't. Having no job, she was still stuck in a pocket-money economy. Her dad made the occasional deposit into her account – 'Get something for yourself, Jocasta,' his text message would say or 'Treat yourself, love,' – and Eve would also occasionally sub her, but she felt like she had reverted to a childlike relationship with Eve when it came to buying stuff for herself, almost having to seek her approval for each purchase. As such, she tended to avoid shopping.

"That's not a problem, Jocasta, as you know. Get what you want."

But it was a problem: that was the whole point.

Eve could probably have written a whole textbook on the need for the modern young woman to be self-empowered and independent, both financially and emotionally, but didn't seem to be able to apply that theory to the practise of parenting her daughter. Cassie knew why – the reason was evident – so she didn't kick too hard against the traces.

It was lucky that they bumped into Dev and Annie – well before the appointed lunchtime rendezvous – because Cassie and Eve were starting to get on each other's nerves. Eve wanted to drink it all in, stop at every stall, speak to every stallholder and Cassie made her disinterest in the whole tiresome process quite evident.

"What's the matter with you, Jocasta?" Eve asked more than once, the edge of irritation in her voice getting more pronounced.

"I'm tired, Mum, and it's hot."

"Well, I did say…"

"I'm not hungover, Mum," Cassie said. She wanted to add, 'Or shagged-out,' but didn't. "Just tired."

Eve didn't believe her – that was obvious from her disapproving look.

They started the polite bickering they often fell into, when Cassie suddenly sighted Annie at a pottery stall, seemingly intent on what Cassie believed was called a 'salt pig'.

"There's your friend, Mum," she said.

Eve seemed transformed. She fixed a smile on her face and brushed a few stray strands of hair off her brow.

"*Our* friend, Jocasta," she said. "Don't forget she got you that job."

Eve seemed less pleased to see Dev, though you had to know her like Cassie did to pick up on that fact. She greeted him nearly as enthusiastically as she greeted Annie. Annie was wearing a long gypsy dress – was that the appropriate adjective? – with a scarf around her head and Dev was wearing a tie-dye T-shirt, cut-off jeans and a battered straw trilby on his head. To Cassie, they looked like a couple of superannuated hippies, but as the market seemed full of superannuated hippies – both customers and stallholders alike – they fitted in well.

There were effusive greetings all around and then the decision was made to get coffee. Cassie wasn't consulted – she wasn't part of the decision-making process, it seemed – but she was glad to sit down under a canvas awning, on rickety chairs, around a battered table. She felt in dire need of caffeine.

Dev and Eve went to get the coffee and Cassie hoped she could just sit in companiable silence with Annie while they were gone. But Annie didn't do companiable silence – or silence, generally, for that matter – and started asking Cassie questions.

"So, Cassie, looking forward to coming back to work on Tuesday?"

Cassie loved the way that both Eve and Annie dignified what she was doing by calling it work. Work to Cassie was something you got paid for. Before Carys died – it was still hard to think of that word in connection with the girl – she'd had a part-time job, as well as studying, and was getting by.

"Well, you seemed to enjoy yourself yesterday," Annie added. "And I'm sure it's good to get out of the house occasionally."

Was it only yesterday? Cassie thought. Time seemed to be passing differently since she'd met Eliza.

Annie smiled at her – she was always smiling – but there was an unasked question in her eyes and Cassie knew what it was. Eve had obviously confided in Annie, told her about what had happened to Cassie after Carys died, how she had hardly left the house or left her room. How her father couldn't cope with it; didn't know what to do. *Thanks Eve*, Cassie thought, *for telling everybody my business.*

It was then that Dev and Eve came back, carrying a tray of disposable cups, and interrupted their conversation, which was fortunate for Cassie as she didn't really have an answer for Annie. And there was somebody else with them: a woman with white hair, cut stylishly around the nape of her neck and framing a face that reminded Cassie of Eliza. They didn't so much as look alike, but rather had similar features. The woman was wearing a shocking pink blouse over black leggings. *Surely they were a bit hot in this weather?* Cassie thought. But the woman, in fact, looked as cool as the proverbial cucumber. Cool in more ways than one, as she looked a little too stylish and chic for the laid-back atmosphere of the market.

"Look who we found in the coffee line," Dev said. "It's Kate."

The woman smiled, but her eyes, while friendly enough, were keen, as if she was taking these strangers in, measuring them.

"This is Eve... you've probably seen her around campus.... and her daughter, Jocasta."

Kate shook hands with them both. Cassie noted that her grip was quite firm, not limp like a lot of women's. Eve would have told her that this was a gendered assumption, but, in Cassie's experience, young girls were discouraged from shaking hands too vigorously in what was perceived as a masculine way.

"Eve has come to join Annie's department from the UK," Dev said.

Cassie zoned out for most of the ensuing conversation – mainly small talk, but also some shop talk about the university, which didn't interest Cassie at all. She noticed that Annie did most of the talking, along with Dev. Eve joined in on occasion, but Kate said very little, just watching the others and listening to them.

Cassie suddenly realised who Kate was. This was Kate Mackinnon, the expert on the Kabiri. She was the one Dev had said to ask about the local indigenous people, but, looking at Kate, seeing how formidable she was, Cassie was suddenly too shy to ask her about anything.

In fact, Cassie was feeling a little strange, almost as if she was underwater, and the voices were coming at her from a distance, from the surface far above her. Then, she realised her vision was shadowed, edged with black circles that were gradually expanding, as if her sight was telescoping down to nothingness. This had happened to her before – once, when she'd given blood – so she knew what was going on. *Fuck, I'm going to faint*, she thought, her eyes flickering shut.

But when Cassie opened her eyes again, she was somewhere else: among trees, with the waters of a stream running close by. It was early, just near dawn, and there was a mist hanging on the branches of the trees and on the bushes, like lace, waiting for the sun to burn it off and start the day. It was a strangely silent, pacific scene, but she had an overwhelming sense of foreboding. She knew something was wrong. She saw that she was on a trail – like a game trail, rather than a path – and she instinctively followed it.

As she walked, she saw that what she had taken for part of the brush, for undergrowth, were, in fact, shelters, with dark forms sleeping in them.

It was peaceful, quiet, so why did she feel so terrified? Then, she heard a noise, a sharp crack rending the morning air, muted by the mist, but still there, insistent. And a smell, a tang of what she knew was gunpowder on the air. She realised that she was hearing shots, coming from upstream. People poured out of their shelters, confused, not knowing what to do. Some of them – well practised – fled. Some looked up the creek in expectation or, perhaps, fear, hoping against hope that they were wrong about what they suspected was happening. That it was just white men out hunting.

But Cassie knew – how did she know? – that the fusillade of shots was not white men hunting. Or if they were after game, it was the human kind.

"No," Cassie said, "they're killing them. Somebody stop them! They're killing them all!"

Almost at her feet, an old, bent woman appeared, as if conjured from the earth. She was almost naked and her skin was like tanned leather. The woman reached out a hand to her and held her arm in an iron grip.

"Eliza, girl, we got to go. They'll be here soon enough."

The old woman tugged her back the way she had come.

Why did she call me Eliza? Cassie thought, then realised that she was seeing out of the girl's eyes. *How could this be?*

The old woman pulled her on, down the creek. The firing was coming nearer. The people were fleeing, but, surprisingly, they were doing so in almost total silence. She could hear cries, harness jingling – riders coming. However, there was hardly a sound from the passing of Eliza's people – because that's who they were – who took to the bush like so many rabbits.

"Eliza, come on!"

The old woman was leading her down to the creek. They waded over it, but suddenly Cassie looked down and let out a cry, which sliced the air around her, like a knife rending a sheet. The water was red... red with blood.

"You're okay," a voice said and she looked up into an unfamiliar face, framed by the whitest of hair.

"Who...?" she started asking.

"Kate. Don't you remember?"

"I do now," Cassie said.

She realised the woman was embracing her, holding her up on her chair.

"I just managed to grab you before you fell," she said, almost embarrassed. "I think you fainted."

"Oh, yes," Cassie said. "Sorry... and thank you for catching me." Cassie laughed. It was her turn to be embarrassed. "I feel so stupid."

"It happens," Kate said. "It's no big deal, but perhaps you should get yourself checked out. Here, take some water."

Kate's grip was firm and very comforting. As Cassie recovered, she let her go.

She could hear Eve in the background whispering to Annie, telling her that she'd had no breakfast, had a heavy night, had brought some girl home – this was said in the merest of whispers – and still wasn't really well.

"Shall we get one of the first aiders?" a voice asked – Dev.

"No, I think she's okay now. How do you feel, Jocasta?" Kate asked.

"I'm fine, thanks." She looked up into Kate's face, seeing Eliza there again. "I just went off there for a minute."

Kate, Cassie noticed, smelled of shower gel and expensive perfume. Chanel No. 5, she hazarded a guess, though she had no idea really, not being a perfume person.

"Well, it could be the heat. Perhaps you're a bit dehydrated, too. You're probably not used to the sun, coming from England... Could be low blood sugar... Anaemia, perhaps."

There were various explanations, but it was decided, almost by committee, that Cassie would be taken home and an appointment booked with the doctor to see if it was anything – perish the thought – more serious.

It was evident to Cassie on the ride home that Eve wasn't pleased with her. To give her mother her due, Eve was obviously concerned, worried even, but she was also irritated by the fact that her day, with her new best friend, had been spoiled because her daughter had been a silly girl, drunk too much the night before, eaten no breakfast, got dehydrated... Or perhaps it was Cassie's decision, which Eve had opposed, to get off her meds, to stop relying on them, which was the cause. Whatever the reason, it was probably Cassie's fault as far as Eve was concerned.

Cassie didn't care; she had too much to think about. She didn't know if what she'd experienced was a dream or a vision, but she'd seen something – something that she felt had really happened – and, what's more, she had seen it through Eliza's eyes.

CHAPTER FOURTEEN

Eve insisted that Cassie should spend the rest of the day in bed.

"You should get some sleep," she said. "You don't look like you got much last night." Eve looked at her closely. "You are really pale, Jocasta."

She didn't say any more, but accusations hung in the air like a bad smell. Cassie knew that Eve couldn't help it. It was easier for her to make Cassie responsible for her present condition – too much drink, too much sex or drug-taking – than to surrender to the underlying fear she harboured that Cassie was really ill.

Cassie didn't want to sleep, of course. There was too much going around in her head. However, she did get some comfort from the fact that she could still smell Eliza in her bed – just faintly, but the girl was still there. And this phantom presence helped her to recall – which she still could, vividly – the dream, vision or hallucination that she had experienced at the market. While she could remember what had happened with some clarity, she in no way understood it. She was convinced that what she had seen – whatever it was – had been through Eliza's eyes. After all, the old woman had called her 'Eliza', hadn't she?

But she knew that the fact the dream or vision had seemed so real and had involved so many of her senses – sight, hearing, smell, taste, even touch – didn't mean it was actually real. She'd had such vivid dreams after Carys died, dreams in which her love was still alive, in which she could feel her in her arms, smell her, taste her, hear Carys's voice whispering to her. Those dreams had been false – tricks her mind had played on her. Her doctor had told her they were an aspect of grief. Dreaming of your dead dears was, apparently, quite normal.

She must have drifted off eventually, because, in the early afternoon, she woke up abruptly from a dreamless slumber to the sound of voices on the veranda. Eve and somebody else. She was suddenly thirsty and walked to the kitchen to get a drink of water. As she did so, she couldn't help hearing what Eve was saying. It was mid-conversation, but she got the gist.

"It was probably a bit naïve of me to think that this move would solve the problem, but… well, what else could I have done?"

"You've done your best, love," the other voice said – it was Annie – "and you can't be taking all this on yourself. It's not going to do you any good in the end."

"But I can't help worrying… I told you she brought someone home last night… Some stranger."

"A boy?" Annie sounded slightly taken aback.

"No, a girl."

"Oh, so… just a friend." There was momentary relief in Annie's voice. "Or…"

"I don't know. I didn't ask… but the girl was strange."

"In what way?"

"I don't know, just weird. And I don't want to sound all middle-class and stuffy," Cassie thought that Eve sounded exactly like that, "but I don't want her hooking up with strangers, exposed to all sorts of bad influences… Oh, God, that sounds terrible, but you know what I mean."

Cassie had heard enough so she clicked the kettle on. The voices were suddenly silent and, within a few moments, Eve stuck her head around the door.

"Oh, so you're up. How are you feeling, darling?"

Cassie gave some non-committal answer. Eve looked a little shamefaced, caught out.

"Annie's here. Come and say hello, if you feel like it."

Tuesday came around, more quickly than Cassie would have liked. She had spent Sunday lounging around the house, using the excuse that she was tired so her mother wouldn't drag her out. She was left alone on Monday, but Eve had obviously made some arrangement with Linda, because the woman called around – to check on her, Cassie thought – and they ended up going to the supermarket together so that 'Cassie could help with the shopping bags'. It was a bit of a lame excuse for keeping an eye on her, but Cassie didn't mind that much. Linda was a chatterbox – quite exhausting, really – but it helped to take Cassie's mind off Eliza and the waking dream for a while, at least.

She travelled into the university with Eve on the Tuesday

morning at an obscenely early time – in Cassie's opinion, anyway – and she felt the usual wave of anxiety as Eve parked the car. She thought of Eliza, conjured up her face, and that got her through the doors of the library and into the pokey office where Lainey was already at work.

"Hi, Cassie, had a good weekend?" she asked.

Cassie just smiled and nodded. Lainey looked like she'd had a good weekend, but not much sleep. She was paler than ever and had dark circles around her eyes, but she also had that slightly self-satisfied air of repletion that suggested she'd enjoyed herself.

"There's some shelving and some labels to be done first…"

Cassie got on with it, relishing the mindlessness of her tasks. She liked these cool library corridors and the stacks of books that hid her from view, like some invisible sprite in a forest. She had drifted off into a reverie, shelving the books from the trolley automatically, when a voice startled her.

"Hi there, Jocasta. How are you feeling?"

It was Kate Mackinnon, dressed in a black linen trouser suit with a white blouse, looking severe and effortlessly stunning.

"Much better, thanks," Cassie said. For some reason, she felt herself blushing, as if she'd been caught doing something she shouldn't have.

"I'm glad about that," Kate said. "You gave us a bit of a scare for a while there."

Cassie shrugged. She didn't know what to say. A part of her hoped Kate would just go; another part of her wanted the woman to stay.

"Jocasta…" Kate started to say.

"Call me Cassie, Doctor Mackinnon," Cassie said. "Only my mum and dad call me Jocasta."

"Yes, quite an interesting name... bit of a mouthful. Cassie's better." Kate smiled, which was a rare occurrence, but worth waiting for. "And you should just call me Kate." She paused, as if thinking of how to put what she wanted to say. "Listen, Cassie... you said something when you were in that faint. Do you remember?"

Cassie wondered how much she should say. Could she trust this woman and, if so, did she want to confide in her? But Kate's eyes looked interested rather than judgemental and something else, too: encouraging.

"Yes, I do remember," Cassie said. "I was having a dream or a hallucination. There were people camping out by a creek—"

"What sort of people?" Kate interrupted.

"Aboriginal people," Cassie replied. "There was danger, people shooting upstream. It was confused but..."

Cassie's words trailed off. How could she tell Kate about Eliza, about seeing through Eliza's eyes? The woman would think she was mad.

"Tell me, Cassie," Kate asked, "had you been reading about this stuff – the displacements, the massacres – by any chance or seen something on TV?"

"No," Cassie said, but she said it hesitantly. She thought that Kate suspected she wasn't telling her everything.

"You know, Cassie, my people set much store by dreams and visions – you know I have Aboriginal heritage, don't you?" Kate didn't wait for an answer but went on. "So, I'm quite intrigued by what you saw."

Kate was looking at Cassie closely, making her feel embarrassed, but then Kate smiled and added, "I mean, look, it could have just been a touch of the sun." She laughed. "Or perhaps you have too much of an overactive imagination, Cassie."

Kate left her words suspended in the air around them like so many dust motes. She looked at her phone for the time, though she had an expensive-looking watch on her wrist.

"I've got to give a lecture in ten minutes, so I can't chat now, but give me a ring if you want to talk some more."

She thrust a card in Cassie's hand and left her there.

CHAPTER FIFTEEN

Cal Armstrong was waiting for her on the road as she made her way back from the mission church. She was among a bunch of girls, but they all fell away when they saw the white man. The stockmen didn't go to church much – they were a godless bunch, Mrs Cleary said – though, according to Jimmy, Cal was a Bible-thumper himself, but of a different sort to the Clearys. Eliza found this confusing, as it was difficult enough dealing with one type of Christian, without thinking that they had a whole lot of other mobs.

Cal was on horseback and he made out that he had just happened along, but Eliza knew that he had been watching for her. It was the one place you were sure to run into Eliza, on the road back from the mission church on a Sunday morning.

"I'll give you a ride, Eliza," Cal said. "Climb up behind me!"

But Eliza shook her head. "No, Mr Armstrong," she said. "I don't like horses."

I don't like you, is what I mean, she thought to herself.

"Come on," Cal said. "He won't bite and neither will I."

Eliza wasn't so sure of that.

"No, Mr Armstrong, horses frighten me," Eliza said, "and it wouldn't be proper."

If Eliza got on the white man's horse, he could take her anywhere, miles into the bush, and she wouldn't be able to stop him. And, like all stockmen, he had his whip and his gun…

"Proper, Eliza!" Cal laughed. "Who taught you that word? Mrs Cleary? Being proper is for white girls, not the likes of you."

He looked ahead of them as he said it, at the straggle of girls, at her friends. They were still loitering, walking slowly. And giggling and looking back at them, as if they were a courting couple. *Stupid girls*, Eliza thought. She knew that there were a few of them who would have accepted Cal's offer of a ride, either from naivety or avidity – white men would buy things for black girls to get in their draws, and to keep them sweet and willing – and they were probably jealous of the attention the foreman was lavishing on her.

"And you should call me Cal, Eliza," the man said. "After all, I'm a friend of your brother's."

Whatever Cal Armstrong thought, Eliza knew that he wasn't a friend of her brother's. James did little more than tolerate the white man.

"And that reminds me, I haven't seen Jimmy for a while. Have you any news of him?"

Eliza shrugged. "Haven't heard from him," she said, noticing that, though he was trying to mask it, Cal was disappointed.

"Isn't he due for a visit soon?" he asked.

"You know Jimmy," Eliza said, though she thought that

Cal probably didn't, "he comes and goes when he takes the notion to."

Cal rode beside her all the way home. He would not have thought of dismounting and walking with her. He would have done this for a white woman, Eliza knew – it would have been polite – but he didn't have to bother with such niceties with her.

Grace was outside the hut when they got to it. Her face wore the usual bland expression – the look she used when dealing with white men – but her eyes were suspicious and Eliza knew that she would have questions to ask her later. And she better have good answers or she would catch the edge of Grace's tongue, if she was lucky, or end up with a slapped face or arse if she wasn't. She would usually be in line for the latter rough treatment, whatever explanations she gave, if she gave her mother cheek, as Grace called it, answering with impudence or disdain. And Eliza often did; she couldn't help herself.

"Got any coffee on the go, Grace?" Cal asked, seeing the pot warming on the fire.

Eliza slipped into the dark interior of the hut, away from the white man's inquisitive eyes, to change out of her Sunday best. Eliza had two dresses and she kept the less shabby one for the mission church. She could hear Cal and her mother talking, laughing occasionally. She knew that Grace had to act that way, to laugh at Armstrong's jokes, allow his teasing and crude remarks. He was her boss, after all, and she had to court his favour, but it made Eliza angry. Sometimes, she wished she had Jimmy's gun – not that she'd have known how to use it – so she could blast away that smug look on

Cal Armstrong's red face. The white man always looked hot, his skin the colour of boiled lobster, and his red hair and mutton-chop whiskers added to the effect.

It was all just a fancy, of course, and she knew that she'd have to go back out into the sun and be civil to Cal Armstrong. And pleasant, but not too pleasant, as she didn't want to give him the wrong idea. When she did go out, she saw that Armstrong had a chipped enamel cup of coffee in his hand and was puffing away on one of the cheroots that he habitually smoked. He saw her looking at him.

"Want one, Eliza?" he asked. "Oh, I forgot, mission girls don't smoke."

Grace laughed, as if on cue, but it sounded false. Eliza knew that Grace wouldn't want her to smoke. She was supposed to be a cut above such behaviour. No rum either. She was meant for better things, or so Grace hoped.

Eliza heard the faintest of sounds from down the creek trail, just like the rustle of leaves in the wind, and she smiled to herself. She thought she knew what the sound foretold and she was right. It was Granny.

The old woman startled Cal Armstrong. He nearly jumped out of his skin.

"For Christ's sake, Grace, can you tell the old woman not to creep up on me like that?"

Grace tried to keep her face neutral, but Eliza could see that she was dying to laugh.

"And you'd better break the rum out for the old bat."

Cal didn't hide his disdain for Granny, but the old woman was singularly unaffected. She came up to the fire and crouched down by it, accepting the cup of coffee that Grace gave her. Cal looked uncomfortable at her closeness to him. He had the same sort of prurience about nudity and naked flesh that Mrs Cleary had, and Granny was hardly clothed.

"Any news of Jimmy, Grace?" Cal asked, making a conscious effort to ignore Granny.

Grace shook her head. "No, but he's due."

"Oh, when's he coming?" Cal asked, his interest piqued.

"Who can tell?" Grace replied.

The answer frustrated Cal, Eliza could see, but he did his best to hide it. "Well, you be sure to tell me if he comes, won't you?" he said.

"You got business with him, boss?" Grace asked. She said it casually, trying not to give offence, but when a white man asked after a black man, it was always a good idea to find out the reason for his interest.

"Me and Jimmy are mates, Grace, as you well know."

But Grace didn't look as if she knew this at all.

"Well, I'd better get on," Cal said, "and I'll see you later, Grace."

He stood up and went to where his horse was tied up to the hanging branch of a gum tree.

"And don't be late!" he added.

"I never am, boss," Grace said.

"Yes, you are – I'll have to start docking your money." He said it with a smile on his face, so Eliza didn't think he was serious.

Cal had a little trouble getting back in the saddle as the horse was skittish – *Perhaps there's a snake around*, Eliza thought – and he cursed the beast. Then, when he was sitting in the saddle, he paused as if remembering something.

"I meant to say, Grace, and seeing the old woman reminded me. Some of my men saw some of your mob around my cows the other day, driving them off, waving their spears at them."

Grace didn't react, but just stared up at the man blank-faced.

"You'd better tell them to back off. Leave the cows alone. If they don't, and if any of my stock come to grief, there'll be consequences."

With that he rode off, still cursing his horse.

"What did he mean, Ma?" Eliza asked, after he had gone.

"Just what he said, Eliza," Grace replied.

She wouldn't say another word on the matter. Soon, she hurried off to get to her work – feeding the stockmen – and Eliza was left with Granny.

"White men do love their cows; those black fellows need to watch out." The old woman said it as if it didn't affect her at all. As if it was somebody else's problem.

"I wish he wouldn't come around here," Eliza said.

"Who?" Granny asked.

"Who do you think, Granny?" Eliza said. The old woman was doing it again, Eliza thought, drifting away somewhere else in her head. "That Cal Armstrong, of course."

Granny laughed. "Oh, I don't think he comes here for you, girl."

"Who, then?" Eliza asked. "For Ma?"

Granny laughed. "No, not for her either," she said.

Eliza was confused. She didn't know what she meant, but the old woman wouldn't say any more.

CHAPTER SIXTEEN

Cal Armstrong wasn't the only one wanting to know when Jimmy was coming home. A few days later, Eliza was on her way home, taking the path up the creek, when she saw Vicky coming towards her, breathing heavily, as if she had been running.

"Eliza, stop there!" she said. "Your ma says not to go home. The police are there, looking for your Jimmy. I ran all the way to warn you."

But Eliza had to see for herself. She made her way up the trail, with Vicky close behind, nagging her, trying to pull her back.

"Come away, Eliza. Your ma said you weren't to come back until they were gone."

She ignored Vicky, pushing her hands away. She left the trail further up the path and crept through the bush, until she could see her house down below her. Vicky had followed her and they both crouched down, under cover, watching what was happening below. Grace was kneeling down on the ground with one of the blue-uniformed figures looming over her, while the other was inside the hut, making a lot of noise, occasionally throwing stuff – her and her ma's traps – out of the door or the window.

"What have they done to Ma?" Eliza asked in a whisper, but the answer was evident. Grace had a black left eye and a cut just above her right eye.

"They roughed her up," Vicky said. "It was that Irishman who did it, O'Halloran. Now he's ransacking your crib."

O'Halloran was one of a number of the white troopers who had been recruited from the Irish Constabulary. What he lacked in local knowledge, he made up for with brutality. His name was known even this far out in the countryside. To someone like O'Halloran, Grace was just a stupid gin, who understood the language of the fist much better than the Queen's English.

The noise from the house ceased and a trooper emerged. *That must be O'Halloran*, Eliza thought. A hulking sort of man with a habitual scowl, as if he heartily disapproved of this country and everyone in it.

"Anything in there, Mick?" the other trooper asked. He was a small, slight man, nervous-looking. He was clasping his carbine and looking around him, as if he expected a mob of black fellows to suddenly emerge from the bush and spear him.

"Nothing to indicate if that fucker has been around," the Irishman said. "Not even anything worth stealing."

"We should go, then, Mick, don't you think?" the other policeman said.

The Irishman looked at his companion with disappointment mingled with scorn.

"I'm not quite finished here, George. I think the old bitch might have some more to tell me."

Eliza knew what was coming. She almost broke cover, wanting to rail at the policeman, to throw rocks at him, but Vicky pulled her back down and put her hand over her mouth.

The Irishman was looking down at Grace, as if deciding what to do, where to start, when Cal Armstrong rode up.

"Can I help you, Constable?" he asked, addressing himself to O'Halloran.

"And you are?" the policeman asked.

"I'm Armstrong, foreman of this station, and this woman works for me."

"Oh, she does, does she?" the Irishman asked. "In what capacity exactly?" He said it with a smile on his face and the other policeman tried to suppress a laugh. It was clear what they were implying, but Cal, to give him his due, stared them down.

"She's the station cook." He looked down at Grace for the first time, then back at the Irishman. "Had an accident, has she?"

"Yes, fell over her own feet, the clumsy dear," the policeman said, smiling again.

Cal didn't return his smile. "What's your business here, exactly, Constable?"

"Well, apart from keeping the peace," O'Halloran replied, "we are looking for this gin's whelp. Black Jimmy by name."

"Black Jimmy, you say. Not the most original of names. Did you coin it yourself?" Cal asked.

O'Halloran was looking uncomfortable. He was of the opinion that the foreman was making fun of him.

"That's what he's known as in the goldfields. And that is the name I have."

"So, is he here?" Cal asked.

"Evidently not," the Irishman replied.

"Well, I suggest you get on your way," Cal said, "as it appears your business here is done."

O'Halloran stared up at Cal but didn't seem about to budge.

"There's a lot of bush between here and Gympie," Cal said. "You'd be advised to get some miles in before the sun goes down."

O'Halloran was still staring, defiantly, but the other constable, weighing up the situation, said, "Let's get going, Mick. He's not here."

O'Halloran did not acknowledge Cal as he rode off, but the other policeman did allow him a curt nod of the head.

Eliza and Vicky came out of hiding. Cal dismounted and lifted Grace to her feet with surprising gentleness.

"Eliza," he said, "bathe your mother's forehead and get a cold compress on that eye."

For once, she rushed to obey him.

"God knows what your brother is involved in," he said, as he mounted again and rode off.

Vicky's mother came over and, between the three of them, they got the crib tidy again. There was no real damage, just mess, so it didn't take too long. Grace sat by the embers of the fire, seemingly deep in thought. Granny appeared out of nowhere and went up to her daughter, closely examining her face.

"He clobbered you good, girl," she said, "but I've got

some stuff that will bring the swelling down and the cut is clean enough."

"Your ma got off lightly," Vicky's mother said.

Eliza knew what she meant. If it had been the black police and not the white troopers, Grace would have more than likely been dead. The black police didn't ask, they told in no uncertain terms. And the words they used – their currency – were bullets.

"What's Jimmy been up to, Granny?" Eliza asked. Their lives were fragile enough, precarious even, without her brother bringing more trouble on them.

"Stealing from the white men," Granny said. "Taking back what they stole already." She laughed, as if she had made the funniest joke.

"What do you mean, Granny?" Eliza asked.

"He's a bushranger, love, didn't you know?" Vicky's mother said.

CHAPTER SEVENTEEN

Sitting there on the slab of rock that jutted out into the creek, Cassie tried to imagine Eliza, to conjure her up. It was strange that she should miss her like this, feel her absence so keenly. It wasn't as if they had more than an acquaintance; they weren't even friends. They'd shared a bed together, that was true, but that fact in itself didn't signify much.

It had been almost a week since Eliza had stayed the night and though the interval had not taken the edge off the longing that she felt to see the girl again – a longing that she didn't fully understand – time was rubbing the shine off things and making the events of that evening seem less strange and more mundane. Perhaps Eliza was just, after all, a peculiar, wild girl, who she had encountered by chance and brought home.

⁂

Eve had asked after Eliza a few days after their visit to the market, when they were coming back from the supermarket. Conversations between them always went better when they weren't looking directly at each other but staring ahead at the traffic.

"Are you seeing your *friend* again this week?" Eve asked, with a certain studied nonchalance. She put a little too much stress on the word 'friend', as if emphasising that Cassie only had the one. It made Cassie feel pathetic.

"I don't know," Cassie answered.

"So, you've made no plans?"

"I don't think Eliza is the kind that make plans," Cassie said, though she didn't know if that was true. She knew hardly anything about the girl.

"Why don't you phone her or text?" Eve soldiered on.

"I don't think she's got a phone, Mum," Cassie said.

"Really?" Eve was surprised. "I thought everyone had phones these days, especially young people."

It struck Cassie, as Eve said the words, that Eliza didn't actually seem to belong to 'these days'. The girl was not only feral, but old-fashioned with it.

"She's off-grid, Mum," Cassie said, to shut Eve up. "Doesn't believe in electronic devices."

"Oh… good for her," Eve replied, which Cassie thought was ironic, because Eve was virtually attached to her phone and wedded to her laptop.

After her fainting fit at the market, Eve had taken Cassie to the doctor. The Australian health system was different from the UK one. It involved something called Medicare, but Cassie had left all the details of registration and billing to Eve. She had, however, insisted on seeing a woman GP as she didn't really want some creepy old man – or young man, for that matter – poking at her.

"Does it matter, Cassie," Eve had said, "the doctor's biological sex? Aren't we past that sort of thing?"

Cassie wasn't. "You tell me, Mum," she said. "You're the Women's Studies lecturer… or whatever it is you teach."

The doctor, Dr Shah, was a middle-aged woman, who told Cassie she had worked in the UK for ten years. "Though I couldn't put up with those cold, damp winters in the end." She was pleasant enough, but her hands were cold even through the latex gloves. "Your blood results won't be back for a couple of days, Cassie, but, as far as I can see, you look pretty healthy to me."

Cassie wondered if that was her professional opinion or more of a guess.

"You could do with putting a bit of weight on, mind," she said, laughing. "I'm usually in the position of telling people to shed a few pounds, but I think you need feeding up."

"I don't have much of an appetite these days," Cassie said.

"I see that you were on an antidepressant, fluoxetine, before you moved here, for six months or so. That can depress the appetite, but the effects should have worn off by now, if you've stopped taking them."

Cassie felt like she had been caught out. She should have thought of this before she came. The doctor was bound to have access to her medical records.

"It's up to you, Cassie, but it might help if you told me why you were prescribed fluoxetine – Prozac, specifically."

Cassie knew it would be there in black and white – that the doctor was just being polite, trying to make her feel she had the power in what was an intrinsically unequal relationship.

"I lost someone," she said.

Dr Shah nodded and said, "You were grieving."

"Yes," Cassie said, but it seemed such a minuscule acknowledgement of what had happened to her: her whole world had been upended and her life had slid away with it.

"Ever thought of counselling, Cassie?"

⁂

"The doctor seemed nice," Eve said when they were back in the car.

"Yes, she did," Cassie replied. 'Seemed' was the operative word. They all *seemed* nice, but they all wanted to pin Cassie down, like a butterfly that was collected and stuck to a card. To explain her. To, in effect, explain Carys away. Everybody was supposed to get over loss, weren't they? But what if you couldn't? What if you didn't want to?

"She doesn't think there's anything wrong with me, Mum," Cassie said. She thought that Eve was owed some reassurance. Eve just nodded gravely. She obviously didn't agree with the doctor's diagnosis, Cassie thought.

⁂

Sitting in the sun by the creek, thinking about Eliza, helped to distract her for a short time, but whatever she did, whatever occupied her mind, her thoughts always came back to Carys. Thinking of her dead dear was painful – sometimes it felt like she was being torn apart from the inside – but it was also pleasant. The memories were all she really had left. She had pictures, of course – who didn't these days? Phones and computers were full of them – but those captured instants, that trapping of ancient light, weren't the same as those memories where all her senses were in play. In them, she could hear Carys's voice, her laugh, smell her, taste her, all in her head. And she was terrified that they would fade, these recollections, and Carys would be irretrievably lost with them.

Suddenly, the sun was too hot, the gentle rush of the creek water no longer soothing, the insects were bothersome. In short, the moment was gone, so she retraced her steps up the creek and then ran back to the house. She was glad that her mother was out at work so there'd be no explanations or discussions. She'd done her stint in the library that week, so she did not have to engage with other people. Or so she thought, because as she came up the drive of her house, she could see Linda in her garden, feeding the kookaburras again.

They're wild birds, Cassie thought, *so why does she bother? Can't they feed themselves?*

She was hoping that she could slip in unobserved, or just exchange a brief greeting, but Linda saw her.

"Morning, Cassie, haven't seen you for a while. Why don't you come over for a catch-up?"

Cassie made an excuse. She was hot and sweaty and needed a shower.

"Well, shower away," Linda said, "and then come over for a coffee, if you like." She smiled. "Unless you're too busy of course…"

That was the decider. If she didn't go, she was basically saying that she couldn't spare a few minutes of her important time for an elderly – perhaps 'older' was the better, politer word – neighbour.

≫

"Any more fainting fits, Cassie?" Linda asked, as soon as she was sitting down on the terrace. Cassie still wasn't used to how direct Australians were: none of that British evasion and understatement when it came to personal issues. Cassie gave a weak smile and said that she was fine now and that she'd been to see the doctor.

"And I bet the doctor didn't tell you much you didn't already know."

Linda, as somebody who believed in alternative medicine, didn't hold much with conventional doctors. She looked closely at Cassie, holding the look a little too long for comfort.

"I bet you haven't had any breakfast. I'm right, aren't I?"

Linda tut-tutted some more and disappeared into her kitchen, coming back with a rather intimidating slice of pastry.

"Macadamia and salt honey tart," she said. "Not my own recipe, mind – got it off a cookery programme."

For all Linda's alternative credentials, she watched an awful lot of telly. The confection, topped with a blob of creamy yoghurt, went down well, but the sheer amount of sugar caused a rush that made Cassie feel as if she'd drunk three espressos, one after the other.

"Better, love?" Linda asked and Cassie nodded, her mouth still full. "Just don't let them get you on any meds!"

Too late for that, Cassie thought. Her body was probably still suffused with the residue of all the Prozac she had taken.

"I can always put you in touch with a yoga teacher or a meditation group," Linda continued. "Much better for you than pills."

"Thanks," Cassie said and smiled at the thought. She didn't think that either activity was for her.

"You don't look convinced, love, but bear it in mind."

Linda made more coffee. Cassie wanted to go, to be by herself, but she didn't want to be rude.

"How's the creek these days?" Linda asked. "No more strange sounds or voices?"

"No," Cassie said, but she hesitated for a moment and Linda picked up on it.

"Something else has happened, hasn't it, Cassie?"

Later, Cassie couldn't figure out why she had told Linda, regarding it as a strange lapse of her resolve, a drawing back of the curtain on something that was hidden. She didn't reveal everything, however. She told Linda about the first time she'd seen Eliza at the creek and describing the encounter reminded her how weird it had actually been. She said that she'd seen her again and spoken to her, glossing over the details and omitting the fact that Eliza had stayed the night. She hesitated before telling Linda about her vision-cum-hallucination at the market, but she did describe it eventually, again omitting some of the information.

On reflection, it all sounded farfetched to Cassie – more a symptom of a confused mind than anything else. To her surprise, though, Linda didn't look embarrassed or sceptical about the revelations. And she didn't scoff or try to explain them away.

"You know, Cassie, it could all just be a figment of your imagination, that's true, but it's possible it's something else…"

"What do you mean?" Cassie asked. "Hallucinations?"

It was as if, for that moment, Linda had drilled down into her innermost fear: that she was going slowly and quietly mad.

"Perhaps what you or someone else might think of as an internal phenomenon is actually an external one. Perhaps Eliza has a separate, but different existence."

"Are you talking about the supernatural?" Cassie asked. "Ghosts?"

That was what Eliza had called her, a ghost, but was it possibly the other way around and Eliza just didn't realise it?

Linda shook her head. "No, something else," she said. "I've always believed there were other realities. Parallel ones. And that time is cyclical. It's possible that Eliza is as real as you are but exists in another reality…"

"I don't really understand," Cassie said.

"I'm not explaining it very well," Linda said, "but I've always thought that there was more to the universe than our mundane little existence. And it's a good idea to keep an open mind about such things."

Cassie slipped away some time later. Linda had a client coming for a reflexology session. Cassie wasn't sure exactly what that entailed and wasn't going to ask, as Linda's explanations usually went into too much detail. She knew that Linda offered various massages – not the kind that led to what she believed was called a 'happy ending'. She could imagine that Linda's elderly but lithe body – a result of all that yoga – along with that wiry frame of hers would acquit itself well in such activity. It wasn't something Cassie particularly fancied herself – she was never good with intimate contact with other people; it tended to embarrass her – but Eve had seemed quite interested when Linda had told her she could sort out her blocked chakras. Cassie didn't know what blocked chakras were, but they sounded painful and perhaps explained her mother's habitually sour expression.

Cassie went home, did the washing up and attempted to clean up. She hated housework and had always left the mundane domestic task to Carys when they lived together. This wasn't completely down to Cassie's laziness; it was more to do with the fact that Carys was one of those domestic goddesses, who liked cleaning and all such ancillary activities. And, what's more, she had high standards: Cassie's attempts at vacuuming, dusting or polishing never quite came up to the mark.

So, after a perfunctory wipe around with a wet cloth – which was the sum total of her attempt at damp dusting – and a quick sweep of the floor, Cassie thought she'd done enough. Then, she filled the washing machine – she hardly had any laundry, but Eve had plenty, including all that fancy and fine lingerie that she had a penchant for and should have been hand-washed – and, when the cycle finished, she put it out on the line. The great thing about this climate was that things dried in a few hours.

Having done all these mundane tasks, Cassie knew that she would have something to offer up when her mother later questioned her on what she had done with her day, why she hadn't gone out and made more of it.

"Well, I did do all the housework," she would say and Eve, who hated domestic labour nearly as much as Cassie, suitably impressed, would give her a reprieve.

It wasn't until later when Cassie was sitting down on the sofa in the living room, blinds drawn, clicking through the various apps on the TV for something to watch, that she thought about what Linda had said about Eliza.

Cassie had just about convinced herself that Eliza was some strange, random girl who had come into her life, erupted into it and then quickly gone. She knew that Eliza was real, because she had shared her bed, slept with her and Eve had seen her. But it had been a long stretch to link Eliza with some of the other strange things that had happened to her: the things she had seen and heard at the creek and, more importantly, that dream or vision she had had when she fainted.

It had been easier for Cassie to dismiss all those experiences as something her troubled mind had conjured up and, in fact, she probably would have explained Eliza away in the same fashion if Eve hadn't happened to encounter her. But what Linda had said, or implied, had provided her with the beginnings of another explanation: that Eliza was intrinsically linked with those other happenings; that Eliza was part of the hallucination at the creek, one of those dark figures she had seen; and that the terrible events that she had experienced through the girl's eyes had happened and weren't just another twisting around of real and unreal things in her head.

And, if it was all real, it helped to explain Eliza's strangeness – that she didn't belong in this world but was part of another version of it, another time. Cassie couldn't help asking herself: *What exactly does it all mean and why is it happening to her?*

CHAPTER EIGHTEEN

Cassie's life drifted on and Cassie drifted with it like flotsam on the ebbing tide. She became used to the routine of her weeks: the Tuesdays and Thursdays spent at the library, then filling her time up as best she could in the intervening days. Weekends were mostly spent with Eve – her mother made an effort to spend time with her – and were usually social and hectic, so Mondays often came as a relief.

Cassie had never held out much hope that the volunteer work in the library would somehow propel her into university life, although she was almost certain that Eve had thought that it would. It hadn't done much more than reveal to her a world that she wasn't really part of. When she wasn't in the library, she passed her time getting lunch, reading a book or wandering around – a loner, or so it seemed to her, among the gregarious bands of students, who all appeared, at least in her imagination, to be having the best of times.

Her fantasy of Lainey spiriting her away and introducing her to the fun-loving party animals of the local sapphic underground – or overground, she should perhaps say, as this was a liberal town – hadn't been realised so far and was unlikely to be. Lainey was friendly enough in a distant way, but – and this was obvious – she saw Cassie as a young, rather awkward girl – not date material – who was only doing the job by the grace and favour of Lainey's personal demi-goddess and head of department, Annie. And Lainey wasn't exactly a laugh a minute, anyway. Cassie came across her more than once, either blowing her nose and wiping her eyes – hay fever, Lainey hastily explained – or staring off moodily into the distance, as if yearning for better times or better places. It was all rather disappointing, Cassie reckoned, but only vaguely so, as she hadn't really expected much from the job. Generally, Cassie didn't expect that much from life these days.

Eve was still pressing her to get a paying job or to enrol on a course at the university or at the local equivalent of a further education college, which made for some awkward car journeys on the way to or from work, but Cassie could never seem to summon up the energy to do anything about it. Instead, she spent her spare time running, laying about the house or talking to Linda.

"Don't you get bored, love?" Eve asked her more than once.

The frank answer would have been – if Cassie ever said any more than that she was okay and her mother shouldn't worry about her – no, she didn't. Painful as it was, she would often spend hours thinking of Carys – her smell, her taste, the sound of her voice – as if trying to conjure her up, to bring the dead back to life. She even thought of the bad times – the arguments, the break-ups, temporary as they always were, the petty bickering and irritations – as if trying to test herself, their relationship, to call it into question, but it never worked. Instead, she remembered those days, difficult as they were, with affection. And then there was Eliza; when she wasn't thinking of Carys, she was thinking about her wild girl, willing her to come back to her, until, one day, she did.

It had happened in the strangest way. A knock on the screen door had woken Cassie up from a day nap on the sofa, from a daydream of other times when she had been happy, and she had padded through the kitchen and blearily peered out at Linda standing on the terrace.

"Just woken up, love?" she asked. You couldn't fool Linda, but she passed no judgement on Cassie sleeping the day away, whereas Eve would have.

"Look, Cassie, me and a mate are taking a picnic down to the lake… It's not too hot today; there's some cloud… So, if you'd like to come along…"

Cassie was going to say no, almost automatically, but the mention of a lake intrigued her. "What lake?" she asked.

Linda looked at her with some amusement.

"Must have been a deep sleep, love. You know… the lake that's right on your doorstep."

In theory, the lake *was* close by, but getting to it from Cassie's house involved a trek through a fringe of bush that was the opposite of welcoming, so Cassie had never gone there. Never so much as glimpsed its waters.

"That would be great," Cassie said, brightening up.

"There we are," Linda said. "Then change out of your jammies and get ready. We leave in twenty minutes."

When Linda had said they were going to the lake, what she had actually meant was that they were going to the western side of the lake, which was a substantial body of water, where there was a strip of shore designated as a public park and a beach for launching canoes and kayaks. Motorised craft were banned because of the abundance of birds and other wildlife. So, though the lake *was* almost on Cassie's doorstep, it took a good forty minutes to actually get there in Linda's car on a circuitous route via back roads. It took longer than it should have, too, because Linda kept getting lost. This was partially due to the fact that her friend, Irene, kept giving her the wrong directions.

"Turn here, love!" she would order and then have second thoughts. "No, not here, love. Back there, I meant."

Linda took it all good-naturedly, laughing and saying, "For God's sake, Irene, stop changing your mind!"

Irene was a small, rather rotund woman with a mass of curly black hair, wearing what Cassie thought was a kaftan, but which, Linda later informed her when Irene had dozed off, was actually a *muumuu*. Whatever it was called, it was a long, shapeless robe, which effectively covered most of Irene, because – so the woman informed them – though she had olive skin – quite dark olive – she was a 'martyr to the sun'. She smoked continuously and, as a result, smelled permanently of fags and perspiration, because she was, as Linda said under her breath, a 'sweater'.

The park was a little disappointing. It was an arid expanse of patchy grass and dirt, shaded by the ubiquitous gum trees, with picnic benches, tables and concrete barbecues. Linda drove almost to the water's edge, parked the car and produced from her rather small boot two sun loungers, a camping chair and all the stuff for the picnic in a couple of cool boxes. Linda set the sun loungers up and Irene decanted herself into one, only moving subsequently to top up her own glass of wine or to shuffle slowly to the toilet for a pee.

Linda's and Irene's idea of a picnic seemed to be quite static: sitting in the sun loungers, chatting and drinking wine from the box they had brought with them.

"Best Aussie invention ever," Linda said, laughing. "The wine box."

It was slightly worrying as Linda was the driver – though, on reflection, Cassie reckoned that she only downed a couple of glasses at most, while Irene, in contrast, gradually drunk herself into a semi-comatose state.

"Lovely being here, isn't it?" Linda said to Cassie, who was perched on the camping chair a few yards from the lake shore.

In truth, it wasn't exactly lovely, but it was different and, in some ways, remarkable. Because the lake wasn't what she'd expected. For a start, it was so shallow that even small rowing dinghies could hardly navigate their way across it without touching the bottom, especially in summer when it almost dried out. Its opalescent greenish-grey waters gave an illusion of depth and had an eerie quality to them, as if strange alien creatures were lurking underneath. It was hemmed in by a fringe of bush that came right down to its shores. In places, mangroves reached out into the lake – a sort of transitionary belt between land and water.

"The creek runs into the lake," Linda said. "Your creek."

It's more Eliza's creek than mine, Cassie thought.

"Right over on the east side," Linda said. "You can just about see it."

Just about and not at all clearly; only a vague smudge of trees in the distance, which might be marking the mouth of Blood Creek.

They ate almost as soon as they arrived. Linda had produced a spread of various salads, as well as a big bowl of couscous, accompanied by marinated tofu. To give the woman her due, it was all quite tasty, except the tofu, but Cassie had never really been able to see the point of tofu. After Linda had cleared the plates away and sealed the remaining salad back in its boxes, she produced, with a conjurer's flourish, some more of her macadamia tart, which Cassie was getting quite partial to.

Irene, by this time, had dozed off and Linda leaned over to Cassie and whispered conspiratorially, "You should tell Irene what's been happening to you, about that girl. She feels things, you know. She's a bit of a medium."

It wasn't something that Cassie really wanted to share with Irene, who seemed to regard her with mild disdain, due to the fact that she obviously considered Cassie to be an intruding and unwelcome presence.

Seeing her reluctance, Linda quickly added, "She goes to a spiritualist church, you know, in Brisbane." She said it as if it made a difference.

When Linda closed her eyes and seemed intent on her own afternoon snooze, Cassie decided to go for a walk. She told Linda, who mumbled, "Okay", then added as an afterthought, "Don't get lost, mind!"

Cassie headed towards a signpost that she could see at the southern end of the car park, which marked the beginning of a trail that followed the lake shore.

CHAPTER NINETEEN

She wasn't lost, Cassie told herself, because she could see the waters of the lake through the trees a little way off in front of her. That meant she could always make her way back – in theory. But the bush was thick, impenetrable in places, and there were the mangroves, which were almost impassable. There was also the feeling she couldn't shake off that somebody – or something – was watching her.

She didn't know how she had wandered off the trail; in fact, it might have been truer to say that the trial had wandered away from her. Because when the path she was on petered out, she had tried to retrace her steps back to what she'd belatedly realised was the main path. She'd inadvertently detoured down a game trail, she thought, and while trying to figure out in her head where it ran, she'd taken a shortcut. That was a mistake. Never try and take a shortcut in the bush – she could almost hear Linda saying it.

When she managed to get over her fear of snakes and any hostile insect life, and having reassured herself that they were too far south for salt-water crocodiles – though there was always a chance that one might have wandered three hundred miles or so off-course and was eyeing her up – she stopped her headlong rush towards the water, which was getting her nowhere fast, to take stock of her situation. She wasn't carrying any food or water and her phone couldn't get a signal. She could have tried a 911 call, hoping that some network might pick it up, but she thought it was a little too soon for that. But stopping, looking around her and listening confirmed her suspicions: there was something or someone out there and that something or someone definitely had her in their sights.

Realising this, she felt scared for the first time in her little adventure. Up until then, she had been hot, bothered and a little dismayed, but all this was replaced with a stark feeling of fear. Trying not to panic, she walked a few paces on and then shrank down in the shadows of a big old gum tree, taking shelter at its base, where there was some cover provided by the undergrowth of grass and shrubs. Listening intently, she heard the sounds of whatever it was stalking her. Just faint rustles and footfalls, but enough to confirm her fears.

Cassie had no sort of weapon and nothing that could be used as one, not even a water bottle. She was dressed in shorts and a T-shirt, with trainers on her feet. She had no choice but to either stay there or to run. Running was probably futile, she thought, but action seemed preferable to inaction at that moment. She rose up a little from her crouch to have a look and got a glimpse of a pair of shadowy figures advancing towards her. The sight was more confusing than frightening, because these figures were barely clothed – or so she thought, as she'd only got a peep at them – and they were armed with spears or harpoons. How could that be? Were they perhaps fishermen hunting fish in the shallows and was it all a misunderstanding? A case of mistaken identity, with them thinking she was... what? A fish? It seemed a rather facile explanation, but how else to explain it?

Just when these possibilities were rinsing around in her mind and stopping her from taking to her feet – in case she got speared by accident – she heard a cry breaking through the silence of the afternoon. It could have been a kookaburra, but it was repeated twice more at regular intervals like a signal. The movement around her stopped and then she heard an exchange of voices. She couldn't understand the language, but whoever was speaking sounded angry. She rose up again to have a look and that's when she saw Eliza, very close it seemed, talking to two young men. They both had the bodies of athletes: lean, sculptured, with each muscle and rib delineated in flesh. This could be seen quite clearly, because both of them were almost naked, apart from brief strips of hide or cloth, which hardly covered their genitals.

They didn't seem pleased to see Cassie, or Eliza for that matter, but they reserved most of their antagonism for Cassie, scowling at her. Cassie looked helplessly at Eliza, who was doing her best to placate the two boys – Cassie thought they looked young, possibly teenagers. The two boys didn't seem to be moved by Eliza's words and kept looking at Cassie. But then, abruptly, they stopped talking and walked off, almost knocking Eliza down in the process as they brushed past her.

Eliza looked at Cassie questioningly. "What are you doing here, ghost girl?"

She didn't exactly sound pleased to see Cassie, but, after a moment's hesitation, she came up and took her hand and led her away. At that moment, Cassie would have followed her anywhere.

Eliza led her to a pool of clean water, just up from the shore. Eliza seemed to find her way easily, whereas Cassie made it heavy going.

"You can drink, Cassie. It's sweet and clean," Eliza said.

Cassie did; she drank deeply. She hadn't realised how thirsty she was. Eliza took a cotton wrap from around her shoulders and wetted it. She rubbed Cassie's face and hair, making her gasp.

"Am I hurting you?" Eliza asked, though she didn't stop.

"No," Cassie replied, "it feels good."

The cloth was cool and so were Eliza's hands.

"What are you doing here, girl?" Eliza asked again. "It's dangerous for you to be here."

"I got lost," Cassie said, finally admitting it.

"Well, you're lucky. If I hadn't been with Granny and if the call hadn't gone up that there was a strange white spirit-girl wandering by the lake, you might have come to grief."

"What do you mean?" Cassie asked.

"Well, those boys might have speared you," Eliza said. "Or fucked you... they'll try and fuck anything. And if they'd fucked you, they'd have probably speared you afterwards."

"No, really," Cassie said. She was having difficulty taking the girl's words in.

"Yes, really," Eliza said. "They'd have thought you were either a bunyip or a white girl ghost and they don't like either of those. Or they might have eaten you."

"Fuck no!" Cassie said, shocked.

Eliza laughed. "No, course not. I was only joking about the eating bit and, besides, you're too scrawny to make a good meal."

She suddenly put her arms around Cassie and hugged her tight. She was incredibly strong for such a slight girl; it was like being hugged by a small bear.

"Still, it's good to see you, Cassie. I've missed you. It's been a while."

Has it been a while? Cassie asked herself. *It's only been a few weeks... was that a long time?*

"I missed you, too, Eliza."

Eliza smiled and took her hand. "Come," she said.

"I should get back," Cassie said.

"Back to where?"

Cassie gestured towards the west. "The park," she said. "There's someone waiting."

Eliza looked at her suspiciously. "You're talking rubbish, girl... you've had a touch of the sun...there's nothing there, no one."

And it was true, Cassie saw, when they came out onto the lake shore. Where the park should have been, off in the distance, was the usual monotonous fringe of trees running all around the lake.

"But what happened?" Cassie asked.

Eliza nodded sympathetically. "The same thing that happened to me, Cassie, do you remember? I ended up in your ghost world and now you've ended up in mine."

"No, that can't be..." Cassie started saying, but she found that she was lost for words.

"Come on, Cassie," Eliza said, "forget about it. We can have fun together."

Fun? Cassie thought. *When did I last have fun?* But then she realised that Eliza was young... younger than she was, she figured... and there was something innocent and childish about her for all her occasional fierceness. Also, why shouldn't they have fun? She didn't know where she was or what had happened, but she was with Eliza and that was the important thing.

"Okay, Eliza," she said and the girl hugged her again.

CHAPTER TWENTY

"You live here?" Cassie asked.

All around, at the mouth of the stream, there were brush shelters and some tents, where people were waiting out the heat of the day; men mending nets and women preparing what Eliza called 'bush bread' – Cassie would have called them 'dampers' – from a mixture of seeds or flour to accompany billy cans of sweet tea.

"No," Eliza said, laughing, "I live with my ma in her crib... her house... just like you do. Remember, I met your ma." Eliza made a face. "I think I gave her a scare that time. These are my ma's people, so I come and visit them."

"They live here?" Cassie asked, because it hardly seemed permanent.

"Sometimes," Eliza replied, "or along the creek. They often up sticks and go to the mountains or down to the coast, though, depending on what they fancy eating."

Eliza was wearing the same dress she'd had on both times Cassie had seen her. She noticed that some of the people around her were dressed traditionally – or what she thought was traditionally – but some of them had western clothes. Old-fashioned western clothes. It was like being in some sort of historical film.

"What year is this?" Cassie asked, a cold feeling spreading from the pit of her stomach, a nausea that was making her feel giddy.

"What do you mean?" Eliza asked, smiling. "White man's year?"

"Yes," Cassie said.

Eliza thought for a moment before answering. "According to Mrs Cleary – she's my teacher – it's 1872."

"Who's on the throne?" Cassie asked, hardly managing to voice the question.

"That one's easy, Cassie," Eliza said. "You should know that, girl. Everybody does, even my granny. It's Queen Victoria, of course."

Cassie felt that familiar feeling: heart racing, breath coming in short rasps. Panic attack, she knew.

"What's the matter, Cassie? You're whiter than ever. And that's saying something." Eliza chuckled, but then stopped, seeing how stricken Cassie looked.

"But how do I get back?" Cassie asked.

Eliza shrugged. "I know, let's ask Granny."

The old woman that Eliza led her to was the same one she had seen in her hallucination. The woman looked at Cassie without any astonishment or curiosity, as if she was as familiar with Cassie as Cassie was with her. She gazed at Cassie for a long time, saying nothing, while Eliza sat expectantly.

Every so often, Eliza attempted to say something, but her granny stopped her, "Shush, girl, stop your babbling."

At last, the old woman announced, "This girl ain't no ghost. She's flesh and blood."

"I knew that, Granny," Eliza said, indignantly, but her granny ignored her.

"And she must get back to her own world."

"Aww, Granny, can't she stay here? At least for a bit," Eliza asked, sounding more like a child than ever.

"No, girl," Granny said, looking at Cassie, "and she knows it. Don't you, white girl?"

"Yes," Cassie said, but she wasn't completely sure. Why not stay here with Eliza in the past? What did the future have to offer her?

Granny shook her head, as if she had intuited Cassie's reluctance. "No, girl. You have to go back, otherwise it's all fucked up. You know that."

Eliza looked upset but the old woman was adamant. "You spend the afternoon with her, girl. And make the most of it. But you get her back to the other side of the lake by sunset, where she tells you she should be. You hear? Someone will be calling her back."

Eliza nodded but didn't seem convinced.

"It's important, Eliza. You do what I say."

⋙

Eliza led her off, away from her people, holding onto her hand again. Like she wasn't going to let go. Cassie was glad to get away from the camp, because, despite Eliza's assurances, she could see that her people were not comfortable about having this strange white girl there. White people were trouble, Eliza had told her before, and Cassie thought that was why people were looking at her so suspiciously.

They walked by the lake shore and Eliza suddenly tugged her hand and said, "I know a place where we can swim."

There was a stream that flowed into the lake further on and, at its mouth, the flow of the water, gentle as it was, had scooped out a pool. Eliza stood on the edge of the water and tugged off her dress. As Cassie expected, she was naked underneath.

"Come on, Cassie," Eliza said. "You're not shy, are you? We're just girls together."

Eliza dived into the water and disappeared.

Cassie hesitated. She *was* shy. And it wasn't just that: she'd never really thought that her body was all that attractive – in fact, she thought it was ugly – and she was scared that Eliza would think so, too. But Eliza surfaced, her wet hair plastered to her head, and said, mockingly scolding her, "Come on, Cassie, get yourself in."

Cassie took a deep breath and stripped off. She was going to keep her pants on, but she thought, *Fuck it!* and waded into the water naked after Eliza.

Eliza was more like a seal than a human being, swimming, diving and frolicking in the water.

⁂

Later, they lay on a strip of sand on the stream bank to dry off. Cassie couldn't help looking at Eliza. She was beautiful.

Eliza saw her looking and smiled. "I'm a brown-skinned girl, Cassie, but you don't seem to mind that."

"Why would I?" Cassie was a little taken aback: Eliza had completely misunderstood her gaze.

"Most white people do," Eliza said. "I think Mrs Cleary does, really, in her heart, though she wouldn't say it to me."

"But why?"

Eliza looked serious for the first time since they'd met that afternoon. "It reminds white people where I came from and that my pa, whoever he was, was white. White people don't like the idea of mixing their blood. White men want to sleep with black women, but they scorn the babies that come from it."

"Oh," Cassie said, "it never crossed my mind."

Eliza sat up and patted Cassie's thigh. She was just being friendly, but the intimacy of the gesture took Cassie's breath away. "I know it didn't, dear Cassie, and I think that perhaps your world may be better than mine… in some ways, at least. Black fellows have a bad time in this one."

"I think it is better, Eliza, in some ways. Not so much in others."

Eliza smiled. "You got a boyfriend, Cassie?"

"No – perish the thought," Cassie said.

Eliza laughed. "I keep away from boys," she said, "for obvious reasons." She made a pregnant belly with a gesture of her hands.

"I keep away from them, too," Cassie said. *Not for the same reason as you*, she thought.

Suddenly, Eliza sat up and looked down at Cassie's body. "I didn't think you could get any whiter," she said. "You look like a pail of milk."

Cassie couldn't help laughing. "I'm not as pretty as you, Eliza," Cassie said, sadly.

"Nonsense, girl. If I was a boy, I'd try and kiss you," Eliza said.

Fuck, thought Cassie, *I wish you would, just once.*

Eliza stood up and shucked her dress on. "I've got to get you back or you'll be stuck here and Granny will tell me off."

She tugged Cassie to her feet and laughed at the strangeness of her clothes as she dressed, asking why Cassie was walking around in her underwear. Cassie couldn't help blushing.

"You've got a bit of colour, now," Eliza said and they both laughed again.

When they got to the western end of the lake, dusk was falling and a mist was hanging on the fringe of the water, draping itself on the mangroves at the edges.

"I don't want to leave you, Eliza," Cassie said. She really didn't. It felt at that moment that Eliza was the only thing anchoring her to the world, to life.

Eliza hugged her and kissed her lightly on the mouth. It was just a brief touch of her lips on Cassie's, like the brush of a butterfly's wings and as delicate. She tasted of salt, like the lake water. "I know, dear Cassie, but you've got to."

"But where... how will I know?" Cassie asked.

She was confused all of a sudden, but then she heard a voice calling, "Cooee, Cassie! Where are you?"

"Go, quickly!" Eliza said.

Cassie looked back once, but Eliza was gone. She stumbled forward into the mist – or was it rather a veil before her eyes, like a membrane? – and then saw the end of the trail. She followed it until it came out at the car park, where Linda was waiting.

"There you are, Cassie. Had a nice walk?"

"How long was I gone?" Cassie asked. Hadn't it been hours?

"I don't know," Linda said. "An hour and a half, perhaps a bit more."

"Really? It seemed longer."

"You okay, Cassie?" Linda asked. "You look like you've seen a ghost."

In a way, I have, Cassie thought.

"I'm okay," she said, "just a bit tired and in need of a drink."

Something strong, she thought, *not water.*

CHAPTER TWENTY-ONE

When she got back to her granny, as the light suddenly faded away like a blind being drawn, Eliza had lots of questions.

"If Cassie isn't a ghost, Granny, what is she?"

"Eliza," Granny said, "you already know the answer. She's a girl like you, not a ghost, a bunyip or any other monstrous creature."

"But how can that be, Granny?" Eliza asked. "And she's similar to me, that's true, but different. She dresses differently, not like other white people, and her house... Well, I've never seen some of the things inside it before. It was like a rich white man's house, like you see in pictures, but I don't think that she's a rich girl, just a normal one."

Her granny was watching her closely, a slight smile on her lips.

"And she asked me what year we were in... white man's year, Granny... and who the queen was."

Granny nodded, as if she understood everything, but didn't deign to explain it all. "Eliza, girl, listen," she said. "White men think that time passes and then it is gone, but you know… you're a clever girl, Eliza… that days and years go in circles. Daylight comes, then night, then day again."

"I know all that, Granny," Eliza said.

"Listen, girl, just listen," Granny continued. "What white men call time doesn't fly straight, but it circles like a buzzard. And these circles of time rub up against each other and sometimes, where they rub, the skin between these different worlds becomes thin…"

"So people can cross, like Cassie did from her world to mine and back again."

"Yes, girl," Granny said, "but not everyone. And I think they can only do so when somebody's spirit calls to them, invites them."

"But I didn't invite Cassie and she didn't invite me."

Granny shook her head. "Pay attention, Eliza! I said your spirit invited her and her spirit invited you. You didn't know anything about it. It could have happened in dream time."

"But if what you say is true, Granny," Eliza said, "why Cassie and why me?"

"I don't know the reason, love, but I do know one thing," Granny said. "If that girl ever calls you again, you go. Without question. Don't look back, just go with her."

The old woman's serious tone rendered Eliza speechless for once.

"Now, Eliza," Granny said, "you go and get me some rum. All this thinking has given me a thirst."

Eliza made her way back to her house in the dark to get a bottle of rum for Granny. Her mother always had some stashed away, traded off the stockmen. In fact, her mother had a little sideline in rum, using it to barter with her own people. Eliza wasn't afraid of the dark. She'd walked this way so many times that her feet would have probably found the path even if she'd been sleeping. There wasn't much to be afraid of: Mrs Cleary had done a good job of clearing her mind of the monsters and demonic creatures that black children were brought up to fear. The white woman had replaced these terrors with fear of Hell and the Devil. But Eliza didn't think the Devil was abroad that night; there was no sulphurous reek in the air.

She still harboured a certain trepidation about the two policemen. She thought that they were long gone, but was concerned that they might have doubled back to wait for Jimmy. However, she knew that white men could never keep quiet, couldn't move through the bush without making noise, or even lay up in cover without some fuss. So, when a dark figure stepped out of the blackness in front of her, blocking her path and making her nearly jump out of her skin, she knew it wasn't a white man.

She was just on the point of bolting into the bush, when a voice said, "Hello, sis, how've you been?"

It was too dangerous to take Jimmy home to Ma – one of the stockmen might have seen him coming or going and sent word to the constables – so they made their way down the creek to the camp and Granny. Jimmy had to retrieve his horse first and they had to go slowly so the horse could pick its way along the creek bed.

Eliza knew it was Jimmy as soon as he opened his mouth, but he seemed much changed, almost a stranger to be shy of. When he hugged her on the path and lifted her off her feet, laughing, he smelled different, like a white man, of leather, tobacco and horse, stale sweat and mildew. And he was also no longer the wild, cheeky boy he had been, always ready to make mischief, to laugh. He seemed much older, quieter, sadder even.

Granny was pleased to see him – she didn't show it much, but her eyes lit up hungrily when he came into the light – and the fact that he produced a bottle of rum from his saddlebag added to the sense of occasion.

"How long you staying, Jimmy?" Granny asked, after she'd fed him – there was fish from the lake, plums and bush bread – and they were settled around the fire, a billy on for tea and the rum bottle uncorked.

"Just tonight, Granny," Jimmy said.

"You on the way to somewhere?" Granny asked.

"Going up to the high country, Granny. Got some fellows on my trail."

Granny just nodded, but Eliza asked, "You in trouble, Jimmy? The police came looking for you."

Jimmy smiled. "Got into some bother, sis, in the goldfields, but those fat-arsed coppers are too slow to keep up with me."

"They were here, Jimmy," Eliza said, without thinking. "They lay hands on Ma. Bashed her about a bit."

Granny darted a glance at Eliza and she realised that she shouldn't have said anything. He'd want to get even with the constables now. Jimmy's face had clouded, some brightness had gone from it.

"Is Ma okay?" he asked. "They didn't hurt her bad, did they?"

"Just roughed her up a bit, Jimmy. It's fine," Granny said, looking darkly at Eliza.

Jimmy didn't look as if he thought it was fine.

"You going to see her, Jimmy?" Eliza asked.

He shook his head, smiling sadly. "Can't risk it, sis, but you'll tell her, won't you? Tell her I'll be thinking of her." He laughed. "Give her a kiss from me, Eliza. A wet, slobbery one."

Eliza didn't kiss her ma much – they were always at odds these days – but in this case, she decided that she'd make an exception.

He left early in the morning, before it got light, while Granny was still asleep. He was quiet and meant to slip out without waking them, but Eliza, even in her sleep, could sense his going.

"Go back to sleep, sis," he said. "I've got to go, but no need for you to stir."

She insisted and walked with him up the creek bed and into the bush, with Jimmy leading his horse.

"A day's good riding and I should be well clear of the coppers." He grinned. "They'll have the devil of a job finding me in the hinterland." He embraced her and then swung up onto his horse.

"Take care of yourself, Jimmy," she said, trying to stop the tears coming.

"Oh, I will, Eliza," he said, tapping his hand on the revolver holstered at his belt. He dug his heels gently into the horse's flank, urging the creature on. As it set off, he shouted back, "Don't forget me!"

He was smiling as he said it, as if it was a joke, but she knew she never would.

CHAPTER TWENTY-TWO

They dropped Irene at her home on the way back to Linda's. She lived in the small town nearby, which seemed mostly to be a sort of suburban dormitory for people working up and down the coast. She lived in a non-descript little house on a street of closely huddled buildings, all looking tired and shabby. *A bit like Irene herself*, Cassie thought, a little unkindly.

Irene had been supposed to come back to Linda's house for dinner, but she was feeling unwell. Quite overcome, according to Linda.

"She felt an atmosphere, Cassie. Some sort of psychic disturbance. It took her funny," Linda said, her face deadly serious.

Cassie thought that Irene had probably been 'taken funny' due to the amount of Sauvignon Blanc she had sloshed down her, but, to be fair to the woman, you could say that there *had* been a psychic disturbance. What else would you call what had happened to Cassie?

"Irene's very sensitive," Linda said as they drove off. "Her Greek grandmother was some sort of witch or wise woman, and she inherited her second sight from her."

Cassie had always regarded such things with a healthy dose of scepticism, but she was starting to have her doubts now. In fact, she was starting to have doubts about most of the things she'd always taken for granted.

They got home as the light was fading. Cassie helped Linda unload the car, putting the chairs back in the garage.

"Cup of tea, love?" Linda asked, but Cassie declined the offer.

"I'd better get home," she said. "Mum will be expecting me."

"Yeah, she looks like she's busy in the kitchen," Linda replied. "Just bear in mind, love... all that stuff we were talking about... you could always have a chat with Irene, you know. She knows a lot about that sort of thing."

Cassie said that she'd think about it, but she had no intention of discussing anything with the woman. As she made her way up her own drive, she started to wonder if Irene's presence was the reason she had been invited to the picnic in the first place. She just hoped Linda hadn't told the woman about what she'd heard and seen. It had all gone beyond talking to people now, whether doctors or psychics.

Eve was cooking their dinner, which was, in itself, a rare occurrence.

"Did you have a good time with Linda?" she asked.

Cassie had texted her mother to tell her where she was going, like a dutiful daughter. There was a bottle of wine in the fridge and she poured herself a glass. She had got out of the habit of drinking while on her prescription drugs, but she felt like she needed one now.

"Want one, Mum?"

Eve raised her eyes in a questioning look. "Do you think you should, Cassie?"

"I'm off the meds, now, Mum," Cassie said, "so it's fine."

Eve looked at her closely and then nodded. "Well, if you're sure."

"It only used to make me sleepy, anyway, if I had a drink," Cassie said.

Eve didn't look too convinced, but she indicated that she did want a glass as well.

"You're going to a lot of trouble, Mum," Cassie said, as a suspicion started growing in her head. "Someone coming over?"

"Yes," Eve said, a little too nonchalantly, "I've invited Annie."

"No Dev?" Cassie asked.

"No, not tonight," Eve said.

"I thought they were joined at the hip," Cassie snapped back.

Eve sighed. "Okay, Cassie," Eve said, "Dev and Annie are going through a bad patch at the moment. Annie wants to talk, but don't let on that I've told you."

"I can eat in my room," Cassie said, relieved that she'd have an excuse.

"You'll do no such thing, darling. This is your home, after all."

⤳

Her mother always did this, Cassie thought while in the shower, washing the salt of the lake off her skin. She always developed these intense, close relationships with other women. She wasn't a lesbian, in terms of physical sexual attraction and wanting to sleep with them; it was all about emotions and empathy. Her father and mother had never seemed to have the sort of closeness that Eve sought with her female friends. They had jogged along as a couple for years, had one child – as if it was expected – but been very much two separate people – almost like colleagues in the childrearing business, rather than lovers. Eve had always got her emotional fixes elsewhere. Or perhaps, Cassie thought, towelling herself down, Eve *was* a lesbian and hadn't realised it yet. For some reason, the thought made Cassie laugh. She hoped not. It was difficult enough dealing with one mother, let alone two.

Cassie had been reluctant to wash the salt off her body. It was a reminder of Eliza – hadn't the girl's lips tasted of this very salt? – but her skin had started to feel itchy and her mother had hinted quite strongly that she needed a wash, finally coming out and saying so: "You're a bit sweaty, love. Why don't you have a wash and change? You'll feel better for it."

Cassie thought it was more to do with what Annie would think rather than anything to do with her own welfare.

To all appearances, Annie, when she eventually arrived, was her usual cheery, friendly self, but if you looked at her more closely – which Cassie did – it was clear that all was not well with the woman. Her eyes were shadowed, as if she wasn't sleeping properly, and her face looked drawn. And she was a bit *too* cheerful, *too* animated, as if she was making an effort.

Cassie thought that she must have come directly from

work, because she had a linen suit on – an expensive-looking one, with loose trousers and a tailored jacket – and the slightly glazed look of someone who had spent too long in the office and at meetings. She took the offered glass of wine and drank it down a little too quickly. Another sign of stress?

Eve – not the most imaginative of cooks – produced a gazpacho for the first course. Cold soup was cold soup, as far as Cassie was concerned, and was thus an oxymoron of a dish. This was then followed by a seafood linguine, which was more linguine than seafood. Annie acted as if she had eaten at the finest of restaurants and Eve lapped up the praise, even blushing modestly.

"You've only picked at your food, love," Eve said to Cassie, when she was helping her to take the plates into the kitchen. "Not hungry?"

The honest answer would have been that she *was* hungry, but just didn't like her mother's cooking, but she just shook her head and said: "No, I ate a lot at lunchtime at the picnic."

Eve didn't do dessert – she never had, regarding the course as just an excuse to ingest more calories – so the meal ended with coffee and some chocolates that Annie had brought with her. They were organic and fairly traded, as expected, but a little too sweet and sickly for Cassie's taste. Cassie was wondering how long it would be until she could slip away to her bedroom without being too obvious, when Annie turned her smile on her. It was like being caught in a searchlight.

"I owe you an apology, Cassie," she said. "Eve and I have been too busy talking shop. You must be bored stiff. How are you, by the way?"

Cassie said she was fine, hoping that would suffice.

"Enjoying the job?"

"Yes," she said. Just that one word, as she couldn't think of anything else to say.

"Getting on with Elaine?"

Cassie nodded.

"She's great, isn't she?" Annie went on. "She's a very promising student, too." Annie chuckled, though she hadn't said anything remotely funny. Cassie thought that she was getting a bit tipsy. "And she's got her own unique sense of fashion. It's almost iconic."

Eve and Annie both laughed at this. It was obviously a private joke of theirs. Cassie could guess why; Lainey's crush on Annie was something of an open secret and invited such comments.

"How are things going with your friend?" Annie asked.

Eve looked pained, as if she wished Annie hadn't brought the subject of Eliza up, and also guilty. It was clear to Cassie that they'd been talking about her. She wasn't at all surprised, but inherent in Annie's question was that implication, again, that she only had one friend, which was galling. All the more so, because it was true.

"You don't see that much of her, do you, Cassie?" Eve said and Cassie realised that Eve was getting drunk, as well, otherwise she wouldn't have said anything about Eliza or poked her nose into her private business, as Cassie saw it.

Cassie probably wouldn't have said anything if she hadn't been irritated by the two women's fascination with her personal life – what they obviously thought was her love life – and if the two large glasses of wine that she'd consumed hadn't gone to her head.

"Actually, I saw Eliza today," Cassie said. "I spent most of the afternoon with her."

"I thought you were with Linda," Eve said, looking disgruntled, as if Cassie had misled her.

"I was… but I went for a walk and bumped into Eliza." She wanted to add, 'And was almost speared,' just to see the effect it would have on them. Instead, she said, "She took me to meet her gran."

Eve seemed lost for words. She'd obviously decided that Eliza was a one-night stand.

"She a local girl?" Annie asked.

"Yes," Cassie said, enjoying her mother's dismay, "her gran is an indigenous Australian and Eliza is of mixed heritage. Her dad is white."

Fuck, Cassie suddenly thought, *why am I telling them this? Annie is bound to want to know more and where will that lead? What if I give too much away?*

But she shouldn't have worried, because Eve quickly changed the subject and soon they were back on university business, discussing this grant and that fellowship. Cassie managed to make her excuses and leave them to it.

In her bedroom, she could hear them talking and guessed from their change of tone that they had got onto those more personal things about Dev and Annie that they couldn't discuss in front of her. Much later, she heard her mother fumbling around in the spare bedroom – sorting the bed out? – and then Annie wishing her goodnight. This was followed by a long silence – a friendly hug or a platonic kiss? – until Eve said goodnight back and all the lights were switched off.

Cassie lay awake thinking of Eliza. Was she a friend as Annie had described her? Perhaps there was more to it than that, but not in the way that Annie and Eve thought. There was some connection between them, some link, that was strong enough to break through the wall of time. Cassie could not even begin to understand it and, perhaps, in the end, it was just a vivid and complicated hallucination, a symptom of her declining mental state or some after-effect of her meds. Even if it was, she didn't care, because Eliza was real to her – more real than the life she lived now.

CHAPTER TWENTY-THREE

Kate Mackinnon breezed into the library in her usual cloud of perfume and crisp linen.

"She's quite something, isn't she?" Lainey said. "Like a force of nature."

But Cassie didn't feel impressed. She felt guilty, as she still had Kate's card at the bottom of her rucksack, untouched and unread.

Cassie was just trying to figure out what her best course of action was – either to avoid the woman or to suck up to her with a profuse apology – when they almost bumped into each other among the stacks. Cassie with an armful of books; Kate distracted by the volume she'd just picked up from the shelf.

"Dr Mackinnon," Cassie said, dropping a couple of the books and crouching down to pick them up. Kate crouched down, too, trying to help, and they almost bumped heads. It was a near miss. *Not a good start*, Cassie thought.

"I've been meaning to come to see you…" Cassie said. But the blank look on Kate's face said it all: she had forgotten who Cassie was. She was just a face among all the other students and staff at the university, but then the cloud of confusion on her face lifted.

"Oh, I remember you now."

So, I am just about memorable, Cassie thought wryly.

"Eve's daughter… Jocasta… No, it's Cassie, isn't it?"

"Yes, Dr Mackinnon," Cassie said.

"Remember, Cassie, it's Kate," Kate said, so emphatically that Cassie would never dare call her Dr Mackinnon again. "You were the one who fainted, weren't you? At the market."

Cassie agreed. The experience had obviously marked her out from the crowd.

"I was intrigued by what you told me," Kate said and looked at her phone, as if considering if she could afford to take the time out of her busy schedule. "Why don't we grab a cup of coffee and have a little chat?"

She had to ask Lainey first – the woman was her supervisor, after all – but the librarian wasn't going to refuse the request of such an eminent member of the teaching staff.

"Of course, Cassie," she said, looking a little bit miffed and slightly jealous, as another one of her innumerable crushes was Kate.

The campus had a countless number of coffee bars and coffee machines. It seemed a particularly contemporary Australian habit to never be far away from a cup of the stuff.

"So," Kate said, when they were sitting with two long blacks in front of them, "remind me of what you saw."

Cassie did. She told her everything, apart from the fact that she knew whose eyes she was seeing the scene through.

"Well, Cassie," Kate said, "leaving aside the content and

context of your... whatever it was... for a moment, I can think of two possible explanations."

Cassie found Kate rather intimidating. There was a fierce honesty about her that she wasn't used to in people.

"The white side of me... you know I have mixed ethnicity, Cassie... would say that you are probably an overimaginative, potentially neurotic young woman..."

Cassie almost winced at the bluntness of her words.

"... but the black side of me would say that you had a vision."

Cassie smiled and said, "So, which side are you going with?"

Kate laughed. "You come over as shy and quiet, Cassie, but I think you're quite a sharp young woman under all that."

Cassie took it as a compliment, though she wasn't completely sure that it was.

"I'm going with my black side, Cassie. The Kabiri side," Kate said. "But the scene you described could be from any of the so-called displacements that took place all over this country, from the landing of the First Fleet right up to the Coniston Massacre of 1928, which was reputedly the last. So, while I don't doubt what you saw, as to where it happened..."

"But I know where it happened," Cassie said and Kate, for once, lost her usual cool composure and looked slightly ruffled.

"It's not far from my house at a place called Blood Creek."

"Okay," Kate said, regaining her usual poise, "you're sure of that? Well... you obviously are or you wouldn't have said it." She looked out of the window onto the green lawns of the campus, as if considering what to say next. "I can't recall any stories from my people or any documentary evidence about a massacre at Blood Creek, but that doesn't mean it didn't happen. I'm a sociologist, not a historian, but I'll do some digging and get back to you." She stood up. "I've got to go, Cassie," she said, "but I think we're on to something here."

Cassie was left with her coffee, basking in the wake of that 'we'.

CHAPTER TWENTY-FOUR

The coppers didn't come back looking for Jimmy – Eliza had been worried that they would – but someone else did. Cal Armstrong. It was almost two weeks after the night that Jimmy had left and word seemed to have got around, in the way that word did, that Jimmy had shot through with O'Halloran hot on his trail.

It was pretty obvious to everyone where Jimmy was heading, up into the high country, the hinterland, where white settlers were few and far between and he could hide out in the forests and the mountains. It would take more than a fat Irish policeman to winkle him out of there, everyone said. They'd need black fellow trackers.

Jimmy passed through, but he left lots of rumours behind. Nobody knew with any clarity what Jimmy had done, but there were plenty of stories: Jimmy had held up a mail coach and taken the strong box; he'd shot a white man dead in a bar fight in Gympie; he'd been ambushed by a party of coppers, shot his way out and killed two of them.

Some of this general curiosity – or nosiness, you could call it, Eliza thought – was satisfied, to a degree, when

Vicky's mother got her hands on a bill that had been posted up outside the post office in the local town. She brought it over, bearing it before her as if it was a sacred item, crouched down on the porch and invited Grace and Granny, who was also there, to stare at the likeness of Jimmy that some jobbing artist had sketched. The women couldn't read it, of course – they had none of the white man's letters and only a utilitarian command of his language – so they had to wait for Eliza and Vicky to interpret it.

Vicky stared at the poster, her eyes as wide as saucers and then passed it to Eliza. "You read it, Eliza. He's your kin, after all."

Eliza did the best she could, but she could feel her eyes welling up with the sadness of the occasion and her belly clenching with the fear that she felt for her brother. "It says: Jimmy… they give him his dad's name, Owen—"

Grace shook her head and said, "Why use that man's name? He's long gone… he never cared about Jimmy…"

When she'd calmed down, Eliza went on, "They say he's also called Black Jimmy, a nickname…"

"No one ever called him that… not here, anyway… that's a stupid name…" Grace again, making a fuss, but then she quietened down, shushed by the others.

Eliza went on once more, "He is wanted for robbery and murder. The magistrates are offering a reward of £200."

"That's because he's a black fellow," Vicky's mother said. "If he was white, the reward would be more."

Granny gave her one of her hostile, snake-eyed stares and the woman shut up. Grace just looked dazed, old and washed out.

"But nobody would sell him out, would they?" Vicky asked plaintively. "None of our people, anyway."

Eliza hoped she was right.

⋙

It was the day after, late in the afternoon, that Cal Armstrong arrived, riding in on a horse that was tired and lathered up.

"See to my horse, Eliza, can't you?" he said with irritation in his voice, handing her the reins and then went straight to Grace.

"What's Jimmy gone and done now?" he asked her, as if it was somehow Grace's fault.

Eliza had only a vague idea what she should do with the animal and she was scared of the big beast, but she tethered it to a fallen log in the shade and brought it water. The horse seemed pleased enough and it didn't bite her, which to Eliza was something of a result.

She went back to the porch and the fire and got Grace and Cal tea from the pot.

"And you haven't seen him, Grace?" Armstrong was asking, his voice was soft, but insistent.

Grace shook her head. "No, boss. He never came to see me."

Her face looked stricken as she said it and Eliza knew that whatever excuse they had given for Jimmy, Grace had been devastated that he hadn't visited her, even briefly, on his way through. They all shared the same question that none of them would voice: what if they never saw Jimmy again?

"I would have come before," Cal said, "but I was away on business in Brisbane... as you well know, Grace."

It sounded like an excuse to Eliza and why was he explaining himself to Grace, his black servant, his cook?

The same thought must have occurred to Cal, because he suddenly became more gruff and formal and added: "Not that my business is anybody's concern."

He asked for more tea, thirsty after his ride, and Eliza poured it for him. He lit a cheroot and seemed to mellow again. "So, you have no news of Jimmy, Grace?" he asked. Seeing the wary look that came over the woman's face, he added, "You can tell me, Grace. I'm not going to go to the coppers. As you know, Jimmy and I are mates."

Grace shook her head, sadly. "There's been no news, boss," she said and Eliza could see that she was on the point of tears.

"Well, if he's hiding out," Cal said, as if trying to reassure her, "if he's gone to ground, he's probably safe enough."

The light was fast going, evening was coming on. Eliza hoped that Cal would go, leave them to their worries, but he showed no sign of budging.

Instead, he called her over. "Eliza," he said, "there's a couple of bottles of rum in my saddlebag. Bring them over, girl."

Grace, like Granny, would never refuse a tot of rum. Cal poured a draft into her tin cup, emptied quickly of tea, and gave himself an equal measure.

"Get yourself a cup, Eliza," he said, looking over at her. "A shot of rum will warm the cockles of your heart, as my old grandmother used to say." He laughed. "My parents never partook of strong drink – abstainers both, they'd signed the pledge – but my old granny used to like a wee dram."

Eliza didn't understand all the words he used, but she got the gist of what he was saying.

≫

Eliza should have kept her eyes on that bottle of rum. Cal topped Grace up more times than he did himself and Grace was not going to complain, being too far gone in her misery. But it was when Cal started giving her *those* looks that she began to get concerned. She was sitting opposite Grace, on the other side of the fire, staring into the flames, feeling uncomfortable, but she was conscious of his eyes on her.

"You know, Eliza," he said, his voice soft and simpering, "when I look at you, I can see the family resemblance." He smiled.

"What do you mean, Mr Armstrong?" she asked.

"Now I told you to call me Cal, Eliza," he said, mock-scolding her. "What I mean is that you look like your brother. You obviously both took after your mother's side of the family and Grace is a handsome woman, black or not."

Grace laughed at this, but her head was nodding and she could hardly keep her eyes open. She was quite drunk, Eliza knew. It wasn't long before she started snoring, her head lolling on her chest.

"Eliza, bring the other bottle over," Cal suddenly said.

The bottle was between them and Eliza didn't know why he couldn't get it himself, but the reason became evident as soon as she handed it to him and he grabbed her wrist.

"Come sit on my lap, Eliza," he said and he wrenched the wrist downwards until she complied and fell onto his lap, almost toppling him over. He quickly righted himself and said, "Now, give me a kiss, Eliza. There's no harm in a kiss, is there?"

Eliza didn't want to kiss him. She struggled, but he pressed his mouth to her lips. His breath stank of tobacco, rum and rotting teeth, and it made her want to throw up. She tried to push herself off him, but he laughed. He held her tight with one arm and put the other on her right breast, squeezing and pinching, hurting her.

"My, what a big girl you've grown into, Eliza," he said and pressed his lips to hers again.

This time, he slipped his free hand under her dress and up between her legs. Eliza, not wearing drawers, was at a disadvantage, but she wriggled too much for him to slip it further than her thighs. He just laughed at her exertions, as if it was all a game to him.

"Come on, Eliza," he said. "Let's have some fun, eh?"

She struggled, but he just laughed some more. In fact, he seemed to enjoy it. She realised that it was getting him aroused. Suddenly, she stopped moving.

"Coming around, are you?" he asked. She could see that he was pretty drunk by now and that made him even more dangerous, but also a bit stupid.

"I need to piss, Mr Armstrong," she said.

"Don't be silly, Eliza. Stop your nonsense!"

"No, I really do," Eliza insisted. "I'm almost wetting myself."

She would have, too – she would have pissed on him, just

to prove the point – but he pushed her off his lap, not keen to get his trousers wet.

"Be quick about it, then," he said, "and come straight back or you'll be sorry."

She stood up and slowly inched away from the fire. She didn't want to start running, until she was sure that he wasn't following.

It seemed to suddenly occur to Armstrong, through his rum-soaked brain, that she might give him the slip, so he got up and started to follow her, but Eliza was quicker than he was and knew the bush better. She started running and dodged into the trees. Armstrong chased her. She could hear his gasping breath behind her, coming closer – she could almost smell that foul breath of his – but suddenly he stumbled and cried out. He lost his footing and lost Eliza in the process.

"You little black bitch," he called after her. "You'll pay for this."

That drunken shout summed it up for Eliza, exactly what he thought of her. In his eyes, she was two things: inferior and animalistic. Two things that made him know he could do what he wanted with her.

A short time later, she was down in the creek, on one of the trails, when she heard his horse approaching in the distance. He wasn't going to give up so easily, she knew. She didn't know where she could go, where she could flee to, but then she had a thought.

She climbed up among the trees on the far side of the creek and huddled down and waited. She could hear him below her – or hear his horse, at least – riding up and down the creek. When she was sure that he had gone down towards the creek's mouth looking for her, she broke cover and headed across country to the place where the bush plums grew. Coming to the stand of trees, she crouched down, hid and listened. She could hear a rider in the distance, but she wasn't sure exactly where Armstrong was. All she was certain of was that he would not stop looking for her.

Her heart was beating fast. She was distracted by fear, but she tried to recall where she had seen Cassie, the exact route the girl had taken, that time when she and her friends had been picking plums. When she was almost sure she knew the way to go, she broke from cover, whispering words that passed for a silent prayer.

"I'm coming to you, Cassie. Help me find you."

CHAPTER TWENTY-FIVE

In Cassie's dream, Carys was calling to her, lost in the distance in the mist, as morning tried to break around them. But just as she got near the girl, just as she put a hand out to reassure her, she saw that it wasn't Carys after all. It was Eliza.

"Help me," Eliza said. "I'm trying to find you, Cassie. Please help me!"

Cassie woke up soaked in sweat and threw the sheet – which was also sodden – off herself. *Fuck*, she thought, *what a horrible dream.*

She padded out to the kitchen, too disturbed to go straight back to sleep, and got herself a glass of water. She nearly had a heart attack when she saw the face at the kitchen window staring in. She nearly called out, woke Eve, but then she recognised who it was and quickly opened the door. Eliza fell into her arms. She was panting, exhausted, her legs and arms all scratched up, twigs tangled in her curls, which were lank with sweat.

"Eliza," Cassie said, "what happened?"

She took Eliza back to her bedroom, helped her onto the

bed. She offered her a glass of wine, but Eliza wanted a cup of tea, which Cassie made for her. She even found a teapot.

"What happened?" Cassie asked again, when she brought the tea back. And Eliza told her, in somewhat halting tones, as if the details somehow embarrassed her. As if it were somehow her fault.

"That's terrible, darling," Cassie said. The 'darling' had just slipped out. "He tried to rape you. Can't you tell anyone?"

The look Eliza gave her told Cassie how redundant her question was. Of course, Cassie thought, in Eliza's time, in her life, there was nobody to tell. She couldn't exactly call the police, could she?

"I could have told Jimmy, if he was still around," Eliza said, after gulping her tea and helping herself to the plate of biscuits Cassie had brought in, "but he'd have got angry—"

"Who's Jimmy?" Cassie asked. Eliza had never mentioned a Jimmy. Cassie felt a sudden, sharp jolt of jealousy.

"My brother," Eliza said, a smile coming to her face at the memory of him, the first time she'd smiled since she'd got there, "but he's gone bush. He's hiding out."

"From who?" Cassie asked, then wished she hadn't.

Eliza looked uncomfortable. "From the police, but I don't believe he did everything that they say he did. Unless he had his reasons, of course."

Cassie tried to suppress the relief she felt, when it became clear that Jimmy was a relative and not a lover. "Well, don't worry about that now, Eliza," she said. "I think you should get some sleep. You look worn out. Do you want a shower first?"

It might wake Eve up, Cassie thought, *but so what?*

"What do you mean?" Eliza asked, having no idea what Cassie meant.

"Sorry," Cassie said, "I meant a bath."

Eliza shook her head. "No, I'm too tired," she said.

"Wait here," Cassie said. She went out and came back with a flannel and a bowl of hot water.

Eliza looked at her suspiciously.

"Keep still," Cassie said and proceeded to wash Eliza's face, her arms and her legs.

Eliza looked slightly stunned by all the attention, but when Cassie got to her toes, she laughed. "You're tickling me, Cassie."

The soles of Eliza's feet were as thick and tough as leather.

"Have you never worn shoes, Eliza?" Cassie asked.

"No, never," Eliza replied, "why would I?"

That's a fair enough question, Cassie thought.

She finished washing Eliza and dried her. Eliza seemed to relax under her hands. Cassie, she had to admit to herself, was enjoying what she was doing, but while it was undoubtedly a sensual experience, it wasn't an erotic one. It was all about caring for Eliza's tired body. This was something of a surprise to Cassie, as she'd never thought of herself as the caring or nurturing type.

"Your hair, Eliza," she said, at last. "You need to brush it. It's full of stuff."

"I'm too tired, Cassie," Eliza said. "I'll do it in the morning."

"Look, let me help," Cassie said.

She was as gentle as she could be, but she couldn't help

hurting Eliza a bit. The girl winced a couple of times, but didn't cry out.

"That's done," Cassie said, "so it's bedtime, unless of course you want a story…"

Eliza looked bemused.

"I'm joking, Eliza. Goodnight."

With one final effort, Eliza took her dress off and rolled over on her stomach. Cassie lay down next to her and covered them with a sheet, after allowing herself a brief, appreciative glance along the perfect curve of Eliza's back.

CHAPTER TWENTY-SIX

This time, Eliza didn't steal off in the early morning light. Instead, she lingered.

Cassie opened her eyes to the sight of Eliza propped up on one elbow, looking at her.

"You sleep really quietly, Cassie... no snoring at all... but you drool a bit."

Cassie was apologetic, but Eliza laughed.

"I bet I snore, don't I?"

She did a bit, Cassie had to admit, and she was a restless sleeper, tossing and turning in the night. It didn't bother Cassie; she just liked having Eliza there beside her. After sleeping alone for over a year, it felt good to have someone by her side, though the notion was not without an attendant feeling of guilt.

"I'll make us a cup of tea, Eliza," Cassie said.

She walked into the kitchen and almost bumped into Eve, who looked embarrassed and concerned in no particular order.

"Morning, dear," she said. "I heard voices..."

"Oh, that's just Eliza. She turned up late last night," Cassie said.

Eve seemed relieved – at least this wasn't some new stranger. "Well, do say hello to her for me, dear," Eve said, all business-like. "Now, I must be off."

Cassie took the tea back to the bedroom. "My mother says hello…" she said.

They both burst out laughing, like two little kids.

Cassie showed Eliza what a shower was and, when she got over the novelty of it, she enjoyed it and didn't want to come out. While she was in the shower, Cassie washed Eliza's dress. It was such an old, pathetic excuse for a garment that Cassie could have almost cried when she put it in the machine with some other stuff. She was hoping that it wouldn't fall to pieces.

Eliza wasn't pleased when she told her what she'd done. "What am I going to wear while it dries?" she asked.

"There are plenty of clothes here, Eliza," Cassie said.

"I don't want your charity, Cassie," Eliza replied, her eyes flashing. She was getting angry, Cassie could tell.

"There's no charity between friends, Eliza. We're just sharing."

Eliza looked suspicious, but seemed to accept the idea.

The problem was that Cassie's wardrobe was, in fact, pretty bare, especially when it came to dresses. Eliza looked despairingly at the shorts and T-shirts and wouldn't even deign to try them on, so she gave Eliza her mother's dressing gown, wore her own and they went in to have some breakfast. This was another potentially problematic situation, because Cassie didn't know what to give Eliza. She tried a concoction of bran flakes and raisins, pronounced that she liked it and ate two bowls with a lot of milk.

Afterwards, they sat on the sofa in the living room and Eliza, looking closely at Cassie, took her hand and asked, "Why are you so sad all the time, Cassie?"

Cassie told her. She hadn't wanted to cry, to give way to tears, but they just came, punctuating her sentences.

Cassie and Carys had been almost inseparable from the day they met in secondary school. It was okay at twelve years old, if you were a girl, to have such a close best friend, to spend nights and weekends in each other's houses. To kiss and hug and share clothes. Even in those times, relatively enlightened though they were, boys couldn't have done the same thing. It was very much the prerogative of girls.

Carys's parents had been quite traditional – Church of England but tending towards the fundamentalist interpretations of the Bible – and had initially been pleased that their daughter was, instead of showing an interest in boys, forming such a firm friendship with another girl. Cassie's parents had been a little more wary. Eve kept telling Cassie that she should widen her circle of friends, socialise a bit more – even if it involved drunken teenage parties – instead of spending all her time with Carys in their respective bedrooms.

But Carys and Cassie were happy with each other, like two pieces of a broken medallion, long separated, which had found each other and fitted themselves together. Carys was studious and this rubbed off on Cassie. Carys sailed through GCSEs and A levels and dragged Cassie with her. Cassie had to put more work in than Carys; she was more of a plodder, but she needed to keep up with her, because they had a plan.

The plan was that they would go to the same university and share a flat or a house, where they could be together and live their own lives out of the restrictive orbits of their families. For Carys, it would present an escape from the stifling atmosphere of her parental home; for Cassie, it was about evading Eve's expectations of her – expectations that she couldn't fulfil and would inevitably end in disappointment for both of them.

Carys's parents were initially quite pleased that the arrangement that kept their daughter out of the way of boys – because everyone knew what boys were like, didn't they? – would go on. Eve was less amenable.

"Cassie, love," she said, "don't you think that you should spread your wings a bit? Take a year out. It's great that you've got such a good friend, but perhaps you both need to step out of the other's shadow – unless, of course…"

"Unless what, Mum?" Cassie asked.

Eve looked uncomfortable. "Unless you are more than friends, Cassie," she said. "Unless you are actually in a relationship."

"But isn't friendship a relationship, Mum?" Cassie asked, being deliberately difficult.

"You know what I mean, Cassie," Eve said.

Cassie did. Because for everyone who knew them in school, saw them together, joined, as it were, at the hip, and said something like, "Oh, that's just Cassie and Carys. You'd think they were twins. That's just what they are like", there were others who would say, "There go the two lezzers." Or dykes or queers or scissor sisters or muff-munchers. Some of their schoolmates had quite a vocabulary when it came to derogatory comments about gay couples.

It didn't seem to bother Carys; she could ignore it. She would ask Cassie what she expected from people. Weren't most of them narrow-minded bastards, after all? It did concern Cassie, though, because she was starting to wonder if there was some truth in their harsh words, the names that they flung at them.

But the worry was fleeting, because there was something she knew that trumped all those petty anxieties about her sexuality – or their sexuality – and that was the fact that she loved Carys. She truly believed that Carys was that soulmate you read about in books – the more romantic gushy ones.

Cassie was suddenly aware of the quizzical look on Eliza's face and the intensity of her gaze as she listened to Cassie's every word.

Fuck, Cassie thought, *I just about forgot that she was there. I've said too much. Does she even understand what I'm telling her?*

Eliza, almost as if intuiting Cassie's question, said, "Cassie, love, I don't really understand everything that you've been saying, but that's because I think your world is so different from mine." She sighed and shook her head. "I don't even understand what you two girls were going to do away from your mas and pas. How were you going to shift for food, for money?"

"The government will give or lend you money to study," Cassie said.

"To go to school, when you are a grown-up girl?" Eliza asked in some amazement.

"Yes," Cassie said, "Carys and I were studying history. What happened in the past."

"People's stories?" Eliza said. "That sounds wonderful."

"It was," Cassie said. "We had our own house."

Eliza's face lit up. "No ma to keep on at you? No boys sniffing around you trying to bed you? No elders wanting to marry you off? No Mrs Cleary on at you to say your prayers and admit all your sins to her?"

Cassie shook her head. "No, we basically did what we wanted."

As she said it, thinking of Eliza's life, she knew that her words smacked of smugness and privilege, but what else could she say? It was, after all, the truth.

"What about boys?" Eliza asked. "When were you girls going to find a husband?"

"Well, we might just have married each other, Eliza," Cassie said.

Eliza looked stunned, for a moment, and then she laughed out loud. "You say such funny things, Cassie," she said and then she grew serious. "What happened, love?"

"Carys died, Eliza," she said. The stark truth of those words were as painful as slashing herself with a sliver of broken glass.

"Oh, Cassie, love… What of?" Eliza's eyes were welling with tears, too.

"Her heart… it just stopped."

Or should she say that her heart betrayed her. That it had harboured a defect since birth that had never been picked up and one day, one morning, Carys had gone for a run, cheerily waved her goodbye and had never come back.

Cassie had been frantic with worry until the phone call came from her mother, from Eve.

"But why didn't anyone tell me, Mum?" Cassie almost screamed the words with the agony of it all. "Why didn't the hospital call me?"

She couldn't understand it. How could Carys go so suddenly, be snuffed out of her life like a flame blown out by some capricious wind?

"Cassie," her mother said, "listen, love. I'm on my way. I'll be with you as soon as I can."

"But why, Mum?" Cassie persisted. She just couldn't understand.

Eve gulped audibly on the other end of the phone, as if something was stuck in her throat. "You weren't her next of kin."

Cassie couldn't understand why time didn't stop in the same way, at the same moment, that Carys's heart did. How could life just go on? Carys was buried on a cold, wet day. There was a flock of black-garbed strangers, none of whom had loved Carys like she had – and Cassie included Carys's parents among these people. And in the funeral oration, the vicar called Carys a beloved daughter and granddaughter – no mention of Cassie at all. She was the invisible woman.

Cassie had wanted to be there, when Carys's mum and dad picked up her stuff from the house, so she could tell them what had belonged to Carys, though in truth they had shared nearly everything, even their clothes. She noted the look the two of them exchanged when they saw that the only bed in the flat was a double – that said it all to them. Cassie knew that they would think their daughter had died in sin, that she had been a sexual invert in their parlance, cruel and twisted as it was. Perversely, she was glad that this would pain them, because she was in so much pain herself. It seemed only fair that they should share some of it.

She never saw them again and she was glad of that, because the look they had exchanged, those thoughts that had crossed their narrow, mean minds, the way they had sought to demean Cassie and Carys's love, had both angered and appalled her.

"Carys died." Cassie repeated the words, as if by saying them again, she might make sense of them.

"Oh, Cassie, love," Eliza said. "Come here!"

Eliza took her in her arms and held her tight and, at that moment, Cassie didn't want her to ever let her go.

CHAPTER TWENTY-SEVEN

Cassie held onto Eliza like a drowning sailor holding onto a spar – or perhaps a mermaid or a siren – but all sailors must come to land eventually or learn to dwell in the deep, and so it was with Cassie.

Lying on the sofa in a tangle of limbs, Cassie was all cried out, when Eliza kissed her gently on the forehead and said, "I have to go back, Cassie."

It wasn't so much that Eliza's words were a surprise, it was just that Cassie hadn't thought about what was going to happen. She was so deep in this present moment with Eliza that she'd started to think it would last forever.

"Of course," Cassie said, trying to hide her disappointment. They disentangled from each other and sat up. "But is it safe to go back, Eliza?"

Eliza made a face and shrugged. "I'm worried about Ma, Cassie," she said. "Worried what that Cal Armstrong might do to her."

"But what about you, dear? What might he do to you?"

"I'll have to take my chance, Cassie," Eliza said. "Sober and in broad daylight, he might think twice before trying it on again." In truth, she didn't believe that, but she didn't want to worry Cassie unduly.

"Can't I come with you?" Cassie asked.

Eliza shook her head. "I don't know, love. I don't even know if I can get back. Granny said something about having to be called back."

"Well, at least I can come part of the way," Cassie said.

They set off in the midday heat, following the road. Cassie had put a hat and sunglasses on, but Eliza was bareheaded. The sun didn't seem to bother her. She kept sniffing at her dress surreptitiously – it still smelled of the washing powder Cassie had used – as if she couldn't make up her mind if the odour was pleasant or overpowering.

"It was along here," Eliza said. "We get off the road here."

They crossed the surface of the road, traversed the verge and then were in the bush.

"You should go back, Cassie," Eliza said. "What if I disappear suddenly and you get lost?"

"No, I'll stay with you…" Cassie replied, looking around her at the tangle of trees and bushes with some trepidation. And when she looked back, the place where Eliza had been just a moment before was now empty space.

⫘

Where the hell had she gone? Eliza asked herself. She called out a couple of times, but didn't want to make too much noise, even though it was the hottest time of the day and anyone sensible would be indoors or in the shade. She didn't want to attract attention to herself. You could never be too sure.

Sadly, she gave up on her friend, hoping that she had found her way back home. Cassie wasn't in Eliza's world, so she must be in her own, she figured. She passed the stand of plum trees and set off across the sparse plain of bush shrubs and long grass towards the creek. She would have dearly liked to have stayed with Cassie, but she had to go back. You couldn't just up and leave everything and everybody.

She reached the creek and crossed it without seeing a soul. Then, she climbed the slope on the other side until she was above her ma's house, looking down on it from cover with bated breath. But, to her surprise, everything looked as it always did: the fire was burning, her ma was pottering about, back from cooking lunch for the stockmen, absorbed by all the little tasks that she got on with, whether they needed to be done or not.

Eliza slipped out of the bush and made her way down to the house.

Grace started in surprise, "God, Eliza, you startled me. You walk so quiet, like your granny." She frowned. "Where you been, girl, out all night?"

"Don't you remember, Ma?" Eliza said. "Cal Armstrong was after me. He chased me half across the country."

"In your dreams, girl," Grace said.

"No, in your dreams, Ma," Eliza replied, "when you were dead drunk."

Grace raised her hand as if to slap Eliza, but thought better of it. "What do you mean…? Did he?"

"He tried to, Ma, but I got away."

Grace sat down, suddenly weary.

"He didn't say anything?" Eliza asked. "Was he angry, Ma?"

"Get me some water, Eliza. I'm parched," Grace said. "No, he didn't say anything, just said his head was pounding after all that rum. And he looked as sick as a dog."

Eliza gave her mother a ladleful of water from the pail.

"He's probably forgotten, Eliza – too drunk to remember," Grace said.

But Eliza wasn't so sure.

CHAPTER TWENTY-EIGHT

It wasn't that Cal Armstrong had forgotten about Eliza, it was just that he had other things on his mind and those things were far more important to him than she was: his stock. Grace told Eliza that the 'black fellows', as she called her own people, were still driving the cattle away from the water whenever they found them unattended. It was summer; the grass and the trees were parched, water was scarce, the lake was almost dry in places. Why should these big beasts of the white fellows' mob drink up all their water? Or so the people thought.

If there were stockmen about, the people had learnt to leave the cattle alone. They feared the stockmen's guns, but, more than that, they were scared of and didn't understand the murderous anger that boiled up in these white men over their cows. Stray cattle, though, were fair game and an extra supply of meat was always welcome. The dumb beasts were easy enough to spear, especially if caught in a thicket or on rough ground – easier than kangaroos, at any rate.

"Mark my words," Grace told Eliza. "The boss don't like losing his cows... they're money on the hoof, see, Eliza...

and he won't stand for the black fellows' mischief for much longer."

But Eliza didn't heed her mother's ominous warning; she also had other things on her mind or, at least, another person and that was Mrs Cleary. The Reverend Cleary was away again 'on church business', as his wife maintained, but Betty, the Cleary's maid, put it about, on scant evidence, that he had gone off to escape his wife's nagging and was probably ensconced in a whorehouse in Brisbane with a flask of rum and a black Judy.

Whatever the reason for his absence, it was a habit of Mrs Cleary's, when left on her own in this way, to enlist one of her girls to keep her company. As Eliza was the current favourite – something of a pet – this task fell to her.

Eliza had mixed feelings about this. On the one hand, she could not help having a certain, rather adolescent, pride in her pre-eminent position, displacing Vicky and the other mission girls who didn't even try to mask their envy. She had nothing against the other girls, didn't hate them or resent them – on the contrary, they were her friends – but she couldn't help feeling that, as *she* had been chosen from among the rest of the flock, she was special – a cut above the others. On the other hand, being Mrs Cleary's companion was stifling and constricting, because it involved being something and someone that Eliza wasn't.

For a start, Eliza had had no warning or notice from Mrs Cleary of what was expected of her. It had just happened on a Monday afternoon. After a day in the classroom and about the many tasks that Mrs Cleary set them – mending, laundry, gardening and anything else she could think of –

Mrs Cleary had suddenly said, as the others were preparing to depart for their homes, "Be a dear, Eliza, and stay with me while the reverend is away."

Eliza knew that it was more an order than a request, so she didn't say no. Mrs Cleary told her that she would send a note to her mother so Grace wouldn't worry, but, of course, sending a note was useless – Grace would just stare at the undecipherable letters – so Vicky was tasked with passing on the message. Sad-eyed Vicky departed, glancing miserably at Eliza as she shuffled away, to convey the news to Grace. Grace, of course, had no choice in the matter, even less than Eliza.

There were advantages to staying with Mrs Cleary. Her house, though relatively modest, was palatial compared to Grace's shack and there was always plenty of food, but Mrs Cleary or Jane ("Call me Jane when we are alone and not in school, Eliza," the woman said. "It's more informal and I think of us as friends") expected Eliza to do exactly as she did. This involved much sewing, mending and reading by candlelight, a modicum of sighing, complaining of the heat and some light chatter about a number of things that didn't remotely interest Eliza, like the latest fashions from Paris or what the queen was up to. To put it bluntly, Eliza was bored and longed to run in the bush, swim in the creek and laugh with her friends, but such things were not allowed in Jane's orbit. Young women had to be decorous – decorative, even – at all times.

And then there was the bedtime routine, after prayers and verses from the Bible – for which Betty would join them but would keep a wry look on her face when her mistress wasn't looking directly at her – Eliza would help Mrs Cleary into a nightgown, one that the girls had worked hard at laundering until it was starched and white as virginal snow. This involved helping Jane to take her dress and her petticoats off, and negotiating the drawstrings of that mysterious item, the corset, loosening it and slipping it off, putting it on a chair where it stood up all on its own, like some self-willed sprite. To Eliza, this garment seemed pointless, some petty torment that white women inflicted on themselves. But not all white women, because she thought of Cassie with her slim white body, her brief draws and that band of cloth she wore to hold up her breasts, rather than all the breadth and weight of Jane's underwear. The question that really concerned Eliza was: how did Jane breath? When fully dressed, she was trussed up like a game cock ready for cooking.

But the corset wasn't the strangest part of her costume. It was the weird pillow of padding she wore above her bottom. This item of clothing – if you could call it clothing – had already been a thing of wonder and some amusement, when Betty, after Mrs Cleary first arrived in the district, had told the other women, the black women that is, about it.

"The missus wears a false arse," she told Grace and the others. "Her bum is so small – shrivelled up like a winter plum – that she wears some stuffing to make it look big under her dress."

They all laughed, but it had worried them. What was the reason for this strange garment? Was it something to do with the Christian God that the Clearys talked so much about?

When the first ritual of the evening – undressing – was done, then would come the final act. Jane would let down her hair and give Eliza her ivory handled brush. This second ritual of brushing Jane's hair went on for some time. Jane would close her eyes and revel in Eliza's touch; she'd get her to rub her neck, telling her how soft her hands were, sighing with pleasure at Eliza's touch. This delighted Eliza, of course, as any praise from Jane would have done. Then, abruptly, she would bid Eliza goodnight, pointing her to the truckle bed that had been prepared for her just a few feet away from her own marital bed.

Every few days, she would help Jane bathe. The tin bath would be dragged from the yard to the tin-roofed shack that was rather grandly called 'the bathroom' and water would be boiled up on the outside fire – this would take an age. Then Betty and Eliza would haul buckets of lukewarm water into the bath house. When the bath was ready – not too hot, not too cold, carefully gauged as if for some princess, rather than a back-country missionary – the same ritual of nightly disrobing would be repeated almost exactly, apart from the fact that everything would come off until Jane's white, fleshy body was draped in a towel ready for the baptism of water. Eventually, and with a sort of shy decorum, the towel would be slipped off and Jane would submerge herself into the water like some oceanic goddess.

Eliza would marvel at the whiteness of Jane's body with its rosy tint – more like cream than Cassie's milk – her breasts floating on the water like twin ship figureheads, cream again with the two coral nipples. But then the time for marvelling would be over and the hard work of scrubbing would start. There was a long, thin, gourd-like object with a rough surface that Eliza would use on Jane's back. The first time she had been urged to do this, she had worried that she would hurt the woman, even scratch her skin off, but Jane seemed to revel in the abrasive qualities of the gourd. Eliza would use the sponge for washing under Jane's arms, her neck and the top of her breasts, though Jane would do the more intimate parts of herself, between her legs and under her breasts.

Then, while Jane soaked her body, in a sleepy state of repletion, Eliza would be expected to kneel on the floor or sit on a low stool like a supplicant, while Jane talked. Sometimes it seemed like the woman was talking to herself rather than to Eliza, but the one subject she would always come back to was Eliza's future.

"Eliza," she would say, "I think you should come and live with me permanently."

This argument was well-rehearsed: Eliza had few prospects in life and the life that she was currently living was precarious and marginal. Would she follow in her mother's footsteps and become a servant for those rough stockmen? If she did, she would be exposed to all their vices, all their unwelcome attentions. If she came to Jane, she would treat her well, train her as a ladies' maid and a companion. Eliza must see that such a future was so much better than the one she faced now, bleak and straitened.

"You see, Eliza," Jane would say, "the black man's day here is nearly over. The sun is setting on him and the night is coming; a cold, despairing night that he is unlikely to survive. The black man is dying out, Eliza. His only chance is to become part of the white man's world, to submerge himself in it and to embrace it. Give up his superstitions and wretched beliefs, and embrace the Lord as his Saviour…"

As Jane said this, Eliza wondered if she meant to include her in this dire prediction, this evocation of a doomed future – and Grace and Granny as well. Were they all to be consigned to darkness, with Mrs Cleary the only one there to guide them in the night, a lantern in her lily-white hands?

CHAPTER TWENTY-NINE

Cassie had tried to follow Eliza – she had dearly wanted to – but somehow, she had lost her. She didn't clearly understand the 'somehow'. She had thought that she was just behind the girl – those glossy, bouncing curls with their hints of bronze just before her – when the shadows of the trees, the glare of the day, seemed to suddenly fill her vision, robbing her of Eliza, who, it seemed, had disappeared somewhere ahead.

She walked on for quite a distance, calling Eliza's name – her voice sounding pathetic, she knew – then, all of a sudden, she started to get anxious about getting lost and began to trace her steps back to the tarmac, to the road and that street of strung-out houses that passed for reality for Cassie.

It was early afternoon when she got back to her house; it appeared that she and Eliza had somehow whiled the morning away. She sat on the couch where, a few moments ago it seemed, she had lain in Eliza's arms. It wasn't just the company she missed; it was the sheer physicality of Eliza's presence. Her absence made Cassie's abiding loneliness – something she lived with almost unconsciously – that much keener.

Cassie couldn't settle to anything that afternoon, with the result that she was still sprawled on the sofa imagining Eliza's phantom arms around her when Eve came home. She knew that this was a rather self-indulgent pleasure and also a rather guilty one.

"What have you been up to today, love?" Eve asked.

"Oh, you know," Cassie said, but, of course, Eve didn't.

Cassie got the feeling that Eve wanted to say something – she knew her mother well enough and could interpret all those little frowns and sidelong glances – but the questions didn't start until after they'd been to the supermarket. Eve had almost dragged a reluctant Cassie out, who would have stayed lying where she was. Eve complained that she couldn't be expected to work all day – she said 'graft', though Cassie couldn't envisage Eve's job involving the sort of effort implied in that word – and do all the shopping on her own as well.

It wasn't the supermarket that Cassie minded – as always, she could happily wander around those sacred aisles for an inordinate amount of time, examining all the things that might come in useful, but she'd never end up buying – it was the having to think about what they were going to eat. Because Eve was terrible at meal planning – it would have been pasta every night, such was the limit of her culinary imagination – and Cassie was similarly unimaginative due to her abiding disinterest in food.

It was when the ordeal was over and they were back in the car on the way home that Eve, after a long sigh, asked what she wanted to know.

"Eliza came over quite late last night, didn't she?"

Cassie had known that the questions were coming, so she wasn't taken aback. "Yes, Mum, it was late," she said. "Sorry if we woke you. We were trying to be quiet."

"That's okay, love. I was just a bit worried," Eve continued. "Anything wrong?"

"No... well, I think she just wanted to get away from things for a bit," Cassie said, being as vague as possible.

Eve seemed to consider this answer. She was glad, Cassie figured, that Eliza was still in the picture, but the hint of trouble or, at least, a troubled life concerned her.

"Jocasta," she said, "you're not getting drawn into anything, are you?"

"Like what, Mum?" Cassie asked.

"Well, does Eliza have family or personal problems?"

Cassie managed to suppress a giggle. The answer was: of course Eliza had problems, both family and personal. She was a girl of mixed ethnicity living in a frontier society in colonial Queensland, where her brown skin drew a mixed response from black and white alike. As she couldn't tell Eve any of this, Cassie just said, "No more than anyone else, Mum."

Eve looked slightly perplexed and not particularly pleased with the almost flippant answer. She sighed again. "Jocasta," she said, "it's not really any of my business who you're seeing or not seeing, I know, but please be careful."

"What do you mean, Mum?" Cassie asked, though she did know what her mother was trying to say.

"I mean..." Eve started and hesitated. "You know what you're like... you get so emotionally attached to people..."

Cassie felt a physical wrenching in her gut. She didn't know if she was getting nauseous or just angry.

"I wasn't just emotionally attached to Carys, Mum," she said, trying to control her temper, her voice. "I loved her more than anything or anyone in the world... as you well know."

"Yes, dear," Eve said quickly. "I didn't mean..."

"What did you mean, Mum?"

"I just meant," Eve spluttered on, "that you're vulnerable... after that... after Carys's death. I just worry for you."

Fuck, Cassie thought, *all this emotion, especially Mum's, I just can't deal with it.*

"Things are different with Eliza, Mum," she said.

'There's no future in it,' she wanted to say, 'because she's in the past.' And the thought came to her, like a chill wind out of nowhere, that Eliza was long dead in this world, in her own time.

Eve put her hand out and touched Cassie's arm. "Sorry, love," she said, "I shouldn't have brought it up."

"Hands on the wheel, Mum! Think of the kangaroos," Cassie said.

Eve's driving scared her at the best of times, let alone when she was distracted and controlling the car with one hand.

"And besides," she added, "this is nothing like Carys. Eliza is just a friend."

But was she answering Eve's question or asking one of her own?

CHAPTER THIRTY

Eliza's sojourn at Mrs Cleary's house ended abruptly when the reverend returned late one afternoon. Eliza and Jane were sitting at a small table under the window that looked out over the yard, making the most of the waning light before they put their needlework away. They heard the jingle of reins, the clopping of hoofs on the road, before the rider turned into the yard.

"Oh," Mrs Cleary said, "Peter is home…"

She smiled at Eliza, but Eliza could see that she was putting it on. It was a false smile, masking disappointment and a barely perceptible flutter of fear. She rose from her chair and went to the door. Eliza stood up, too, trying to look attentive.

Peter Cleary was a tall, rangy, nervous-looking man with a head of straw-like fair hair. It was usually unruly, but he'd obviously found a barber in Brisbane, who had trimmed and tidied it and left narrow margins of white skin, where his hair used to formerly meet his tanned face. This face of his was narrow with a thin, longish nose and he had the habit of cocking his head backwards and looking down the extended snout. This physical trait matched a mental one, because he habitually looked down at people, feeling that most of them were inferior to him. In contrast, if he met someone he thought superior – a bishop, for instance, or a magistrate – he adopted the most wheedling of tones, which Betty described in her own inimitable way as 'arse-licking'.

If the settlers and stockmen of the white population didn't live up to the reverend's exacting standards, it goes without saying that the black population didn't either. He didn't only look down on the black fellows, he regarded them as a lesser race, even a lesser species. Therefore, it was odd, strange even, that he had set himself to bring the Lord's word to them and save their souls. But, of course, as far as the reverend was concerned, he hadn't chosen this life, but rather he had *been* chosen for it by God, who Eliza always imagined as some old white man with a long beard living on a cloud.

In Peter Cleary's hierarchy of the unworthy: after poor, ignorant whites and childlike blacks, there came the half-castes like Eliza, right at the bottom. He had that fear that many white men had at the time, including the most educated and 'civilised', of the mixing of black and white blood. His nightmare was a khaki or mud-coloured race of such people displacing both the black and white races. So, the look he gave Eliza, when he brushed past his wife at the door, was one of pure disdain.

He pulled his long coat off – Jane tried to help him, but he was impatient of her slow fingers – spreading a miasma of dust in the air and flung himself onto the sofa.

"Girl," he said to Eliza, his watery blue eyes fixing her, slightly and scarily magnified by his little round glasses, "help me off with these boots."

This task took a time – the boots just wouldn't come – and Eliza ended up covered in the dust of the road.

"Take them out the back and brush them along with my coat," the reverend ordered Eliza, as Jane bustled around helping Betty prepare afternoon tea in the English fashion. The back door was open, so Eliza could hear exactly what was said.

"I don't understand your penchant for these girls, Jane – rough beggarly slatterns, all of them."

Betty came out with the pot to make tea from the kettle on the fire and whispered to Eliza, "Master's in a filthy mood, girl. Too much rum and not enough brown sugar."

The woman tittered and, as always, Eliza was shocked by how disrespectful she was to the reverend gentleman – but, as Betty always said when challenged on this particular issue, "You lose respect for a man when you have to scrub his shitty smalls."

Eliza could hear Jane defending her charges. "Surely, Peter, we should encourage the girls to be industrious, to act like young ladies…"

"Young ladies, Jane?" the reverend snorted. "Come on! You know what they are like."

Jane's voice became low and serious. "We're here to bring them the Lord's word, Peter, to save their souls…"

"Exactly, Jane," the reverend snapped back, "you put it in a nutshell, but saving their souls doesn't mean petting them the way you do."

Eliza was listening avidly, but then Betty came back and said, "Better get along now, Eliza."

"But the mistress..." Eliza started.

"She won't need you anymore today, Eliza," Betty said. "Go home."

Eliza did as she was told, but not without a backwards glance or two in the direction of the house, feeling all the while that she had been ejected from a minor sort of Eden. Dusk was coming on and she didn't want to be out on the roads after dark, so she hurried back home.

⤳

Grace was outside by the fire, her work finished for the day. There was an open bottle of rum by her and no sign of any supper. Grace would have eaten the white men's leftovers, Eliza knew, and she hadn't been expected, so she couldn't really complain.

"You back, girl?" Grace stated the obvious. Her voice was slurred, so Eliza knew she was well on the way to oblivion.

"Yes, Ma, the reverend came back, so I had to go."

Grace laughed, but then looked seriously at Eliza, crouching by her beside the fire. "That white woman is trying to steal you away from me, Eliza." She nodded emphatically at her own words.

"She's not, Ma. She's just a kind lady..."

Grace laughed again, but it came out like a snort. "Kind lady, my arse. She just wants to take you off me."

Eliza knew that it was no use arguing with her mother when she was drunk, so she muffled her protestations.

"That white woman got no children, so she wants one," Grace said. "She don't want a black kid like Vicky, but a pretty brown-skinned girl like you…"

"I don't think so, Ma," Eliza said, but she was wondering if Grace, for all the fact she was half-cut, wasn't that far from the mark.

"If it's a child she wants and not something else…" Grace said, looking furtively at Eliza.

"What do you mean, Ma?" Eliza asked, but Grace would say no more on the subject.

"Anyway," she said, "I got no food for you and the boss is due soon, so it's best if you get away to your granny's. She can feed you and keep you out of the boss's way."

Eliza felt dejected; it was the second time that she'd been chucked out that day, once by her ma and once by the woman she had come to regard as something akin to a second mother. It was getting dark, but she could have found her way down to the creek and the camp even if she had been blindfolded.

Granny was there and sober for once – though probably not for long – and cooked her a fish she'd caught earlier in the day, with other tucker to go with it. Eliza told the old woman what had happened to her. Granny laughed.

"You're feeling sorry for yourself, aren't you, girl?" she said. "Like a joey abandoned by his ma – or two mas in your case."

Eliza agreed, almost in tears.

"Well, buck up, girl," Granny said. "It's not that bad. Grace is just keeping you safe – a pretty girl like you – from that boss of hers. And as for the white woman… well, I think you're better away from her. She treats you like a doll she can play with."

Granny's *humpy*, her bark-covered shelter, was small, so Eliza cuddled up close to the old woman. Sleeping there by the side of the lake, the wind carrying a faint trace of the water's coolness in the still, hot night, Eliza felt safe. The people's camp wasn't quiet, there were all sorts of night-time sounds, but they were familiar sounds, comfortable ones. She couldn't help thinking about Cassie, her big soft bed and that strange empty house of hers, with just the two women in it.

"Granny, I saw that white girl again, my friend," she said.

Granny grunted, as if she wanted to sleep, not to talk, but her interest was piqued and she asked, "Where did you see her, Eliza? By the creek?"

"No... I was running away from the boss, that Cal Armstrong, and I sought her out."

"She saved you from him?" the old woman asked.

"Not exactly, Granny, but she took me in again. Helped me."

Granny nodded; not questioning Eliza about the details of what happened, just accepting that it had. "You and that girl got some kind of link," the old woman said. "Some cord stretching out between you. A cord with which you can pull each other in."

"And I think I sort of helped her, too, Granny," Eliza said. "She is very sad and lonely and she likes having me there. She lost someone..."

"Who did she lose? Her parents, her husband?" Granny asked.

"No, a girl," Eliza answered. She thought she understood what Carys had meant to Cassie, but she wondered if Granny would.

"I'm glad you were a help to her, Eliza. I think you are meant to help her and she, you."

"How so, Granny?"

"You mind what I told you before, Eliza," the old woman said. "When you're in trouble and she calls you, you go to her without hesitation."

"Alright, Granny," Eliza said, rather nonchalantly.

"I meant it, girl! You go to her! Now, get some sleep. I can't have you chattering away all night."

CHAPTER THIRTY-ONE

Cassie decided that missing Eliza was becoming a habit and she couldn't decide if it was a good one or a bad one. She still wondered, sometimes, if she had conjured the girl up out of a combination of loneliness and desire. As if she had taken the raw clay and shaped an effigy of Eliza, which had, by some magic, been brought to life. But Eliza was real, she knew, warm-fleshed, human, if a little lost in time. Thinking about how it all worked didn't help, but thinking about Eliza did.

It wasn't that Eliza had in any way replaced Carys in her affections. She loved Carys, would always love Carys, of that she was determined and that wasn't going to ever change. What was happening with Eliza was altogether different. There was something pulling them towards each other, some force, and Cassie didn't know exactly what it was. It wasn't just friendship, attraction, whatever you wanted to call it. She had the sense that it was way more important than that. There was a reason for it, she was sure, even if she couldn't fathom it.

While Cassie had resigned herself to the fact that Eliza only appeared infrequently and unpredictably, Eve unfortunately hadn't. Though they didn't really talk about it, Cassie suspected that Eve had Eliza down as Cassie's girlfriend. The result of this assumption was that Eve kept asking when she was seeing Eliza next or, conversely, why she saw her so seldom.

"She's got a lot on, Mum," Cassie would say, one of a number of excuses. "I'm sure she'll turn up one of these days."

"Does she work?" Eve asked, trying to glean as much information as she could to fill the blank space where her knowledge of Eliza should have been.

"Not as such," Cassie said, but remembered what Eliza had told her of the mission school. "She's studying."

"Oh, where?" Eve asked, her interest piqued. "Is she in college?"

"No, it's far away," Cassie said, which wasn't totally untrue if you were talking of time and not distance. "I think it's some sort of Bible college."

Eve tried hard to hide her surprise and her disapproval. "Is she religious then?" she asked.

"No, not particularly," Cassie said confusingly. "And she takes care of her granny as well."

Cassie wasn't sure this was entirely true. She thought it was more than likely that Eliza's Granny took care of her.

It was evident to Cassie that Eliza had become a fixture, if not exactly in their household, at least in Eve's mind. And the reason for this was clear: Eve so wanted Cassie to live something that might pass for a normal existence, however tenuous that normality might be. This was partly altruistic – after all, Cassie was her daughter and she wanted her to be happy – but also partly selfish. If Cassie had someone, had something in life, Eve could stop worrying so much about her.

If it wasn't for Eliza, Cassie's life would have been, if not exactly tedious, routine and uneventful almost to the point of monotony. She existed on what she thought of as a giant hamster wheel with various spokes: the university library, home, cups of tea and outings with Linda, more home, days out with Eve, and the occasional dinner or barbie with Dev and Annie – who were now seemingly reconciled – and, of course, yet more home. Her running was an illuminated point on the map of this routine, but runs to the creek were always bittersweet, because she never saw Eliza there, but always longed to.

Routine and monotony have a tendency to numb the brain, so when Kate stopped her in the library during the eternal task of shelving, Cassie couldn't think why she would seek her out.

"Hi, Cassie," Kate said. She was, as usual, dressed immaculately; that day, she had tapered grey jeans on – obviously expensive, because they fitted like a glove – and a black leather jacket that screamed 'designer'. "Fancy a coffee or a drink later? I've got something for you."

Cassie agreed – you couldn't say no to someone like Kate – and they met in the lobby of the university by the reception desk.

"Shall we get out of here?" Kate said. "Let's go somewhere a bit quieter."

The woman, for once, looked tired and serious.

If Cassie had had any pretensions to sophistication, they were totally destroyed by what Kate said next.

"Text your mother, Cassie. Tell her I'll drop you home."

Kate's car was surprisingly unflashy – unlike the woman

herself – a mid-range Toyota, the sort of solid dependable family car that anyone might have. They travelled towards the coast in silence. Cassie knew that there was only one thing the 'something' could be about: Blood Creek. The fact that Kate wanted to go somewhere to tell her what she had found out and the additional fact that they drove in silence told Cassie that it was something unpleasant. This wasn't a surprise, as she'd always known it would be. She had, after all, seen what had happened through Eliza's eyes or, at least, seen part of what had happened.

They drove into the car park of a surf life-saving club. Cassie had noticed before that these places – primarily bases for lifeguards – had bars and even restaurants. The bar here was almost empty and they took a seat on a balcony looking out over the Coral Sea, which stretched in front of them for countless miles.

"What do you want to drink, Cassie?" Kate asked. "And I should warn you, you might need an alcoholic drink after what I've got to tell you."

Kate brought back two big glasses of wine.

"As I told you, Cassie," she said, when they were both sitting down again, "I'm a sociologist not a historian, but I've had discussions with one of my colleagues about what you told me... what you saw."

Cassie suddenly felt a panic rising inside her. She wanted, of course, to find out that nothing had happened, no atrocity to spoil the ageless calm of the creek, its shady banks and the lake shore. But if nothing had happened, did that make her a fraud or worse?

"I don't know if you've come across it, Cassie, but the

University of Newcastle – in New South Wales, north of Sydney – has created an interactive map of massacres by colonists of Aboriginal peoples from the First Fleet up until the twentieth century. Blood Creek isn't currently on it."

Cassie was now certain that Kate was going to tell her she was just an over-imaginative, hysterical young girl.

"The map, however, isn't comprehensive. The people working on it are quite aware of that fact – and there is, as always, more work to be done on it. There's a friend of mine, John Morgan, a doctor in the history department at the university, who has been doing some research about local events: violent clashes between settlers and Aborigines, so-called 'displacements' and so on. So, I had a chat with him."

Kate paused and took a sip of wine.

"Well, to cut a long story short, he found two documents referring to an event at Blood Creek in 1872..." Kate suddenly stopped and looked at Cassie. "Are you alright, love?" she asked. "You've gone terribly pale."

"I'm fine," Cassie said, but she wasn't feeling fine. "Please carry on."

"Well," Kate said, "the first document was a newspaper report – I can email you a PDF of it, if you like – which talks of a clash between some stockmen and the local Kabiri people... that's my people, Cassie." Kate gulped and paused.

She's looking a bit white, too, Cassie thought.

"It was a bland report," Kate continued. "A few lines about a clash between stockmen and tribal people because of some dead cattle. Four 'black fellows' – as they put it – were killed, supposedly in self-defence, of course. The stockmen were unscathed. The reporter talks in the usual trite phrases about the need to chastise the blacks and bring them into line like naughty children. Regrettable, but necessary."

"Is that all?" Cassie asked and immediately felt guilty.

Kate gave her a questioning look. Four people dead wasn't exactly a minor event.

"No, it's not," Kate said. "Now we come to the second document, which was found in the papers of an old man. Well, not exactly in his papers… It was secreted in a book and the book found its way to an antiquarian bookseller, before it was passed to a local amateur historian."

Kate gulped some more wine.

"I won't go into all the circumstances and chances that led to the document ending up in John's hands, which is quite a saga in itself. Suffice it to say that it did eventually, after being filed away on top of somebody's wardrobe for many years and going unremarked."

Kate paused, looked at her phone and then sighed.

"I should have brought my laptop with me. I thought I'd copied it to my phone, but I haven't. Again, I can send it you, so you can read it yourself."

Cassie didn't think she wanted to. It was enough for Kate to interpret it, to keep it at a distance.

"The document is a letter or testament, headed 'To whom it may concern', written in 1911 by a local man, James Johnson, who was a stockman on the Montrose Station, or cattle ranch, which was very near to where you currently live, though the range land has been almost covered up by suburban housing.

"Johnson was a member of the party that clashed with the local people on that day in February 1872, but his account differs quite markedly from the newspaper report. He says that the station manager, who was sick of what he calls the Aboriginal 'depredations', told his men that they were going on a 'nigger' hunt – the actual words he used – early the next morning and to get their rifles and other firearms ready.

"Johnson goes on to say that they left before dawn and laid an ambush at the mouth of Peregian Creek – 'peregian' is the local indigenous word for 'emu' – knowing that the Aboriginal people would start fishing at first light. When a number of men and women appeared at the creek mouth with nets and lines, the boss, as he calls the station manager, ordered them to open fire. He says that he did not like the idea of killing women – he uses the word 'gins', a pejorative term for indigenous women – but they were mixed in with the men. The 'black fellows', as he calls them, had no chance, and Johnson thought it was all over, but the boss ordered them to mount their horses and ride down the creek to drive off all the remaining Aboriginal people.

"Johnson says that he didn't fire his carbine again, but many of the stockmen did and, he admits, many men, women and children were killed or wounded and driven into the bush. He says that he counted twenty-two dead afterwards but was convinced that the casualty rate was much higher, because of the thick bush on the creek sides where the wounded had crawled off to die. None of the stockmen were injured and he puts this down to the speed and surprise of the attack. He, in fact, seems quite proud of this aspect of it.

"The boss told them to leave the bodies – he said,

according to Johnson, that any living 'niggers' could deal with them – and gave them the afternoon off. The boss broke out the rum when they got back to the station and told them what to say if they were asked, by any settler or policeman, what had happened. That cover story was, in essence, the newspaper report.

"White men very seldom got prosecuted for killing Aboriginal people and the Queensland Native Police – recruited from Aboriginal tribes outside the area – were little more than a death squad, but the station manager was probably trying to avoid awkward questions from missionaries or other sympathetic whites.

"Johnson goes on to say that because there were Kabiri people working as servants at the station, word of the massacre soon got out, as some of the victims were relatives of the domestic staff. This didn't bother his boss, who said that he'd taught the 'niggers' the lesson that they were due and that no one would take the word of a 'black fellow' over that of a white man, anyway."

Kate sighed and finished her glass of wine.

"God, I wish I wasn't driving," she said. "I could do with another one of those."

Cassie got them some water instead. When she came back from the bar, Kate went on.

"Where was I? Oh, yes… It appears that Johnson wrote this testament because, in old age, he was feeling guilty about participating in the massacre, particularly about the women and children killed. He seemed to have had no problem with killing men. It was obviously some sort of attempt at personal contrition, but not enough of one to go public with it. And one other thing, a detail that definitely places this massacre at your creek – on the day of the killing, the waters ran red with blood, so the local Kabiri referred to it from that day forth as Blood Creek."

Cassie thought she was going to faint again; the revelation was what she had expected, but it was still devasting. To think of Eliza caught up in that and, worse, that Eliza might have been one of the victims didn't bear thinking about – but she couldn't stop thinking about it.

"Cassie, are you alright?" Kate asked.

"It's just…" Cassie said but couldn't finish the sentence. "I think I need some air."

They drove back in silence, but when they got to Cassie's house, they both stayed sitting in their seats, as if they knew there was more that had to be said.

"It's not unusual, you know, Cassie, for such incidents to be either hushed up or underreported. It's part of a pattern, really, that started quite early on, to gloss over or hide… a better word for it… the number of deaths inflicted on the native people by the whites. Even when the scale of the deaths was known, the perpetrators were never brought to justice.

"I think I mentioned the Coniston Massacre to you before. It was a series of killings of Aboriginal people in 1928 in the Northern Territories. After an Aboriginal man had killed a white man, a dingo hunter, who had sexually harassed or assaulted one of his wives – quite a legitimate reaction under Aboriginal law – a posse led by a policeman took the law into their own hands and killed approximately two hundred Aboriginal people in a serious of punitive raids. The Aboriginal men they arrested for the white man's murder were acquitted by a Darwin court, because the evidence against them was so flimsy.

"Pressure from the federal government, the church and the British newspapers led to a Board of Enquiry in 1929, which was little more than a cover-up. It found that the members of the posse, despite all the killings they had carried out, had acted in self-defence. And that was in relatively modern times, so you can see how the events at Blood Creek in 1872 were not only tolerated but sanctioned by the attitudes of white society."

Cassie put her hand on the handle of the door, but Kate hadn't finished.

"But what I couldn't quite understand, when John told me about what had happened, was how the massacre slipped from the memories of my own people. I had never heard anything about it growing up. And when I started talking to old aunties and other elders, there was a marked reluctance to discuss anything about it. They would say that Blood Creek was a bad place, that bad things happened there, but they didn't seem to know what."

Kate bowed her head; she looked upset and vulnerable, smaller and older than she usually appeared. Cassie had never seen her like that before.

"I could understand that the whites would want to forget what had happened, consign it to history and do what they always do: make a bland statement acknowledging the traditional owners of the land and the past wrongs inflicted on them, but not get into too much gory detail, before quickly moving on – but not my people. Why would they want to forget something like that?"

Kate paused again, looking out of the window. Eve had come out onto the terrace and was waving, but Kate ignored her.

"But then John told me that there are examples from history of this happening. That sometimes such events are so traumatic that even the victims want to forget them. It's a form of cultural amnesia. The fact of remembering, of bearing witness, is always painful; sometimes people want to escape from pain, from the evils of the past, especially if they are a powerless minority in a dominant society that would also rather forget such events."

Kate looked up and smiled at Cassie.

"Well, I'd better stop talking and let you get back. You look shattered and I feel emotionally exhausted. We'll talk later in the week."

Kate looked closely at Cassie, with something like wonder in her eyes. And people didn't usually look at Cassie that way.

"And we haven't even started on why you saw something that had been hidden from history for so long... but I think we've had enough for today."

Cassie waved to Kate as she headed off down the drive, but Kate was staring ahead, fixed on some point in front of her, some destination that Cassie could only guess at.

"You did ask Kate in, didn't you?" Eve asked.

Kate was another member of the university staff that Eve had an academic crush on. *Who wouldn't?*

"Yes, I did, Mum, but she had to go."

Eve smiled. "What were you two talking about for so long?" She was obviously intrigued.

"About the local Aboriginal people and their history," Cassie said blandly.

"Well, you'll have to tell me all about it," Eve said, but Cassie doubted she meant it.

Eve then whittered on about dinner: what were they going to eat? Was Cassie hungry? What about a takeaway? But Cassie didn't really hear her. She was thinking about Eliza. She had to warn her, to tell her to keep away from the creek on that day. And not only her, but all the rest of the Kabiri.

But how would that work? Could she change the past? And, just as importantly, how was she ever going to contact Eliza?

CHAPTER THIRTY-TWO

It wasn't until dusk, with night coming on, that Grace told her the secret she had been harbouring all day.

"Jimmy's been back."

When Eliza arrived back from the mission school that afternoon, she could tell that something was up with Grace. The woman was smiling and singing to herself – and Grace was usually a miserable woman with a face, as Betty put it, like a 'slapped arse' – and she even seemed on occasion to be hugging herself.

Seeing this change in her mother, Eliza started wondering if there was a man involved and whether that would mean she would have to contend with some new male presence hanging around the shack. Grace had, over the years, drifted from man to man, often on a transactional basis – when you had two kids to feed, it usually came down to who was the best provider. And she was still young enough and bonny enough – as Cal Armstrong said, when he was trying to flatter her – to attract the odd male glance.

Eliza had a moment or two of panic when she thought the new man might be the boss himself, as she wasn't sure that he would settle for Grace, but might want her, too, as part of the package. It was likely to be a white man – like her father and Jimmy's father had been – as the stockmen were always avid for female company, and white women were very few and far between in the district. And black fellows, even those of her own mob, would steer clear of Grace. It was widely known that she'd shacked up with two white men in her time – which was a transgression of tribal law and custom – and working for the white men, the bane of the Kabiri's existence, made her all the more suspect.

It wasn't, after all, a new lover who had made her so happy, but it was love, an old abiding love, because Jimmy, her firstborn, her only son, was and had always been her favourite child. This had been clear to Eliza for so long that she just took it as a fact of life. There was some bond between her mother and her brother that had existed before she was even born, which had inextricably cemented them together. Even at a distance, it still held.

But Eliza loved Jimmy, too, and the idea that he had been there, however briefly, and she hadn't seen him was devastating.

"Why didn't he wait to see me, Ma? I miss him as well," she said.

Grace looked at her with disappointment, if not disdain, as if Eliza should have known the reason and didn't have to ask. "Stop your whining, Eliza," she snapped. "You know your brother is a wanted man. He can't tarry in one place for overlong."

The way Grace was looking at Eliza told her everything: her ma was wishing that *she* was the one hiding in the bush and that Jimmy was the one at home, where she could take care of him, be his willing slave.

"But where is he now, Ma?" Eliza asked plaintively.

Grace shook her head and lowered her eyes, but, eventually, glancing up at her again, she told her, "He's camped on the far side of the lake, on that hill they call the Turtle's Back. In a stand of coolabahs. If you hurry, you might catch him."

Grace said it as if she didn't care one way or the other.

Eliza set off at once, even though it was dark. She knew it was a fair distance, but even if being abroad at night had its dangers and hazards, she couldn't miss out on the chance of seeing Jimmy one more time.

Rather than work her way around the bush that fringed the lake, which was tangled and tortuous, she headed westwards, cutting across grassland and past stands of gum trees. She passed close to the grove of plum trees – thinking ruefully of Cassie as she did so – and bore north to cut the shore of the lake again, working down another creek. The Turtle's Back stood out clear in the vestiges of light that hung above the horizon like a luminous cloud.

She knew there was a fold of land just north of the hill, where the waters of a stream pooled on their way to the lake. It had been a favourite spot when they were kids and wanted to get away from their ma. They would disappear in this childhood world of theirs, where there were no worries or cares, and there was no one to call them 'brown-skinned bastards' or 'mongrel by-blows'.

It was a hidden spot, concealed from the hill above and the land around, and you would have to know exactly where it was to discover it. She was just finding her path through the trees, the smile already on her face at the prospect of seeing her brother, when she heard voices ahead of her. She froze with fear, stood stock still and listened: two voices. Had the policemen come back and caught Jimmy? But it was Jimmy's voice she could hear. She could only just make out what he was saying, his voice was so low and insistent.

"I don't know what you want me to say to you, mate," Jimmy said. "It was just one of those things that happen on the trail… and we'd both had too much to drink."

"I haven't told anybody where you are, Jimmy," the other person said and she suddenly knew who it was: Cal Armstrong.

"Well, fair dos for that, Cal, but I don't know what you want from me. You know I've got to keep moving."

"You could come back, Jimmy," Cal said. "I could square it with the law somehow…"

"How the fuck would you do that, Cal?" Jimmy asked. "That's just a pipe dream of yours."

"Or I could come with you," Cal said, sounding desperate and something else. His voice was breaking, as if he was on the verge of crying, which was strange in itself, as white men weren't allowed to cry – or so Eliza understood from Jane.

"Don't see you as bushranger, Cal. Besides," Jimmy said, "I'm not like you, I prefer to go with girls."

"And so do I," Cal answered him back, quickly and loudly, "but I thought we had something special between us, unique…" His words trailed off.

Eliza was having difficulty understanding what was going on. She had wriggled closer and could now see Cal clearly from where she was hiding. The man stood up and moved towards Jimmy. He tried to take Jimmy in his arms, moving his lips towards her brother's.

"Leave it out, Cal," Jimmy said, pushing him off. "You'd better just fuck off and get going."

Armstrong, his face as white and drained as a dead man's, fetched his horse and vaulted into the saddle. He took a last, long look at Jimmy and said, "You get a favour this time, Jimmy. I won't tell the coppers you've been back, but next time I see you, I'll shoot you myself." He turned to go, but he had something else to say, "You'll rue the day that you wronged me, Jimmy. Mark it well!"

Jimmy's hand hovered around his holstered revolver as Cal rode off. Everyone knew that the boss had bought one of those new-fangled Henry repeating rifles from America – he boasted so much about it – so he was a man to watch, what with both his armament and his fiery red-headed temper. Jimmy watched him closely until he faded from view in the undergrowth.

"You can come out now, Eliza," he said.

"How did you know it was me?" Eliza asked.

"I could smell you," Jimmy said.

"No, you didn't," Eliza said, putting her nose to her armpits and sniffing. "I'm not even that sweaty... No, really, how could you tell?"

Jimmy laughed. "I don't know, sis," he said. "I just could. I always know when you are around."

She wanted to ask him what all that had been about, but was afraid of the answer she might get.

He smiled and sort of explained it anyway. "Had you not

suspected that beneath that manly aspect, Cal Armstrong was hiding something of a girlish nature?"

But he's been after me, Eliza thought. And then she suddenly realised the meaning of what she had just seen. Cal wanted Jimmy, not her; she was just second-best, hence his reference to the family resemblance.

"You shouldn't have come, sis. It's too dangerous," Jimmy said, "but I'm glad you did."

Eliza was disappointed; she could see that Jimmy was packing up his few traps in his saddlebags, rolling up his bedroll and tying his billy can on behind.

"Are you not staying a while longer, Jimmy?" she asked.

She was trying not to cry, because in her heart of hearts she knew that he had to go, but it was difficult. Too difficult.

"Ah, sis," Jimmy said. "Come on, don't cry! Your face is wrinkled enough already, it'll look like a shrivelled plum if you carry on like that."

She couldn't help laughing through her tears. Jimmy was always like this – teasing her. And she'd tease him back. It was the way they rubbed along together.

"I was going to shoot through in the morning, anyway, Eliza," Jimmy said, "but that little altercation with Cal Armstrong has decided me on a swifter departure."

"But where are you going to go, Jimmy?" Eliza asked, trying to mask the sadness she felt.

"I'll head north, sis," he said smiling at her. "It's better if you don't know exactly where, just in case…"

He didn't have to spell it out. She knew what he meant. O'Halloran would think nothing of beating the information out of her.

"I shook off the coppers up in the hills," Jimmy continued. "They sent a black tracker after me, but it turned out that he was less good at the job than they thought. I doubled back on them and shot up their camp. You should have seen their faces, Eliza."

Jimmy laughed as he told her and, in this laughter, she saw another side of Jimmy: a fierce, fatal side of him that she wasn't sure she wanted to know.

"Hopefully they might leave me alone for a while as the trail is cold... unless Cal makes it hot again."

He had carried on with his packing while he talked and he was now almost ready. Eliza saw that, apart from the revolver, he also had a police carbine holstered by the saddle horn and she wondered where he'd got it from.

"Well, I must be off, sis," he said, "but I'll not leave you alone out here. Climb up behind me and I'll take you part of the way home." He helped her up into the saddle behind him. "When did you get so big, Eliza?" he said. "You used to be a little scrap of a thing."

She smiled to herself. It was just like Jimmy not to see what was in front of his eyes, how his little sister had turned into a woman. She held her arms tightly around him, as they rode. Even through his corduroy jacket, he gave off a comforting warmth, and though he smelled of the horse and the trail, it was a good smell. It was Jimmy's own personal smell and she breathed it in, making a conscious effort to remember it.

He dismounted and helped her down by the plum tree grove. "I can't risk getting closer, Eliza," he said, "but you should be alright from here." Then he hugged her tight as if he didn't want to let her go and kissed her hair – but he did let her go.

"Take care of yourself, sis," he said, "and take care of Ma."

Then he was gone, a shadow among other shadows, disappearing into the night.

CHAPTER THIRTY-THREE

The worst thing for Cassie was that there was no one she could talk to about Eliza and what she feared might have happened to her. Even someone like Kate, who was at least sympathetic to her propensity for visions of past events, would baulk at the idea of Cassie conjuring up an actual flesh and blood figure from that past.

Kate might be part Kabiri, but she was also a successful academic; that was the other side of her, with a strong aversion to purveyors of nonsense and bullshit. And Cassie couldn't help thinking that by even broaching the subject, Kate would consign her to the ranks of the latter.

Even if she was willing to risk telling someone – risk the possibility that whoever it was would think she was mentally unbalanced – she wasn't sure that she would be able to find the words, if she actually had the vocabulary, to describe what was happening to her without falling back on the language of lurid sci-fi dramas, using phrases like 'temporal anomalies' or 'time slips'. And using this type of jargon would inevitably trivialise, or even fictionalise, something that was so real to her.

Eve still kept asking about Eliza – mainly, Cassie thought out of politeness rather than any real interest in the girl – though less often, as it became clear to her that Cassie was being even more tight-lipped than usual about her friend, which didn't, as far as Eve was concerned, bode well for the putative relationship.

The truth was, however, that Cassie couldn't bear to have trivial conversations about Eliza with her mother, with the prospect of the massacre hanging over her friend. Such conversations had always been difficult anyway, since, not really knowing a great deal about Eliza and not being able to divulge what she did know, she often had to fall back on making things up or, at least, twisting the truth into an acceptable shape. But it felt impossible now and Eve's questions, however well meant, received terse, non-committal replies.

The only thing that helped Cassie was running and most early mornings, when the day was still cool, found her on her way to the creek and the bridge, where she would inevitably stop and wait, sometimes venturing down to the water, just in case she might see or hear Eliza and hopefully pull her out from her time into Cassie's, where she would be safe, at least temporarily.

Cassie would often stand on the bridge racking her brains, trying to think of something she could do, but she never came up with a solution. She had the actual date in February 1872 of the massacre, but she wasn't quite sure if Eliza's calendar coincided with her own. And she wondered if Eliza, even if she saw her, would have any concept of what the date actually was in her own time. She didn't think that Eliza's people went by the white Australian calendar. However, running to the bridge and the creek made her feel that she was doing something rather than sitting at home brooding impotently on the sofa.

It was a week or so after Eliza's visit that Cassie saw Linda on her driveway, just as she was returning from one of her runs. Cassie had been avoiding Linda, ever since the picnic at the lake, and the reason for this was Irene. When Linda had told her that Irene had sensed an atmosphere on the day of the picnic and that she was some sort of medium, Cassie had been worried that Linda would tell Irene some of the things Cassie had told her and pull the woman into some uncomfortable collective séance to contact those spirits at the creek. She could just imagine it: the three of them sitting in Irene's musty, hot living room, curtains drawn, joss sticks burning and, of course, a wine box on the go. Irene calling up various presences, with Linda providing the commentary, "Not that one, Irene. That's the wrong bloody spirit." And, of course, keeping Irene's wine glass topped up.

But coming face to face with her neighbour, Cassie couldn't help feeling guilty, as she knew that the woman had only introduced her to Irene to be helpful. Linda, after all, had believed Cassie when she told her about hearing and seeing things at the creek, rather than questioning her sanity.

"Fancy a coffee, love?" Linda asked and Cassie couldn't say no.

⫸

They sat on the terrace and Cassie was suddenly struck by how much smaller and older Linda looked.

"I've been ill, love," she said, seeing the stricken look on Cassie's face. "Been off form for a few days."

"You should have said," Cassie replied. "I could have…" – *What could I have done?* Cassie asked herself. She wasn't that good with sick people – "… at least got your shopping."

Even to Cassie, it sounded a rather pathetic offer of help. And it suddenly struck Cassie how self-absorbed she'd been, not only about Eliza, but ever since Carys had died. Grief was, however natural and legitimate, a particularly selfish emotion.

"That's okay, love," Linda said, trying to assuage Cassie's guilt. "I would have asked if I'd needed anything, but I'm like an animal. I like to curl up on my own, away from people, when I'm sick. Besides, I wouldn't go to a doctor. I take care of myself."

Cassie knew that Linda had a whole cabinet of homeopathic remedies in her bathroom. Linda had showed her.

"Anyway," Linda added, "I'm much better now. So, drink your coffee and I'll pour you some more."

But Cassie insisted on doing it herself, topping up her own cup with the regular coffee from the coffee plunger that Linda kept for guests, and making more of the hemp coffee substitute that Linda habitually drank.

"I'm afraid I haven't had the energy to bake anything, Cassie, but there are biscuits in the tin."

Cassie said that she was alright, though she hadn't eaten anything that day.

"I saw your friend the other morning," Linda said

unexpectedly and Cassie was a little taken aback. Almost embarrassed. As if Eliza was some sort of guilty secret.

"Yes," Cassie said, flustered, "she stayed over…"

Her words trailed off, but Linda didn't seem to notice. Instead, she smiled and chuckled.

"She looked just like I used to look in the seventies: op shop dress, bare feet and a frizz of hair. It took me back."

Cassie just smiled, as she didn't know what to say.

"Anyway, dear, I'm glad you're making friends. I know it's been tough."

It wasn't a surprise to Cassie that Linda knew this: she, herself, had told the woman a certain amount and Eve was loose tongued enough to have told more, but she wasn't sure how much Linda actually did know.

"She an indigenous Australian?" Linda asked.

"Yes, on her mother's side."

Linda nodded. "A very pretty girl," she said and then looked curiously at Cassie. "None of my business, love… And you can tell me off for even asking… But is she more than just a friend?"

Cassie knew that she should have expected the question – Linda had that Australian directness – but she was taken aback and didn't know how to reply.

"I mean, it doesn't bother me, Cassie," Linda continued. "I was a hippy chick and when we said free love, we meant it. Biological sex was irrelevant."

Cassie was silent, still not knowing what to say.

"Sorry, love, if I've offended you and it is, of course, your private business, but I'd just presumed… after what Eve said about your partner…"

It took a lot to embarrass Linda, but it seemed that Cassie had succeeded.

And it was odd to think about Carys in that way, as her 'partner.' She'd thought of the girl as part of her, an indivisible part that had been ripped away when she died. Like the double Venus necklace that Lainey wore: two souls never to be pulled asunder. Cassie had loved a woman wholeheartedly, in every sense of the word, but she wasn't sure that this fact could be so easily, and perhaps trivially, categorised as being a gay or lesbian thing.

"No," Cassie replied at last, "I'm not offended, Linda." She smiled. "I'm just not sure how to define my relationship with Eliza."

CHAPTER THIRTY-FOUR

Ever since Eliza had stayed with Mrs Cleary, she had noticed that the woman's attitude to her had changed. Where she had previously been warm and had often smiled at Eliza, touched her on the arm or the face when praising her, or asked her to stay after class to help with something, she was now cold and distant. She still praised Eliza's work if she did well, but with a formality that was hurtful.

Vicky and the other girls couldn't help but notice and, although they didn't say anything directly, the giggles and the arch looks they exchanged told it all. Eliza's position as teacher's pet was becoming increasingly tenuous.

It was Betty, who, in her own inimitable way, explained the reason to Eliza one night when the old woman was sharing a bottle of rum with Grace.

"The master gave the mistress a right talking to that day he came back from Brisbane." Then she chuckled, as if enjoying the memory. "He said that she shouldn't have a girl like you helping her bathe and dress. Said it wasn't seemly."

"What did he mean?" Eliza asked. She could see no harm in it.

Betty exchanged a glance with Grace and they both laughed.

"No, really," Eliza persisted. "I don't understand."

"Well," Betty said, attempting to explain through the fog of rum that was clouding her thinking, "the master has a particular dislike of girls like you, Eliza…"

"Girls like me?" Eliza almost wailed the words. "What do you mean?"

"What I mean, girl," Betty said, "is that he don't like the fact that you're a brown-skinned girl – white daddy, black mammy. He is one of those white men who can't abide black and white having babies."

Betty hiccupped and paused for a moment. Grace offered her water, but she took more rum instead. "But I don't think that is all the reason, Eliza," she said.

Eliza waited avidly for her next words.

"I think the master is jealous. After all, you've seen and touched more of the mistress's body than Reverend Cleary has for years, if ever."

Betty and Grace hooted with laughter, but Eliza still didn't really understand. She did, however, know that the Reverend Cleary thought that way about her, that he saw children like Eliza as the living embodiment of that dilution of the white race. But it was hardly her fault that white men couldn't leave black women alone.

As the weeks went past, things got better. Mrs Cleary's attitude to her underwent a slow thaw, which speeded up in those frequent periods that Mr Cleary was absent. Eliza had just about regained her status as the woman's favourite, much to the chagrin of Vicky and the other girls, within a couple of weeks.

So, it wasn't a surprise when Mrs Cleary asked Eliza to stay behind after lessons to help her tidy up the schoolroom. When she had said help, what she really meant was for Eliza to do the actual work – tidy away the tatty, dog-eared books that had been donated by the mission's supporters, empty the ink wells back into the big ink bottle and make sure all the copy books were stacked and put in the cupboard, while Mrs Cleary sat at her desk and completed the school log.

Eliza was just sweeping the floor, the last of her tasks, when she became conscious of the fact that Mrs Cleary had looked up from her ledger and was watching her. Eliza smiled shyly at Mrs Cleary, but the woman did not return the smile. She just kept staring sadly at her.

"Can I go now, Mrs Cleary?" Eliza asked when the job was finished. She was starting to feel uncomfortable. Mrs Cleary was behaving rather oddly.

"I wish you had come to me when I asked you, Eliza," Mrs Cleary suddenly said. "It's much harder now, almost impossible."

Eliza wasn't quite sure what she was talking about. "What's that, Mrs Cleary?" she asked.

The woman sighed. "I told you to call me Jane when we were alone, Eliza. Why won't you? Have I somehow lost your affection?"

Mrs Cleary – Jane – seemed to be on the verge of tears.

Eliza didn't know what to do. "But I thought…" she said.

"What did you think, Eliza?" Jane asked softly, her eyes gleaming in the light from the oil lamp.

"That I'd done something wrong, Mrs… Jane," Eliza answered and she gulped, all the emotion of the woman's earlier rejection of her rising in her throat. "That you didn't like me anymore."

"It was just...." Jane started saying. "It was no longer so easy... and Peter..."

She suddenly rose from her desk and came towards Eliza. She stopped a few feet away and looked at her, before saying, in a voice as thick as molasses, "Come here, girl."

Eliza did as she was told – why wouldn't she? – and Jane folded her into her arms. She sighed and buried her head against Eliza's shoulder.

"I have missed you, Eliza, did you know that?"

Eliza couldn't deny that it felt good to be held and that particular smell of eau de cologne, soap and starch that emanated from Jane was familiar and comforting. It was also rather disturbing, especially since Jane's embrace had an insistent, almost fierce quality to it. It was even more discomforting when Jane lifted her head and kissed Eliza full on the lips.

"My beautiful girl," Jane said and seemed to be enraptured.

Eliza could smell something else on Jane's breath, something sweet but cloying. She could also taste it on her lips. She suddenly realised what it was: that strong wine they called sherry.

Jane pressed Eliza closer, her lips insistent, her tongue pushing against Eliza's closed mouth, as if trying to gain entry.

"Jane... Mrs Cleary... I can't breathe," Eliza said, pulling away.

Jane suddenly stopped and looked at Eliza with surprise.

As if she, like in that story of a sleeping princess that she had once read to the girls, had woken up from a spell and suddenly realised that Eliza was really there and not some dream. Jane closed her eyes and shook her head, swaying slightly as she did so. She then seemed to make an effort to gather herself together, along with her voluminous skirts. She opened her eyes once more and took Eliza's hand firmly.

"Come, we will go and pray together," she said, "for forgiveness."

Eliza didn't want to follow her, but she tugged her along, across the yard to the tin-roofed mission church and pulled her down with her, to kneel on the bare dusty boards.

"Lord, forgive us our sins..." Jane started. When she realised that Eliza was silent, she insisted, "Eliza, say the words with me."

Eliza did, though, as far as she was concerned, the words meant nothing. She didn't understand the nature of their collective sin.

When the prayer was finished, Jane took her hand again and tugged Eliza to her feet. "You must go home now, Eliza. Your mother will be worried."

Eliza thought that it was more than likely that Grace was already well into the rum bottle, so was past worrying.

"I think I had too much sun today," Jane added, "which is why I was feeling faint earlier." She shot a shy look at Eliza – and Jane wasn't usually shy with her girls – and said, "I think that was why I was acting a little strangely... I will retire early, as I think I need to rest."

"I could stay and help you, Mrs Cleary... Jane," Eliza said, quite innocently.

Jane smiled but shook her head vigorously. "No, Eliza, it's best if you go home. I can call Betty if I need help."

Jane suddenly seemed unable to meet Eliza's eyes, but when she finally did, Eliza saw that her expression was pained.

"I am very fond of you, Eliza, you know," she said and then she hugged her again. This time, it was a just a brief, chaste clasping of bodies – all passion banished.

On the way home, Eliza thought over what had happened. She was innocent, but not completely naïve. Even before she had found out about Cal and her brother, she had known that men could lie with other men. There used, in fact, to be a long-standing joke among her people about this particular predilection of white men when there were no women around.

But she would have been surprised by the ardour of Jane's embraces, if not shocked, if it hadn't been for her friend, Cassie. Because Cassie, or so she had said, had loved another woman and even lived with her. Cassie had also said that, in her world, two women could get married.

Eliza did wonder, though, how two women would go about the business of fucking. Perhaps it was something like that tight embrace of Jane's and the insistent kisses. She told herself that she must ask Cassie about it when she next saw her, if it wasn't too rude a question.

CHAPTER THIRTY-FIVE

It was another barbecue at Dev and Annie's and though Cassie had made any number of excuses to her mother to get out of going, Eve, for once, had insisted that she came.

"Annie's been very kind to you, Cassie, and Dev, too, so at least make an effort," Eve said.

On the way there in the car, Cassie tried to figure out what Eve meant exactly. Apart from the voluntary job, which was fast becoming as repetitive as some short avant-garde film on a video loop, the sort you saw in those galleries dedicated to what they called 'modern art', there didn't seem to be much else to be grateful for. But she knew that it was just Eve's way of cementing that friendship she craved so much. A permanent state of gratitude, deserved or not, would make her wayward daughter beholden to her new friend.

It was difficult being at Dev and Annie's without interpreting every wry look or arch glance as having a hidden meaning, knowing what Cassie knew about the state of their relationship. From what she'd gleaned from Eve – and Eve would always talk a little bit too much when she'd had a couple of glasses of wine – the relationship had always been rocky and given to shaky periods. And both Dev and Annie had been involved in various emotional entanglements with other people during the course of the marriage.

Cassie couldn't really understand these 'grown-up relationships', as she thought of them. Her relationship with Carys had been that much simpler: they liked being together on their own and didn't need anyone else to bolster their sense of self or worth. She did wonder, though, if her memory was shining a rather golden light on the way things had been between them and whether, if they had ended up being together as many years as Dev and Annie, they would have come up against the same sort of obstacles on that long road.

Cassie was parked on a sofa on the veranda with a glass of wine – her mother had managed to look disapproving as Annie poured it – away from the small, random crowd of guests on the lawn. It was a Saturday afternoon, a little early for a party in her opinion, but the timing had given her a ready excuse: she had a headache and had to keep out of the sun. Of course, no one there, apart perhaps from Eve, really cared whether Cassie socialised or not, so nobody, she was sure, was going to bother her.

Lainey was there – there were a few post-grad students of Dev's and some of Annie's – but they'd only exchanged greetings. Lainey had spent most of the afternoon hanging on Annie's every word, in nearly the same way that Eve had, although Eve was a more sophisticated fangirl, not as blatant as Lainey.

For once, Cassie wasn't thinking about Eliza; she had something else on her mind. She'd spoken to her dad earlier in the day – there was almost a twelve-hour difference so it had been evening in Oxford. He had told her – 'prepared her', as he put it – that the woman he was seeing was moving in. They were going to try to make a go of it, he said, which was a rather underwhelming way of putting it.

The fact he was seeing someone hadn't been a surprise to Cassie, though all she knew about the woman was that she was called Sharon and was 'in sales'. Eve seemed quite content that her husband would now be someone else's emotional responsibility, but the fact that cohabitation had suddenly been factored in had floored Cassie. Because it effectively closed off her escape route.

She had come to Australia on the understanding that she could – and probably would – return to the UK in the future, but the advent of Sharon, in the family home, meant that such a prospect was looking exceedingly unlikely. Cassie didn't want to share a house – or her father – with the updated, newer model of Eve. It was bad enough sharing a house on the other side of the world with the old model. And it wasn't that she disliked Queensland particularly, she just felt unmoored. Part of her had considered a move back to that same country where Carys lay in the black, merciless soil as a possible answer to her problems.

"You had the same idea as me," a voice suddenly said and brought her out of her reverie. It was Kate Mackinnon, dressed effortlessly and elegantly as usual in a linen ensemble.

"Sorry?" Cassie asked.

Kate smiled. "What I mean is that I can't stand these sorts of events – all that shop talk and small talk – so I thought I'd find a piece of shade and have a sit down, but you beat me to it."

"Oh," Cassie said, rather gormlessly. She had expected that someone like Kate would take this sort of social event in her stride.

"Budge up, then," Kate said, "if you don't mind being disturbed, that is."

Cassie moved along the bamboo sofa and Kate sat down.

"Your mum is in her element," Kate said and Cassie detected just a hint of disdain in her voice.

"Yes," Cassie said. "Well, she doesn't get out much, so she laps up parties like this."

Kate laughed. "I don't know if Eve would appreciate your frankness, Cassie," she said, "but I get your meaning. To me, these departmental parties are a chore, but others, like Dev and Annie, seem to thrive on them."

Kate looked at Cassie a little too long for comfort, before she glanced away.

"I'm still trying to take in all that stuff about Blood Creek... to come to terms with it," Kate continued, taking a sip of her gin and tonic. "I think it's because of the local connection that it got to me... you know, in all likelihood, those people were my ancestors."

Cassie hadn't really thought of this before. She suddenly realised that Eliza and Kate could possibly be related.

"Not that it's something that's particularly easy to find out," Kate continued, "as most indigenous people were undocumented, unless they worked for the settlers or had contact with the missions."

Cassie remembered that Eliza had talked about a mission school and her teacher, but only in passing.

"So, it comes down to memory and while my people

have a great tradition of oral history, we are talking of the passing of a hundred and fifty years or so. And there's another complication…"

Kate paused and looked at Cassie, as if she was worried that she was boring her. Cassie, however, was listening avidly.

"Well, I don't know if you are familiar with the tradition of most of the indigenous mobs – that you mustn't mention the names of the dead, to spare the pain of the relatives?"

"No, I wasn't," Cassie said. And she wondered if that would have helped or hindered her in her own grief. If, instead of referring to Carys, people had said 'your friend' or 'your partner', but then she realised that, effectively, that was what people did say. Very few people mentioned Carys by name.

"It's still a tradition in some communities and the period involved can last from at least a year up to a number of years, depending on the particular cultural rules. These can make it difficult, especially after so many years, to trace the family histories of specific individuals." Kate shrugged. "I've talked to some of the elders of our mob and all I could ascertain was that when they were children – as far back as the Second World War in a couple of cases – there was a cultural or religious restriction… a taboo, you could call it… against them playing or even going to Blood Creek. It was rumoured to be a place where something bad happened, but they were told nothing more."

"So, we'll never know anything more about those people," Cassie said, thinking of Eliza and her granny; those laughing, chatting women she had seen; the children splashing in the water; and those still, silent men fishing in the lake.

"That's the way it goes, Cassie, I'm afraid," Kate said. "Most of the indigenous people killed in these sorts of incidents were nameless and faceless, whereas, in the case of white people killed by the Aboriginals, we often get not only their names, but their stories."

Kate took another gulp of her drink.

"Because you know, Cassie, it wasn't always one-sided. Some of the mobs mounted a quite effective campaign of guerrilla warfare against the settlers, picking them off one by one. But the reprisals, when they came, tended to be disproportionate and devastating."

Kate looked out towards the people grouped on the lawn in front of her, chatting away, voices and laughter getting higher and shriller as more alcohol was consumed.

"I think I need another drink... but there is something else I want to tell you before I go and try to be sociable," she said. "My friend, John... you know, the history lecturer I told you about... he's found out that there was a short-lived mission station not far for the creek. It was run by a couple from England, the Clearys. It was a small establishment, funded by some obscure missionary society, so not closely linked to the established churches. He's trying to see if he can find any records—"

"Cassie," a voice said, interrupting their conversation.

It was Eve, but she seemed taken aback to find Kate with her daughter.

"Hi, Eve," Kate said. "How are you?"

"I'm fine, thanks," Eve said. "I just came over to tell Cassie that the food is ready."

Kate said that she was going to get herself a drink

and would see them later. Eve watched her go. There was something in the way she looked at the woman, but Cassie couldn't figure out if it was a sort of grudging admiration or just jealousy.

"You two seem to be getting on well these days," Eve said to Cassie. "I didn't know you were interested in sociology – or whatever it is she teaches." Eve smiled pleasantly as she said it, but there was no disguising the hint of bitchiness in her voice as she spoke.

"We were just having a chat about other stuff," Cassie replied.

"Oh, what other stuff?" Eve asked.

But Cassie wouldn't say and eventually Eve gave up, as she all but pulled her out onto the lawn to join the party.

CHAPTER THIRTY-SIX

When the hot weather came, the mission school was just about the worst place to be. The tin roof heated up the schoolroom below it as if it was effectively an oven and the low narrow windows didn't help to cool it down at all, especially as there was hardly a breath of wind blowing most days. The girls, in their patched dresses and the occasional tattered hat or bonnet – trying to look like the insipid little white girls they saw in the storybooks on the plank shelves around the walls – wilted in the heat like so many hothouse flowers.

They knew that if they'd been down at the creek or by the lake, they could have sat in the shade, slouched out of their dresses when they wanted to, and bathed their hot bodies in the cool water. But they were stuck at school and most of them had no firm idea why. Often it was their mas and pas who had sent them, out of a sense of religious duty – in the case of the people who had been converted to Christianity by Peter Cleary – or in an attempt to better their prospects in life in this white man's world. But mostly it came down to the fact that the girls, with their ever-hungry mouths, were fed at the school, given enough tucker to fill their bellies, with a bit left over to bring home, if they were lucky. To the girls, though, it was just all a series of painful constrictions of discipline and duty, and they were jealous of their sisters whose families, the traditional hold-outs, didn't make them dress up in white man's clothes or sit in stupid white man's houses, being baked like those bread rolls that Betty was tasked to make for the reverend each morning and always ended up burning.

The girls had little choice in the matter but to sweat it out. The one concession that Mrs Cleary had made to the weather was to start school early, at first light, and to let them nap in the afternoon, on their benches, before more study and work in the cool of the evening. But none of this really mattered to Eliza. Although she experienced as much discomfort as the rest of the girls, her mind was full of other concerns, other worries.

Eliza had always liked going to school. She had always enjoyed the work involved and the praise she received from Jane when she did well. She had gained a sense of achievement and of pride, unlike anything she had ever experienced before, and also something else: she had felt valued by Jane and even loved. As if Jane was another mother to her, a different mother, one unlike Grace, who tended to let Eliza get on with things without demonstrating much affection for, or appreciation of, her daughter.

And now things had changed. Whatever it was that had happened between Jane and Eliza – if something *had* actually happened; Eliza wasn't really sure that it had – spoiled everything else. Because Eliza had always felt comfortable with Jane, safe and secure in an uncertain world. Now, an uncertainty had crept in between them and Eliza would always have to be on her guard.

She wasn't sure what it all meant and particularly what Jane wanted from her, because, as always with white people, she did want something – that was clear. And, again, as always in such cases, it would be mean trouble of some kind. She already knew, courtesy of Betty, that Peter Cleary didn't particularly like her and was jealous of her, and Eliza had no doubt that, in the end, if it came to it, Jane would always have to take her husband's side, to do what he wanted. It was just the way things were.

Despite the way Eliza felt, Jane was, in fact, treating her with more affection and consideration than ever. But this in itself gave Eliza no comfort; it was as if the woman was making up for something, Eliza decided, like you would bribe a child you'd just spanked with sweets.

The one change in Jane's behaviour was that she would, when she asked Eliza to stay late after school, also ask Vicky. Vicky was too pleased to be picked to ask why Jane didn't want to be left alone with Eliza. But to Eliza, it was clear. She, Eliza, had done something wrong, transgressed in some way.

Vicky and Eliza fell into their usual comfortable companionship. They'd known each other since they were babies and, though they had the occasional spat, they were easy enough in each other's company. And Eliza had to admit that it did make the time go more quickly, the work more enjoyable and it was good to have someone to walk home with.

Sometimes they would forget themselves and get too loud, or even laugh, but though Jane would ask them to quieten down, she would be gentle about it, not scolding them the way she used to do.

"What's up with Mrs Cleary?" Vicky asked, after one of these occasions. "She gone soft?"

"You think so?" Eliza said.

"Yes, Eliza," Vicky went on, "and she hasn't used her stick for a while."

Jane had a cane and if one of the girls misbehaved, they would have to hold their hand out to receive their punishment. The cane was thin, but as flexible as a whip, and Jane was practised enough to use it to maximum effect. It hurt like hell, as Eliza knew from experience. And if one of them did something really naughty, she would lift up their skirts and cane them on the back of their thighs, which was equally painful. She never beat their bare arses – as Grace had done to Eliza enough times – because, apparently, it wasn't seemly to chastise girls in that way.

"Perhaps we're just all behaving ourselves," Eliza said, but Vicky shook her head.

"No... I think something's up... And she's been at the grog lately, you can see that. She can hardly stand some of the time."

Eliza knew what Vicky said was true. Jane was going through a lot of sherry. It was more socially acceptable than rum, but it was still turning her into a drunk. Both girls, however, took this in their stride – they were used to drinking and drunks. It was how most of the white people coped with life out there and rum, once it had been introduced to the black fellows, had become almost as much of a necessity for them.

However much they tried to figure out Jane's behaviour, it was Betty who solved the mystery for them late one afternoon as they were about to leave for the day.

"The reverend wants to move further north to a new mission, where he's been offered a position, and the mistress doesn't want to go. She prefers your black arses to any other black arses." Betty laughed, as usual, as if she'd said the wittiest thing.

"No!" Eliza exclaimed. "She wouldn't go and leave us, would she?"

She couldn't believe it and neither could Vicky, who looked equally upset.

"Well, girls, it's always the same," Betty said. "White people don't stay put for long. They can only pass a few years here before they want to move on somewhere else more civilised or back to England." She laughed again. "Us savages get too much for them."

As she walked home with Vicky afterwards, Eliza was quiet. Vicky tried to engage her in conversation, but eventually gave up and sulked the rest of the way home. Eliza could only think of one thing: Mrs Cleary was leaving and it was all her fault.

CHAPTER THIRTY-SEVEN

"Where you been, girl?" Grace asked when Eliza got home.

"I stayed after school, Ma. What did you think?" Eliza said.

Grace got up from the fire and lunged at Eliza. She grabbed her by both shoulders and shook her. "Less of your cheek, girl, or I'll tan your arse for you until you can't sit down for a week."

But Grace didn't scare Eliza, because, by the dim, flaring light of the fire, she could see that Grace wasn't really angry, she was terrified. Grace sobbed and the shake turned into a hug. Then, her ma let her go and quickly stepped back.

"I was worried, Eliza. I thought something had happened to you, with all that was going on."

Eliza was oblivious; she had no idea what her mother was talking about.

"That's just like you, Eliza," Grace said. "Walking around in a dream. Haven't you heard?"

Eliza's heart seemed to skip a beat. She went icy cold and felt unsteady on her legs. *Jimmy*, she thought.

"Sit down, Eliza," Grace said. "You've gone pale."

Her ma poured her a cup of tea and added rum to it – just a shot – and put a hunk of bread and cheese on a tin plate. It was food she'd brought back from the station and not particularly to Eliza's liking, but it was grub, so she ate it.

"The boss found another of his beasts dead, tangled up in the mangroves by the edge of the lake. Some black fellows had speared it. He's spitting blood over it, but that's not the worst of it."

Even Eliza, in her own dream world, knew that her people were waging their own sneaky sort of war on the stockmen, cutting out and killing cattle, keeping the thirsty beasts from the precious waters of the creek and the lake.

"There's a shepherd been killed over at Barrow Creek by the local mob," Grace continued.

Eliza could see how serious that was. "But, Ma, that's a fair way away. They can't blame our people."

"That don't matter, girl. When have they ever needed an excuse? The boss and his men are all rummed up and riding the country all around. God help any black fellow they come across."

"But we have to warn our people down at the creek, Ma," Eliza said. "We've got to warn granny."

But Grace wasn't having it. "You stay put, Eliza, or you'll be the one that takes a bullet. Our mob will have to look out for themselves."

They passed a sleepless night. Eliza, in her crib in the corner of the hut – they didn't dare sleep outside in case some drunken stockman, seeing enemy warriors in the shadows, blasted away at them – had a feeling that Grace was watching her every time she stirred, making sure she didn't try and slip away down to the creek.

꙳

Morning came and, tired though she was, Grace had to go to work. Even hungover stockmen had to be fed. She told Eliza to stay put in the hut; she wasn't to risk the road on the way to school. In the middle of the morning, Vicky slipped through the trees and joined her.

"None of the girls have gone to school today, Eliza," she said. "Their families won't let them."

"So why did you come out, girl?" Eliza asked. "Why did you risk it?"

"Because I'm scared, Eliza. I didn't want to be on my own." Vicky crawled into Eliza's crib and was soon asleep beside her. She hadn't slept last night either.

Eliza must have dozed off, because she came awake when she heard a noise outside. It was only Grace.

"You can come out, you two girls," Grace said. "It's all died down."

They sat by the fire, drinking tea and eating the snap that Grace had brought back – white man's leftovers.

"The police arrested a man from the Barrow Hill mob. Lucky they got to him first or he would have been shot down. Black tracker found him, hiding in the bush."

The story was that the man had found the shepherd, a rather dissolute character called Grant, molesting one of his daughters. They'd fought and the shepherd had come off worse: dead, in fact. That was what Grace had heard, anyway.

"I think, if it was me," Vicky said, though it was hard to think of this big, soft girl engaged in any act of violence, "I think I'd rather be shot down in the bush than hung. They say they deliberately use short ropes for our mob."

Eliza knew what that meant: slow strangulation.

"Dead is dead," Grace said. "Makes no difference."

But Eliza agreed with Vicky; the way you died mattered.

None of them doubted that the black fellow would be found guilty, taken from his reeking cell and hung in front of a band of white men, howling for his blood. *Much better to go down fighting*, Eliza thought. She hoped Jimmy would think so, too, when they caught up with him. She couldn't bear to think of him dangling from the end of a rope.

CHAPTER THIRTY-EIGHT

The date was lodged in Cassie's head. She saw it when she closed her eyes. It was like being back in school, when you got your exam timetable, and the day and date of the particular exam that you hated, the subject that you just couldn't get, would be there in bold ink on the white page, inevitable and unavoidable. The anticipation would make you feel physically and mentally sick. Only this was much worse, more like a prisoner waiting for their execution, if that was even imaginable.

The 14th of February, an ironic date for what happened. She wondered if they even had Valentine's Day then, but she thought they must have at least marked it as a saint's day. Did they send those silly cards in the 1870s? She vaguely remembered reading something about the Victorians sending such tokens, more symbols of affection than of romantic love. It went without saying that Valentine's Day had never been a day that Cassie had looked forward to. When she was younger, she had never been the sort of girl that people sent Valentines to. And when she was with Carys, they had never celebrated the day, staying aloof, regarding it as a trivial and superficial occasion – another one of those excuses for people to spend money.

The date itself was problematic. Reading over the newspaper report and the confession of the stockman – or whatever you wanted to call it – there was no way of knowing if it was accurate. The newspaper article – and it was a very brief report, at the bottom of one of the dense columns that marched down the page – referred to the 'incident', as it called it, as happening on, 'Wednesday last'. The report was dated Saturday 17th February, so that would have made it Wednesday the 14th. Johnson's account didn't mention the actual date or the day of the week, just referred to 'a day in February'. And considering that the newspaper report was inaccurate, anyway, when it came to what had actually happened on the day, there was no reason to suppose that it was any more precise about the exact date.

The fact that there was no clarity over the actual date just added to the confusion that dogged Cassie. She was just not sure what she could do and whether, in fact, she could do anything. Remembering those few brief times that she had spent with Eliza, she thought that she could be reasonably sure that their days and nights were aligned. The time that Eliza had chased and caught her in the twilight – her elbow still occasionally ached – had, according to what Eliza had said or, at least, hinted at, also been at the end of the day for her. When Cassie had got lost at the lake in the afternoon, it had also clearly been afternoon in Eliza's reality. And that night Eliza had come to her house – the night she remembered so fondly – it had been Eliza's night-time, too.

She'd been fleeing in darkness. However, that still left the problem of whether their calendar dates aligned in the same way that their times did. She could make the assumption that they did, but as there was no logical explanation for any of the things that had occurred between them, it didn't necessarily follow.

She remembered that conversation she had once had with Linda, about time being cyclical not linear. At the time, she had thought that her neighbour was voicing more of her 'half-baked hippy theories' – as Eve called them when Linda was out of earshot – but now she thought that the woman's words made a lot of sense. If time was cyclical, periods from the past and future might align with each other and the membrane – the wall, the layer, whatever you wanted to call it – between them could perhaps become porous or, at least, breachable. But though this would explain some of the things that had happened to Eliza and herself, it didn't necessarily follow that the alignment was exact, especially when it came to calendar dates, which were, anyway, artificial and essentially man-made.

Though Cassie entertained only a vague hope of being able to break through to Eliza when she needed her, she decided that it was better to actually do something rather than just sit at home fretting, so, after another unremarkable week had slipped by, she made her plan.

⁂

On Saturday 11th February in her time, she took to her bed in the afternoon, telling her mother that she felt ill.

Eve followed her in with a glass of water. "What's the matter, sweetie?" she asked.

Eve always called her 'sweetie' when she was ill – it went back to her childhood, when Eve had been a more nurturing, if anxious, parent – even though Cassie hated it. However, this time, she didn't let herself react negatively to the endearment.

"I'm just not feeling too good, Mum," she said, trying to sound feeble. "Probably a cold or something."

Eve felt her brow. "You do feel hot, Cassie," she said, though everyone felt hot as the day was sweltering. "Have a rest and call me if you need anything."

Eve was terrible at nursing sick people – Cassie wasn't that good at it herself – and you could see that she resented the waste of time (as she saw it) that such ministrations involved. But she did her best.

⁂

On the Sunday, Cassie just stayed in bed. Eve popped in and out, but, thankfully, went out for a few hours in the afternoon. In the evening, when she returned, she made Cassie something to eat and brought it in.

"Any better, dear?" she asked.

"Well, no worse, Mum," Cassie said. "I'm sure that I'll shake it off in a couple of days."

"Oh," Eve said, not being entirely successful in hiding her disappointment, "so you don't think you'll be better for work on Tuesday?"

"No, I don't think so," Cassie said weakly. "Could you

get a message to Lainey for me?" She thought Eve was going to protest – gently, but firmly – but Cassie quickly added, "If it's a virus, I don't want to give it to anyone."

And Eve couldn't really argue with that.

CHAPTER THIRTY-NINE

Cassie sat on the shelf of rock that jutted out into the waters of the creek. At that particular moment, she thought it must be the most beautiful place in the world; the dark shadowed banks, the soft murmur of the creek water, a pink glow just suffusing the eastern sky and giving the ragged clouds that hung high up over the lake a pearlescent lustre.

The air was cool and rich with all the night-time scents of the bush around her. She knew that, in an hour or so, the sun would shine down implacably on the scene and it would become a slumbering world of shadow and retreat.

For five consecutive mornings, she had come down to the creek as soon after dawn as she could. This hadn't always been easy; she'd had to wait until her mother left for work before leaving the house. Then she would pull her running gear on and jog down to the creek and the bridge, inevitably seeking out that ledge of rock, where she would sit listening and, occasionally, when she was sure there was no one around, call out Eliza's name.

But nothing happened: Eliza hadn't come. She hadn't

heard anything at all. The creek was as quiet and lonely as it had always been. She'd sit there until it got too hot to bear and then make her way home. Then she would shower and lounge around the house for the rest of the day, making sure she was in, or within easy reach of, her bed, when her mother was due home.

⋙

On the Tuesday, when Eve came back, the talk had taken place – the one that Cassie had been expecting.

"Darling," Eve said, "are you sure you're ill?"

"Of course I am, Mum," Cassie replied. "What do you mean?"

"Well, sweetie…" Eve said, looking at Cassie. She was sitting next to her on the bed, her warmth and the weight of her body a little too intrusive for Cassie's liking. "I'm just worried that it's happening again…"

"What, Mum?" Cassie asked, though she knew what Eve was getting at.

"That you're depressed… I could make an appointment with the doctor, you know."

"I'm not depressed, Mum," Cassie said, "just ill." She gave an involuntary shudder at the thought of being on meds again, living that half-life.

"You're sure, dear?" Eve persisted. "It's just that I haven't seen Eliza lately… she hasn't come around… I wondered if—"

"Mum," Cassie said, interrupting. She wanted to be angry, but she couldn't. Eve looked so anxious, forlorn even.

"It's not like that. Eliza's just a friend and she comes and goes… what I mean is, she comes when she can."

"Are you sure, dear?" Eve asked. There were tears in her eyes.

"It's not like before, Mum," Cassie said and they both knew what she meant.

※

Linda caught her on the Wednesday morning, coming home.

"You don't look that sick," she said, a smile on her face.

"I'm feeling much better, Linda," Cassie said, tempted to tell the old woman to mind her own business, but unable to be so impolite.

"Well, I'm sure a bit of exercise won't hurt you, Cassie, if you're up to it," Linda said, "but don't push yourself."

Cassie nodded and was going to pass her, to go back into her house, when Linda added, "It's none of my concern, love, but you know you don't have to skive off. If you don't want to go and do that job, just don't go."

"It's not that simple," Cassie said.

"It probably is, love," Linda replied. "You're just too obliging, sometimes. And you don't have to keep doing things because Eve wants you to."

Cassie shrugged. "Okay, Linda, just don't tell Eve that I've had a miraculous recovery."

"My lips are sealed, Cassie," Linda replied. "As I said, it's none of my concern anyway."

When had that ever stopped Linda from getting involved? Cassie asked herself. She had been tempted to tell Linda what she was doing – it would have been nice to tell someone – but there was always Irene hovering in the background, ready for that impromptu séance, so she didn't.

⫸

On the Friday morning, she sat on the rock until the sun got too hot for her, then moved into the shade. By noon, she decided to give up and she made her way back to her house. She tried to run, but, for once, her heart wasn't in it and she ended up walking the last mile or so.

She knew that that was it: her chances had all run out. There was no point in going back for any more mornings. What had happened, had happened and there was no way she could change Eliza's fate. After all, Eliza was dead and had been for so many years. There wasn't anything Cassie could do about it and she had a horrible feeling that she would never see Eliza again.

CHAPTER FORTY

Eliza carried the folded piece of paper close to her heart, tucked in her dress, as she walked home. Vicky, walking beside her, looked at her with covetous eyes, flicking from her face to her breast, where they both knew that the paper rested.

"Let me see, Eliza," Vicky entreated, her eyes moist, her voice thin, so avid was she to read what was written there, to drink it all in.

Eliza shook her head. "I can't be bothered to dig it out again, Vicky," she said. "Besides, I showed it to you once."

Vicky stopped in front of Eliza, impeding her progress. "Please, Eliza," she said, walking backwards. "I only saw it for a moment back in class. Let me have a good look at it."

Eliza took her time about it, a frown on her face, as if she was carefully considering the matter. She was deriving a perverse sort of pleasure from Vicky's obsessive desire to cradle the piece of paper in her hands, to read those few brief words again. It was just a momentary pause, though, because Eliza, while enjoying this unusual sense of power, wasn't cruel and she wouldn't deny her friend for too long.

"Well, just make sure your hands are clean, Vicky," she said. "Yes, that's right, wipe them on your kerchief."

Vicky tried her best to clean her hands of sweat and dust, while Eliza dug around in the folds of her dress, soon producing the now crumpled paper. She unfolded it carefully, as if she was unfurling the delicate petals of a wildflower. She did not yet place it in Vicky's hands but instead held it out for her to see. This was too much for Vicky, who attempted to grab the paper with her right hand.

"Don't, Vicky," Eliza said. "You'll rip it!"

Vicky looked crestfallen, as chastened as a whipped dog.

Eliza felt guilty. "Here," she said, holding the paper out, "but be careful."

Vicky took it and smiled, but her pleasure was tempered by an evident sorrow. "It's beautiful, Eliza," she said, "but what flower is it?"

The folded paper had a flower as its centrepiece, painted in watercolours. Neither of the girls recognised the clumsiness of the rendition, its amateur nature – to them, it was a minor masterpiece.

"It's a rose, Vicky," Eliza said, revelling in her new-found know-it-all status. "You know, like Mrs Cleary tried to grow in her garden."

They had all felt a little guilty about Jane's floral experiment. The English seemed to have a particular affection for roses and took them wherever they went. There was no reason, Jane had told them – and she had it on good advice, she'd said – that roses shouldn't grow well in the tropics. And they did, up to a point, but the roses that flourished didn't have an over-enthusiastic troupe of mission girls to contend with. Mission girls who didn't know that you could over-water even these thirsty blooms. They'd killed the flowers with kindness, Jane had concluded.

"And what's she written?" Vicky asked. She then proceeded to read out the words, "'With love and affection for my dusky rose'."

Eliza felt pleased by the words, but also embarrassed. She put her hand out and took the letter back.

"But what does it mean?" Vicky asked and Eliza couldn't answer her, because she didn't really know.

Neither of them had ever heard of a Valentine's card before or even of Saint Valentine himself, whoever he might be. It had been in the afternoon, when they had finished their schoolwork – the painful forming of letters, the rote reading and reciting of mathematical tables – that Jane had told them what the day signified back in England.

They were about their mending and sewing, sitting in and around the porch in any shade they could find, hoping that there might be a breath of cooler wind in the damp, dusty heat of the afternoon.

"In England," Jane had said, "we mark this day by sending tokens of affection to those we love. We send cards or letters by the post."

"She's always going on about England," one of the girls complained, when Jane had excused herself to go to the lavatory – her word for the 'dunny'. "Why doesn't she go back there if it's so good?"

Eliza thought that this would be a terrible prospect, thousands of miles of wild seas separating her from her friend. A waste of water she could never cross.

When Jane came back, she started telling them about what she called 'the language of flowers'. How the flower pictures that your card bore had a meaning. So, if you valued a friend's loyalty, you would send them carnations. Lilies were for a devoted friend. Daisies represented innocence and orchids refined beauty. The concept of refined beauty was a hard one for Jane to explain, but Eliza understood it. It described Jane perfectly, at least in Eliza's eyes.

If Jane had thought that this subject would pique the girls' interest, she was mistaken – the problem being that they mostly had little idea what the flowers actually looked like, there being nothing that grew locally to compare them with. They had to fall back on the illustrations in the dog-eared books in the school library, not the most satisfactory educational experience.

Vicky, who had always been one of the brightest girls in the class, suddenly said, "You left a flower out, Mrs Cleary."

"Which one?" Jane asked.

"The rose, Mrs Cleary," Vicky piped up, guiltily remembering Mrs Cleary's love for those dead flowers from her garden.

Mrs Cleary suddenly looked taken aback. "Ah, yes," she said. "The rose is a symbol for love."

Some of the girls tittered.

Jane reddened. "That's enough," she said, bringing the discussion to an abrupt end. "Get back to your sewing."

But now, looking down at the painting of the rose, Eliza recalled her words. The rose was telling Eliza that Jane loved her, a prospect that made Eliza both pleased and uncomfortable.

"One thing I don't understand," Vicky said, "is why didn't she give me a card? Call *me* her dusky rose?"

"Oh, Vicky, don't go on so. It's just a card," Eliza said, but she wasn't so sure about that.

CHAPTER FORTY-ONE

From the mission school, all that Eliza and Vicky had to do to get home was follow the road – which was little more than a dirt track – down to the junction where the wider road from the coast bisected the track. This road was little better than the track from the school and regularly washed out in the wet season, but it carried the contractor's mail coach on its regular journeys inland, as well as wagons and drays carrying goods up from the coast and wool down to the sea.

When they got to the crossroads, the girls had two choices. They could carry on straight ahead towards the cattle station and then cut down to the huddle of huts on the edge of the station where they both lived, or they could turn left, follow the road down towards the creek, almost to the point it forded the watercourse, and make their way home that way, traversing a tract of bush and then descending to the banks of the creek. It was quicker to go straight ahead, but ever since the killing of the shepherd, the stockmen had been suffused with an anger that they regarded as righteous and which they couldn't wait to unleash on any black fellows they came across, so the second route was probably the safer one.

At the crossroads, an enterprising individual had built a general store to take advantage of any passing trade, but as passers-by were few and far between, there was scant opportunity for commerce. Or enterprise, for that matter. The result was that the general store had become less general, not much of a store and increasingly ramshackle.

The enterprising individual – a one-legged Welshman called Lewis, who was purportedly an ex-seafarer, but was suspected of being an ex-convict – had hung on in his establishment, taking his only solace from rum and his Aboriginal wife, Mary. There were some white settlers, particularly the more upright and Christian ones, like Peter Cleary, who regarded any such relationship between white and black as abhorrent, especially one that resulted in children, and would shun the establishment, even though Lewis would always maintain that he and Mary were legally married. But Mary's presence was fortuitous in another way, because it meant that her close relatives and extended family felt much more inclined to patronise the store than they would other white establishments.

Many of these relatives worked for the whites in some capacity and were most often paid in kind rather than money. Those who worked at the cattle station, like Grace, were paid in the currency of food, rum, blankets or cloth, but sometimes they had the odd spare penny for little luxuries or fripperies and Mr Lewis's store would get their custom.

Jane Cleary had told Eliza and Vicky, as they left the mission after the other girls, to hurry home quickly. "Go straight home, girls," she had said, "and if you see anyone on the way, try not to offer them any offence."

Jane looked worried as she watched them go and Eliza knew what she was trying to say, what her words really meant: Don't give any white men you meet any excuse to beat you or abuse you. Unfortunately, what Jane didn't, or wasn't willing to understand, was that the colour of their skin, their very existence, was often offence or excuse enough.

They should have left the track behind the store and cut off the corner where the two roads met by walking the boundary of Mary's garden, but Vicky, disappointed as she was at not being the object of Mrs Cleary's affection, had a sudden hankering to enter the store, having an English farthing in the cloth pocket she wore under her dress. Where she had obtained this coin, or for what service, was a mystery that Vicky was tight-lipped about and Eliza wasn't sure she wanted to know.

Eliza would have pulled her away – Vicky was always intending to spend the farthing, but never did – but Mr Lewis's daughter, Gwen, another of the mission girls, was on the back porch and waved to them.

"Vicky," she said, "come and see these new ribbons!"

They were in the dark interior of the shop, delving deep in the draw of ribbons, when Cal Armstrong came in.

"Eliza," he said, "I need to have a word with you."

She didn't want to leave her friends – Cal was red in the face and looked vicious – but he grabbed her arm tightly, hurting her, and pulled her out onto the rickety porch at the front of the building. He had a crumpled piece of paper in his hand and waved it at her.

"Did you have anything to do with this, Eliza?" he asked.

She could see that he was making an effort to control himself, that his body was tensed, as if ready to pounce on her, to slap her or worse.

"Sorry, Mr Armstrong," she said, "I don't know what that is."

She put a hand out tentatively towards the paper, but he snatched it away.

"Come, Eliza," he said, "I know they teach you girls to read and write at the mission and Grace is always telling me what a good scholar you are. So, I think you are quite capable of producing something like this."

She was starting to get frightened now and it was made worse by the fact that she had no idea what he was talking about. His horse was hitched to the rail outside and his whip and rifle – the one that fired all those bullets without having to be reloaded – were hanging off his saddle. They were a reminder of the power he wielded over her and her mother.

Cal Armstrong looked at her, disdain and disgust clearly written in his face, and his grip tightened. "I've a good mind to give you a thrashing to get the truth out of you."

"Mr Armstrong… boss," Eliza said, "I don't know what you are talking about."

The slap when it came was quick and unexpected. A shock that set her eyes to crying. Her right cheek stung. His hand – the left hand he had slapped her with – was still raised, as if there was more coming.

"You cheeky little bitch," he said. "I'm going to—"

But Eliza didn't find out what Cal was going to do,

because a voice suddenly interrupted him. "Mr Armstrong," it said, "what's going on here?"

It was Mr Lewis and behind him, in the shadows of the store, Eliza could see Vicky and Gwen, with Mary peering out from behind the counter.

"It's none of your business, Lewis," Cal said. "Keep your nose out of it."

Mr Lewis was a small, dark man, ungainly and limping from the loss of his limb. He was much smaller than Cal Armstrong, but – and this surprised Eliza – seemed unafraid of the Scotsman.

"It *is* my business, Armstrong," he said in his sing-song voice, "as this is my store and the girl is a friend of my daughter."

Cal looked suddenly confused. He was used to being able to do what he wanted with – and to – his black employees, and that included their families, without anyone intervening.

Eliza could smell the rum on him, which scared her, because drunk men, whether white or black, were always worse than sober ones. However, the drink that Cal had taken made him uncertain, not so sure of himself.

"Look at this, Lewis," he said, pushing the paper up into Mr Lewis's face. "This slur, this insult I received, and I suspect that this little doxy is responsible."

Lewis scrutinised the paper and handed it back to Cal, who crumpled it up in his fist before throwing it down onto the road. "I suggest to you, *Mr* Armstrong," the emphasis that Lewis put on that 'Mr' made clear how little he thought of the title in this particular case, "that this is someone's idea of a joke and that Eliza is not the culprit. She's a good girl, not a doxy, and I doubt that she would even come close to understanding the subtleties of what the writer implies."

"Still…" Cal blustered, but ran out of steam and words.

"Go home and sleep it off, man!" Lewis said. "And don't make such a fuss of a joke. I agree that it is in poor taste, but you should rise above it."

Eliza was afraid that Cal was going to get his gun and shoot them all, but instead he mounted his horse, quite meekly, and rode off down the track to the station. Mr Lewis looked after him and spat out onto the dust of the road.

"What a to-do," he said. Then he looked at Eliza, not without kindness, and told her, "Best get home, girl, as fast as you can and do your best to avoid Mr Armstrong."

It wasn't until they were off the road and following a track through the bush down to the creek that Vicky stopped Eliza and held out her hand.

"Look," she said, unclasping her fist, showing the ball of paper that it held. She smiled, as if she was pleased with herself. "I picked it up from the road when no one was looking."

They sat down on a fallen branch and scrutinised it.

"It's a Valentine's message," Eliza said.

But they could both see that it was actually a rather crude attempt at a Valentine: a stick-like drawing of a black fellow holding what appeared to be a rose. The message read:

A Valentine from your brown Adonis.
Roses are red, violets are blue,
Black Jimmy Owen has had the measure of you.

The spelling was bad, the writing was atrocious. Eliza was rather disgruntled; how could Cal have thought that she was responsible for something so shoddy?

"What does it mean?" Vicky asked. "Is it from your Jimmy?"

"No," Eliza said, "Jimmy can't write. Somebody else wrote it."

"I don't understand," Vicky said, her beautiful dark eyes clouded, her eyebrows drawn into a frown.

"No, I don't know what it's all about either," Eliza said.

But she wasn't telling the truth. She suspected that she did know.

CHAPTER FORTY-TWO

"Eliza, girl, what have you done now?" Grace asked her when she came back from work late that evening.

Eliza had dutifully come straight home from the store and stayed in and about the cabin, being careful whenever anyone passed by and hiding from any of the stockmen who came that way. She'd done all her chores; brushed the dried mud floor – a thankless task, which just raised a cloud of dust – washed her mother's spare dress out in the creek and hung it to dry on a bush, hauled water to fill the kettle and gathered wood to get the fire going.

She'd been particularly industrious and this was because, however much she told herself that she had nothing to do with the Valentine that Cal had received – Jane had told them, with some reluctance, that such perverse missives, insulting and jeering were called 'vinegar Valentines' – she still had an ominous sense that, guilty or not, she had brought trouble on them.

And she was not wrong, because when Grace came home, looking not only tired, but fretful, she immediately, without any greeting, asked that question.

"I've done nothing, Ma," Eliza replied, tears coming to her eyes because of the unfairness of the accusation. "That letter was nothing to do with me."

Grace disappeared into the hut, coming back with a flask of rum. She sat on a log by the fire and swigged it straight from the bottle. "That's not what the boss says," Grace went on. "And he also told me that you were cheeky to him at the store. That I should tan your hide good and proper."

"I wasn't cheeky to him, Ma," Eliza protested. "I just told him that I didn't know anything about it."

Grace looked at her, thoughtfully, but Eliza wasn't sure her mother believed her or, indeed, whether it actually mattered if she did or not.

"The boss said that he had a mind to put us off his land," Grace said, "to pack us off."

Eliza was sobbing, not so much at her mother's words, but at the unfairness of it all. She'd done nothing, but it didn't seem to matter. Only what Cal Armstrong said mattered.

"But he said," Grace went on, "that he might consider keeping us if I took you in hand. Took you down a peg or two."

"What does that mean, Ma?" Eliza asked, but she thought that she already knew.

"He told me that you had gotten above yourself at that mission. Acquired airs and graces, he said – whatever that means."

A cold chill was creeping over Eliza, because she was sure she knew what was coming.

"The boss says that you are old enough to leave the school and come and help me around the station. There's plenty of work to be done: cooking, cleaning, washing. He said that would fix you proper."

"But, Ma," Eliza said, "I thought you wanted me to get some learning, to make a better life for myself."

Grace shook her head violently, as if she was trying to shake Eliza's words out of her ears, as if there were buzzing insects around her. "That's in the past now, girl. I have to do what the boss says or we'll have no place to live. No way to put food in our mouths."

Grace took another swig of rum. She didn't look angry anymore, just tired and something else – defeated, brought low. "Oh Eliza," she asked, "how have we come to this?"

Eliza was weeping uncontrollably now, watching her future slip away. It hadn't been much of a future in the first place – a decent position as a servant in some white woman's house, if she was lucky – but it was better than being a stockman's drudge, the prey of those white men, who'd feel entitled to touch and maul her. She tried to think of something she could say, in her defence, and came up with the only words that she thought might hold off Grace's hand.

"Jimmy wouldn't like it, Ma," she said. "He wouldn't like Cal Armstrong laying down the law about me."

"Jimmy's got nothing to do with this," Grace snapped back.

"But he has, Ma. That letter that made the boss mad was about him and Jimmy," Eliza said, "and he's taking it out on me, because I'm Jimmy's sister."

Grace looked at Eliza with something bordering on hate. That look was more frightening than the prospect of a hiding, but it showed that Grace knew more than she was letting on, Eliza suspected. "Jimmy isn't here to speak for himself," Grace said, "so don't bring him into it. Anyway, he's not a burden to me like you are." She took another slug of rum. "But you won't be no more. You'll pay your way from now on, girl. No more Mrs Cleary this, Mrs Cleary that." She laughed, but with bitterness rather than amusement. "Now, fetch me my cane."

It was part of the ritual of punishment that had grown up between them that, when Eliza was due a beating, Grace would make her fetch the stick. Sometimes, the very act of fetching the stick was deemed punishment enough, but not that often. The stick was a thin, flexible length of bamboo that Grace had acquired from some unknown source years ago. It was smooth and polished with use.

In the normal run of things, Eliza wouldn't have questioned Grace's right to chastise her. It was just what was done by a parent like Grace. Even Mrs Cleary would occasionally smack the hands or legs of the girls in her care – Eliza, of course, seldom did anything to merit such punishment. It was just part of life in the white world. In contrast, Granny's people hardly ever resorted to such physical chastisement of their children. It was a habit that Grace had acquired when she left her mob, when she'd abandoned them along with their ways.

"No, I won't," Eliza said, wiping her face on her dress and suddenly fierce, "because I didn't do anything wrong, Ma. I don't deserve a hiding."

"You'll do as I say, girl," Grace said, but there was just a hint of uncertainty in her voice.

"No, Ma," Eliza said, defiant but still fearful.

Grace looked at her angrily. "Then you can go. Get out!"

She waved the gin bottle at Eliza, as if she was tempted to throw it. Eliza knew she wouldn't want to waste the grog.

"Ma... please," Eliza pleaded.

"Get out, I said!" Grace repeated and turned her face away.

⋙

The camp was mostly asleep, but Granny was wide awake, sitting outside her *humpy* as if she was waiting for her.

"Ma threw me out," Eliza said.

Granny just nodded. "She'll come around," she said, but Eliza wondered if she would.

Eliza tried to explain it to Granny, but the old woman didn't look all that interested in the involved tale of Valentine's cards and aggrieved white men. When Eliza had rather tearfully drawn the story to a conclusion, Granny just laughed.

Looking down into the smouldering embers of her fire, she said, "That Jimmy was always too good-looking for his own good."

"It's not Jimmy's fault, though, Granny," Eliza said, defending her brother, but Granny laughed even more. Eliza wanted to tell the old woman about the Valentine she had received from Jane and how it had confused her, but she was afraid that this revelation would be greeted with amusement, as well, so she held her peace.

Instead, she put the question that had been eating at her into words, "What am I going to do now, Granny?"

"I told you, girl," Granny said. "Grace will come around."

"But what about school, Granny?" Eliza asked.

Granny laughed again. Eliza was started to wonder if she'd already had a bellyful of rum that evening.

"You like that white man's learning, I know, girl, but it's not just about the learning, is it?"

"What do you mean, Granny?" Eliza said.

Granny looked at her closely. "I mean that the white woman, that Jane Cleary, you see her as your future."

Do I? Eliza asked herself.

"You think she will take you away from your life now and give you a different one."

Eliza was going protest, to say it wasn't true, but then she realised that Granny had seen what she hadn't, what she wouldn't. Granny had figured out the truth about Jane. A truth that Eliza, though she wouldn't admit to herself, knew in her heart: Jane – poor, lonely Jane; solitary even within that constricting marriage – wanted her not only as a lady's maid, but as a companion. Someone to fill that empty space in her life, where feeling and passion should be; a gap that her cold husband couldn't or wouldn't bridge. And not only that. There was more to it, something intimate and strange to Eliza that she did not want to examine too closely, because it might get in the way of all her hopes and expectations. *Yes, Granny is right*, she thought. She had been counting on Jane to take her with her, when she went, though Eliza was loath to admit it to herself.

"You told me, girl," Granny went on, "that you didn't want to be a drudge for those stockmen and I don't blame you." Granny paused, as if drawing breath. She didn't usually talk this much, Eliza knew. "That was the path your mother took and why she is what she is now, neither really white nor really black, on the margin of both."

"Yes, Granny, I know," Eliza said, "and I don't want to be like her." It felt disloyal to say so, but it was true.

Granny had a serious look on her face now. "I was told, girl, that white men keep birds in cages and try and make them speak. It's true, isn't it?" the old woman asked.

"Yes, Granny," Eliza said. "They keep them as creatures to spoil and pet." She wondered if the old woman was drifting off on another subject.

"And I hear that some of the cages are made of sticks and some of the cages, of kings and queens, are even made of gold," Granny said, pausing. She looked at Eliza before adding, "But a cage is a cage, Eliza, whatever it is made of."

"Then what should I do?" Eliza asked, confused. "Live here with you?"

Granny smiled again. "You're too soft for that, girl," the old woman said. "You've got all those white woman ways now."

But as they lay down to sleep, Eliza knew that Granny was joking. She'd never turn Eliza away. She could always come back to her people, her mob.

CHAPTER FORTY-THREE

"Eliza, child, you must wake up."

A hand was shaking Eliza, pulling at her. She knew it wasn't time for school, as it was still dark outside, with the light only just beginning to soften towards dawn. It was too early to roll out of her blanket.

"Eliza, wake up," the voice was insistent.

And this time she did. As she awoke, she remembered where she was: sleeping next to Granny.

"What's the matter, Granny?" she asked, but the old woman didn't answer. She couldn't see Granny's face clearly yet, but something in her voice told her that she must obey her. Something terrible was happening.

"Come on," Granny said, pulling her to her feet.

There were some complaining voices. One shouted to her that she should get the old woman back to bed, but she could also see, near them in the dark, that others were taking heed. A woman close to them, the alarm on her face just visible in the embers of her fire, rolled out of her bedding, quickly waking and lifting up the child who slept beside her. In silence, others were joining her, taking only what they could carry, what would not impede them.

They had already started down the creek when they heard the shots, strangely flat, muted by the low mist that hung over the waters, but sharp and insistent at the same time. And the unmistakeable sulphurous tang of gunpowder was in the air and riding down water on the mist.

Everyone was awake now and most of them were heading off down the creek, away from the shots. Some of the mob were hesitating, either through fear for the men who had gone up to the lake early to fish or out of disbelief, hoping against hope that the white men – for white men it must be – were hunting game. But Eliza knew that such a volley of shots was not the sound of hunting. If it was, the game was human.

"No," Eliza said, as she realised what was truly happening, "they're killing them. Somebody stop them! They're killing them all."

She looked around for a weapon, but there wasn't one. And even if there had been – a spear, a throwing stick or a gun – she wouldn't have known how to use it.

"Eliza, girl, we got to go," Granny said. "They'll be here soon enough." Granny grabbed her arm and pulled her on with an iron grip.

The firing was coming closer and she could hear other sounds: cries, harness jingling, the heavy clump of hoofs on mud that signified riders were approaching. The mob were splitting off in many directions, taking to the bush in silence, the only sound the occasional rustle of a branch or the stifled cry of a child. Her people were used to running away and doing it stealthily.

"Eliza, come on!" Granny shouted.

Eliza was dazed. She was only half awake and the scene around her, while terrifying, was also somehow unreal.

Granny pulled her down to the creek. They waded over it, but suddenly Eliza looked down and let out an involuntary cry, which sliced the air around her like a knife rending a sheet. The water was red... red with blood. And Eliza suddenly realised that some of the shots that she'd heard must have come from up the creek. The way the sound moved along the notch of the valley had deceived them.

"They're already ahead of us, Granny," Eliza whispered.

But Granny kept pulling her on, down the trail and along the bank of the creek, over the water again in a sinuous, serpentine route dodging the stockmen, who had ridden down the creek once and were riding up again.

An angry bee whizzed past Eliza's head and she suddenly realised that it was a lead bullet. It struck a gum tree just to the side of her. As they scrambled up the stream bank, a horseman loomed in front of them, pointing a revolver, like the one Jimmy had, at them. But his horse reared and spoiled his aim as one of her mob, a grey-bearded old man, reared up from the undergrowth and lunged with a spear in the man's direction. Eliza pulled Granny on and didn't see what happened to the old man.

They went to ground behind a tea tree bush to get their bearings, but it was just a temporary refuge. The stockmen were firing randomly, so nowhere was safe. Any small movement or sound drew one or more shots in its direction.

"Eliza," Granny said, "you call to that white girl."

"Which white girl, Granny? Mrs Cleary?"

What use would the missionary be? Eliza thought, with her Bible and her teachings of love and fellowship, against this band of assassins – Christians to a man.

"No, that other girl."

"Cassie?"

"Yes, call her, but not with your voice, with your spirit."

And in her head, Eliza did as Granny asked, saying Cassie's name, over and over again, as a silent prayer. Even though Cassie, she knew, couldn't help her: she was too far away in both time and distance.

Soon they were on their feet again, heading down the creek, keeping to the bush. They did not dare head westwards, as the slope flattened into a plain of scrub and grass where they would easily be spotted. Eastwards was the direction of the cattle station, which was equally perilous.

Everything seemed to suddenly go quiet, so Eliza started to hope that it was over, that the stockmen had had enough of their sport, tired of shedding blood. They were at a turn in the trail, when Cassie heard hoofs and harness behind them: a rider was coming up fast. She looked at Granny. The old woman, though tough as her leather cloak, was done in. She didn't have any more running in her. Eliza made a snap decision. She kissed Granny on her cheek – wrinkled and rough as a dried plum – and pushed her off the trail into a cluster of bushes.

"What are you doing, girl?" the old woman asked, trying to extricate herself from the foliage that was on the point of enveloping her.

"Stay put, Granny. Go to the ground," Eliza said. "I'll draw them off."

Granny started to argue. They were both whispering furiously, but it was too late. The rider came around the bend and saw Eliza.

"There's one over here," he shouted and put his spurs to his horse.

Eliza ran. In the normal course of things, she would not have been able to outrun a horse, but the creature, despite the urgings of its rider, was nervous of the uneven trail with its tangled vegetation and protruding roots. Eliza could hear shouts from the far side of the creek, a rider paralleling her course, calling enthusiastically, as if he was hunting a roo not a girl. She knew that she would shortly be at the ford, where the trail ended at the road, and, as soon as she was clear of the bush, the men would catch her before she had a chance to cross into the trees on the other side. It was inevitable.

The rider behind her had holstered his carbine on his saddle and was holding his stock whip. He couldn't use it while he rode down the trial, there was no room to wield it, but as soon as they were in the open, he would be able to reach her with it. She'd seen stockmen using their whips and knew what they could do with them. The glimpses she got of the rider as she ran told her that it was a young man, hardly older than herself – one of those men she had seen around the station, but always avoided.

She could hear no firing now, so she wondered if they had run out of bullets, but with that thought came another one: the stockmen were just as likely to use a knife or a hatchet on her as a gun. It didn't bear thinking about, so she ran. All her senses seemed heightened. She was terrified, it was true, but also as vital and quick as she had ever been.

As she saw the line of sky where the bush ran out and the road started, she noticed that the mist had pooled in the creek, hanging strangely and eerily before her. However, she couldn't afford to hesitate, so she just ran on, sure that these were the last moments of her young life. But where the ford should have been, there was the low, rough planking of a bridge. She couldn't stop to wonder at this. Instead, she scrambled up on the bank besides the bridge, intending to head over the road and onwards, ever onwards, till she ran out of trail or life. But suddenly a hand grabbed her arm. She shrugged it off angrily and screamed at the figure besides her.

She would fight; she would claw, rend flesh, kick like a roo, use every fibre of her being to hurt them before they finally brought her down.

"Eliza," the figure said – she could hardly focus on it, discern it, so overwrought was she – "it's me, Cassie. You're safe."

And then, abruptly, she collapsed into Cassie's embrace, feeling the girl's arms encircle her, hold her up. Frail as they looked, they were strong.

"You called to me and I came," Cassie said.

CHAPTER FORTY-FOUR

Cassie had been in the car with her mother when she had heard Eliza. They had left the house early – it was a Thursday and they were both heading into work – and were just approaching the T-junction at the end of their road.

The voice had been so clear in her head – as if Eliza was sitting in the back seat behind her – that she almost asked Eve if she had heard it, but she decided against it. She knew where that would have led: a one-way ticket to the psychiatrist.

"Cassie, come to me at the creek," the voice was repeating, over and over again.

Cassie closed her eyes, suddenly feeling nauseous. Though Eliza's voice was familiar, the experience was still weird and unearthly. It was as if her world, everything that held her on the planet, gravity itself, had been unanchored. She had no handle on what was real or unreal anymore. But it was a feeling she was increasingly familiar with these days and what did it ultimately matter? To her, Eliza was more real than almost anyone or anything else in her life.

Eve had seen the change that had come over Cassie's face; the way that she screwed her eyes up, as if she was in pain, the whitening pallor, the sweat that was breaking out on her brow. She slowed the car.

"What's wrong, dear?" she asked.

Cassie was going to lie, say she was ill, but she was tired of pretending. "Stop the car, Mum," she said. "Eliza needs me."

Eve was flabbergasted, her mouth dropping open in astonishment. "What new nonsense is this, Jocasta?" she asked, irritated, but also disconcerted. "How could you possibly know that?"

"I can't explain it, Mum. I just do." Cassie opened the door.

"Wait," Eve said. "Where are you going?"

"Down to the creek," Cassie said. "She's there."

"I'll come with you," Eve said.

"No, Mum, no need to..."

"But I can't leave you like this..." Eve said, for once looking unsure of herself. "Are you quite sure you're well?"

Eve's hands were shaking on the wheel and worry was written all over her face under her make-up, making her look older than she actually was.

"No, Mum," Cassie said. "You go to work. I'm better than I've been for a long time, but I have to go."

Eve stayed there, undecided, in the car.

"Go to work, Mum," Cassie said. "I'll find Eliza and then I'll text you."

Cassie set off down the road to the creek. She wasn't dressed for running – linen trousers and a blouse, borrowed from Eve – but she went as fast as she could.

But when she got to the creek, she didn't know where to go: upstream or downstream? She was standing on the bridge, thinking, when she heard a noise just behind her and Eliza scrambled up out of the creek bed and onto the track.

"Eliza," Cassie said. "It's me, Cassie. You're safe."

Eliza looked more like a wild animal than a young woman. Her eyes stared, but in a glassy way that told Cassie that she wasn't actually seeing her. Cassie put her hand out towards Eliza, touching her arm. Eliza shrieked and recoiled from her touch. The look she gave Cassie was one of pain and anger, mixed with confusion. But then, abruptly, the girl staggered and fell into Cassie's arms.

"You're safe," Cassie repeated, but then she had the uncomfortable notion that she wasn't really sure of that. What if the people who were pursuing Eliza – and Cassie knew their nature by now – were going to burst through that rupture in time, the same way that Eliza had?

"We've got to go, Eliza," Cassie said. "Can you walk?"

Eliza looked at her and nodded, then she kissed her on the cheek.

"Come on," Cassie said. She took Eliza's hand and pulled her along up the road, back to the house.

Eve was there, waiting for them.

"God, Cassie," she said, "what happened?" She turned to Eliza. "You poor girl." Then, she reached for her mobile.

"What are you doing, Mum?" Cassie asked.

"I'm going to call the police."

"Don't," Cassie said.

Eliza, understanding what Eve meant, shook her head violently. "Don't," she said, echoing Cassie.

"But…" Eve said.

Cassie found a convenient lie. "It's not a police matter,

Mum," she said. "Eliza had an accident. She's shaken up. She just needs a shower and a change of clothes and then she'll be fine. You just go to work and I'll sort it."

"But..." Eve repeated. Cassie's new-found assertiveness had quite floored her. She looked at her watch. "Well, if you're sure," she said.

"Yes, missus," Eliza said, "Cassie is right. I'll be fine. I just need what she told you."

Cassie didn't think that Eliza had quite understood all that she had said, but she had obviously got the drift.

They watched as Eve drove away and then Cassie took Eliza in her arms and held her for a long time. Eliza didn't weep, which worried Cassie. She should be sad or angry, she thought, but instead she was numb.

Cassie hadn't really looked at Eliza – really looked, that is – too intent was she in getting the girl home, but now she saw how wild Eliza appeared. Her dress was ripped in places, her legs and arms were scratched, her face wore a mask-like layer of sweat-streaked dust and blood from small cuts. Her hair seemed to be tangled up with half of the forest.

"Let's get you in the bath, love," Cassie said. It was the only thing she could think of.

While she ran the bath, she made Eliza a cup of tea. She'd read somewhere that hot, sweet tea was good for shock. And she thought that shock was the only explanation for the trance-like state that Eliza was in. Thankfully, Eliza drank the tea and attempted to eat one of the biscuits she'd put out, though she just nibbled at it and didn't manage to finish it.

When the bath was ready, Cassie led Eliza to the

bathroom. She undressed her, while Eliza just stood there with doll-like passivity.

"That's not too hot, is it, Eliza?"

Eliza shook her head and Cassie helped her in. Eliza allowed Cassie to wash her and try to sort the tangles in her hair with a brush. Once or twice, when Cassie hurt her, Eliza whimpered and gave Cassie a hurt look, just as a child would. She soaked for a long time and then, suddenly, seemed to wake from her trance.

"You came for me, Cassie," Eliza said.

"I heard you, Eliza, calling to me," Cassie replied.

"Granny told me to call you..." Eliza said and trailed off, her face suddenly stricken. "Granny..." she repeated.

"Is she alright?" Cassie asked. The words that framed the question felt so inadequate.

Eliza shook her head. "I don't know, Cassie. I left her there, hiding, but I don't know." Then Eliza looked at her with an almost hostile curiosity. "You know what happened?"

Cassie nodded. "I do. I found out and I tried to contact you. To warn you." Cassie hung her head; she felt that she'd failed Eliza in some way.

Eliza put her hand up and cupped Cassie's cheek. "Don't, Cassie," she said, "you saved me, girl. Can you believe that? I'd have been a goner."

Eliza's eyes sparkled with some of her old energy and she rose up in the bath and flung her arms around Cassie.

Cassie laughed. "I'm soaking wet now, Eliza."

➤

They both wrapped up in towels and sat on the terrace, careful to keep out of Linda's eyeline. There'd be too much to explain to Linda and Cassie felt that she just didn't have the energy to make up all those neat excuses.

"What did happen, Cassie?" Eliza asked. "I mean, what do all those books of your people say?"

Your people, Cassie thought, *is that how Eliza sees me, as one of* them – *the settlers and the missionaries?* She told Eliza what she knew about the massacre.

"That makes sense," Eliza said. "Cal Armstrong's men must have been waiting there for the mob. They wouldn't have stood a chance." Eliza closed her eyes. Her face looked pained. "I don't know how many of my people are dead, Cassie, but you know that the creek ran red."

"I know, Eliza," Cassie said. "I know."

Cassie didn't know what more to say and, indeed, what words could form an adequate response to the terrible events that had engulfed Eliza?

When Eve came back in the late afternoon, it was almost a relief – something to distract them from their collective knowledge of what had happened.

"Hello, Eliza," Eve said, stepping onto the terrace. "Are you feeling a bit better, now?"

"I'm fair enough, missus," Eliza said in her usual guarded way, so Eve didn't try to press her further.

"I bought something home for dinner, Jocasta," Eve said. "I thought Eliza might be hungry."

Cassie tried to control her face and not to laugh. The last thing on Eliza's mind was food. Eve looked at her questioningly so she quickly said, "Thanks, Mum. That's kind of you."

Eliza looked aghast at the bags of foods Eve was bringing in – the sheer excess of them. "Cassie," she suddenly said, "I feel done in. Can I have a lie down in your bed?"

Cassie took her to her room, but though she would have liked to lie down with Eliza, she knew she had to go back to Eve.

They unpacked the shopping together; there seemed to be a lot of it.

Eve looked at Cassie and said, "Look, Jocasta, I was having a chat with Annie about this…"

It figured, Cassie thought, but she just listened.

"She said that you should be careful about what you are getting into," Eve continued. "A lot of indigenous Australians come from troubled backgrounds, have experienced abuse and over-dependence on alcohol and drugs…"

She sounded like a textbook, Cassie thought.

"Don't worry, Mum," Cassie said, "I know exactly what I'm getting into…. Now, shall I leave the cheesecake out to defrost or put it in the fridge?"

Eve shut up, put off her stride by the mundane details of food storage.

CHAPTER FORTY-FIVE

Dinner was more of an ordeal than a pleasure. Eve had cooked pasta – Eve always cooked pasta – and Eliza, unused to the dish, just picked at it. Because of this, Cassie felt that she had to make an effort, so she ate more of it than she wanted to. Eliza did rather better with the cheesecake that Eve served as dessert, initially being suspicious of it, but then managing to polish off two helpings. Cassie, in contrast, ate hardly any of the sweet, uncomfortably full from the first course.

Eve opened a bottle of white wine and offered a glass to Eliza.

"Is that grog, missus?" Eliza asked and Eve looked bemused by the question.

"Eliza doesn't drink, Mum," Cassie quickly interceded. When Eve went to pour a glass of water for Eliza instead, Cassie whispered, "You don't, do you?"

Eliza shook her head.

"Call me Eve, Eliza," Eve said as she brought the water back. She had been as bemused by being called 'missus', as by any other of Eliza's strange eccentricities.

"Alright... Eve," Eliza said.

The conversation was as difficult to negotiate as the food. Eve did her best to ask Eliza questions, but the girl's guarded answers did little to encourage her.

"Jocasta says that you are at college," Eve said.

"Who's Jocasta?" Eliza asked, but then realised, after hand signals from Cassie, who Eve meant.

"Yes, missus... I mean Eve... I'm at school."

"Are you enjoying it?" Eve persisted.

"Yes, I am," Eliza said, answering as tersely as she could, in order to close down the conversation.

"What are you thinking of doing afterwards?" Eve asked.

Eliza was stumped: she hadn't thought about it, of course. It wasn't as if she would have much choice in the matter.

"I don't know, Eve," she eventually replied. "Get a job or go and live with my granny and her people."

"Oh, where does your granny live?" Eve asked. She looked confused, rather than intrigued.

"She lives in the bush, Eve." But then it occurred to Eliza that she was talking about the past. She didn't know any longer where granny lived or even if she was still alive.

"In the bush..." Eve was starting to ask a question, but Eliza ignored her and looked at Cassie.

"Cassie, I'm tired. Can I go and lie down?"

"Of course," Cassie answered. "You know where the bedroom is."

When Eliza had gone, Eve filled her wine glass up and took a deep swallow. "Is she alright, Jocasta?" Eve asked. "She doesn't exactly seem... with it."

"She's had a shock, Mum, and she's tired," Cassie answered.

Eve looked like she had more to add on the subject, but, in the end, she just said, "Don't worry about clearing up, darling. I think Eliza needs you."

⤜

Eliza was lying there in the dark, the cover pulled up over her face, leaving just her two eyes staring out at the fading light.

"Are you alright, love?" Cassie asked, knowing how feeble a question it was.

In answer, Eliza lifted up the cover and said, "Just hold me, Cassie."

Eliza snuggled into Cassie, in the innocent, unselfconscious way a child would, but she held on to her tightly, as if time and place were hurricane-force gales that were threatening to blow her away and Cassie was the only fixed point.

They must have fallen asleep, because the next thing that Cassie knew was that it was full dark and she was hot and sweating from the clothes that she was still wearing. She tried to gently push Eliza off her, so that she could undress, but the girl clung on all the tighter, whimpering, as if she was having a bad dream. Suddenly, sensing Cassie's movements, her eyes flickered open.

"Eliza," Cassie said, "I just need to take my clothes off."

Disconcertingly, Eliza sat up and watched Cassie closely as she undressed. "You're much skinnier than Jane," Eliza said.

Cassie had a sudden flash of jealousy. "Who's Jane?" she asked.

"You know, Mrs Cleary," Eliza said.

"You mean the missionary?" Cassie asked. "When did you see her naked?"

Eliza laughed. "When she was having a bath, of course."

"You were there?" Cassie said indignantly. She knew that she was being irrational, but she couldn't help it.

"Yes, she used to like me to bathe her, so what?" Eliza was smiling in a rather irritating way.

"Nothing…" Cassie said. "It's just that…"

"Just what, Cassie?" Eliza asked, surprised and more than a little amused by Cassie's discomfort.

"Well, it sounds like she was taking advantage of you," Cassie said.

Eliza laughed again. "You are a funny girl sometimes, Cassie," she said. "It's no different from what we girls do down at the creek when we swim there, helping each other wash." But Eliza wondered if she was being completely honest. She suspected that it was different but didn't want to admit it.

"Anyway, it's nothing to do with me," Cassie said.

Eliza shook her head. "Of course it is, Cassie," she said. "You're my friend, so you can say what you want."

"Well, I say we should get some sleep."

⇶

Eliza woke in a sweat from a dream where men on horses were chasing her. She was holding Granny's hand, but Granny slipped away in the darkness and amid the pursuing shadows, however hard she tried to hold on. She sat up bolt upright, crying out, but Cassie was there, awake, and put her arms around her.

"You're okay, dear," Cassie said. "You're here with me."

But suddenly Cassie's embrace seemed too stifling, too cloying. Eliza sat up on the edge of the bed. Cassie reached out a tentative hand.

"Leave me be, just for a minute, Cassie, love," Eliza said. She knew Cassie would be disappointed, upset, but she just needed to feel the air around her, not someone's arms.

"I feel lost," Eliza said, at last. "I *am* lost." In this strange elsewhere, she thought, like one of those pirates that she had read about in Mrs Cleary's books, marooned on a desert island.

Eventually, she lay back down, but neither of them could get back to sleep. They lay in silence, each alone with their thoughts, but there was one question that loomed over them both, if in a slightly different way for each of them: what would they do?

Cassie took Eliza's hand and said, "We could go somewhere together, get jobs, somewhere to live." She wanted to add, 'We could be happy together.'

"What do you mean, Cassie?" Eliza asked.

"Start a new life together, dear," Cassie said, holding Eliza's hand tightly. "We could both put our old lives behind us, go somewhere no one knows us."

Eliza looked at Cassie. Her eyes were filled with so much hope and expectation. It was tempting, Eliza thought, what Cassie was saying. Like Eve and that snake and that apple. But Cassie, if she was a snake, was a good snake, with a good spirit inside her. And why couldn't Eve have walked out of the Garden of Eden with that snake and lived happily ever after, with no Adam to make demands?

She remembered when she had told Granny that story, after Mrs Cleary had read it to the mission girls, from that Bible she always had at hand, and how Granny had said: "You'd have to drink a bellyful of rum before snakes started talking to you…"

And with that thought, and the sound of Granny's laughter echoing in the halls of her memory, Eliza knew what she had to do. She kissed Cassie on the cheek, kissed away those tears that had sprung to her eyes.

"You know that I have to go back, love?" she said. "Don't you?"

"Why?" Cassie asked. "What is there left for you in that other place?"

Eliza smiled and brushed Cassie's hair back from her forehead. "I don't belong here, Cassie, you know that," she said. "My story doesn't end here. I have to go back and let it find its way."

Cassie did know this; Eliza could see the truth of it written in her eyes. She was well aware that a new life together was just a dream: a beautiful dream, as thin as spider silk. One hard tug and it fell apart.

"All creeks have got to flow to the sea, Cassie," Eliza said. "You can't dam them up for long."

Cassie lay back down. "When will you go?" she asked.

"Tomorrow morning," Eliza said. "If I can. We don't know if it's even possible."

"I hope it's not," Cassie said.

Eliza couldn't help but smile. "I know, love," she said.

The next morning, Cassie and Eliza found themselves at the bridge.

Where it all started, Cassie thought. "How will you get back?" she asked.

Eliza smiled. "When we got back to sleep last night, I had a dream. Granny was calling me, telling me that I had to come back."

"So, Granny is okay?" Cassie asked, heartened by the news that there would still be someone to look out for Eliza.

Eliza shook her head. "I don't know. She may be a spirit now, for all I know, but she's hanging around for me to get me back."

They had moments left; Cassie knew. "I don't know what I'll do without you, Eliza," she said.

"Yes, you do, girl," Eliza said, taking Cassie's hands. "You'll live and you'll live well."

"But…" Cassie said.

"No buts, Cassie. We never have people for long – not as long as we think, anyway – but people stay with us. They don't go away as long as we remember them."

"Will you remember me?" Cassie asked.

"Of course I will, Cassie. I'll never forget you. You saved my life. I'll think of you every single day. Now, stop crying!"

"I can't help it," Cassie said.

Eliza hugged her. "I'll bet that you'll forget me, though, Cassie," she teased.

"Only your snoring," Cassie said.

"See, you can smile and laugh still, Cassie," Eliza said.

It was suddenly time, their last moment together.

"Give me a hug, Cassie."

She let Eliza enfold her, feeling those strong little arms for the last time, inhaling Eliza's scent, trying to imprint it on her senses, so she could recall it later.

"It's time," Eliza said.

"Whenever I'm…" Cassie started, but Eliza put her hand up to her lips to stop her words.

"Shush, Cassie love, let me remember you just like this…"

She stared at Cassie for what seemed an age – an age that Cassie didn't want to end – and then Eliza turned and was gone.

CHAPTER FORTY-SIX

Eliza walked through a strange, alien landscape, which had seemed so familiar just a day or so before. The path was all cut up by the passage of the horses. Dark, tell-tale patches and trails, where people had died or had dragged themselves off wounded, marked where the blood had already been soaked up by the soil. Soon, even these stains would be gone, absorbed by the ground and by memory. There were no bodies: either the people had taken their dead or the stockmen had got rid of the evidence of their crimes out of guilt or shame.

Crossing the creek, Eliza was struck by the near silence around her. Even the birds were quiet, as if they also knew what had happened, as if they could no more find their voices than Eliza could find hers. And Eliza's people, who had always filled this valley with the sound of their everyday lives were mute, too. They had died or had fled and would not come back again.

The hut that she shared with her mother was untouched and looked the same as ever. She had almost expected that it would be changed; if not burnt down, then somehow bearing witness, in some way, to what had happened nearby. She sat in the shadows of the hut until Grace came back from work. The sight of Eliza gave Grace a shock.

"For God's sake, child," Grace said. "I almost jumped out of my skin." Then, she looked more closely at Eliza. "You are real, girl? Not a ghost come back to haunt me?"

She didn't wait for an answer, but just held Eliza tight, rocking against her. There was a strange noise and Eliza realised, rather uncomfortably, that Grace was sobbing.

"I thought you were dead, Eliza darling," she said, "though the men who went down didn't find you among the bodies. I feared you'd crawled off somewhere to die."

Eliza gently pushed her mother away. She wasn't used to such physical affection from Grace. It felt odd.

"What about Granny?" she asked, though she was scared to hear the answer to the question.

Grace shook her head. "No trace," she said, "of that old woman." Grace, though she inhabited a white man's world, still wouldn't utter her mother's name, in case she was actually dead. "No body, at least, but most of the people who were left after the killing are long gone, up into the hinterland."

"I heard her in my dreams last night, Ma," Eliza said and Grace nodded.

"That doesn't mean anything, Eliza. The old woman's spirit might linger."

But Granny was out there, somewhere, Eliza knew. If not in the flesh, then in the birds, the trees, the very water that flowed in the creek, watching her, watching over her.

"Sit down, girl, I'll fix us some breakfast," Grace said, bustling about.

Bread and bacon brought back from the station and cold coffee warmed up over the fire sufficed. Eliza had thought that she wasn't hungry, couldn't even contemplate food, but she ate enough in the end.

"You finish that, girl," Grace said. "Pick up your traps and then you'd better get going."

"Going, Ma?" Eliza said. "What do you mean?"

What had she done? Was Grace going to throw her out again?

"You get yourself off to Mrs Cleary. She's being asking about you."

As news of the killings at Blood Creek had got out the day before, Jane Cleary had thought it best to keep her girls – as she called them – close. They'd bunked down in the schoolroom, but there was one conspicuous absence: Eliza. Jane had sent Betty in the evening to seek news of the girl and to urge Grace to send her to the refuge of the mission.

"Why can't I stay with you, Ma?" Eliza asked, but it was a pointless question. Even Eliza knew that she couldn't stick around.

"It's not safe, girl. Those white men think they can do anything," Grace said. "They think that they are above the law of man and that of God." Grace was a notional and convenient Christian, but not an enthusiastic one. "Besides," she continued, "you were down there at the creek. Someone might have seen you and they wouldn't want you telling any tales."

Who was there to tell? Eliza asked herself. Not the police or the magistrates. The law was for white fellows, not black fellows.

Eliza had few possessions, so it didn't take long.

"You'll tell Jimmy where I am, Ma?" Eliza asked. "If he comes home."

Grace shook her head, sadly. "There's little chance he'll be back, Eliza, and you'd better hope that he doesn't turn up."

"Why, Ma?"

"Because he won't let things lie. He'll want blood for blood," Grace said, "and you know where that would finish."

She didn't have to spell it out: however many of them Jimmy got, they'd get him in the end.

"There's nothing for you here, girl," Grace said, almost apologetically, as Eliza stood ready. "Just trouble, so it's best if you get on."

"But what about you, Ma?" Eliza asked.

"It's too late for me, girl," Grace said, "but not for you. You've still got a chance."

Grace watched her go, disappearing into the bush as she traced her way back to the creek. Her mother raised one hand in farewell and held it up, until Eliza was nearly out of sight. Then she lowered it and let her head drop down on her chest, as if she was in mortal pain.

⋙

The mission was stirring when Eliza arrived. Girls were washing at the pump, building up the fires and getting about the making of food. It was Vicky who saw Eliza first and enfolded her in her arms.

"Eliza," she said, tears of relief pouring from her cow-like eyes, "I thought you were dead... we all did."

The girls surrounded her, hugging and kissing and patting her arms, her back. She looked up though the flurry of arms and heads and saw a tall, straight figure standing on the porch of the house, a hand shielding her eyes.

"Lord be praised," Jane Cleary said. "He has brought you back to us."

Eliza wondered who Jane meant by 'he', but then she realised.

⇛

Eliza had always enjoyed her days at the mission, the mixture of reading and writing and chores, but on that day the time dragged and she couldn't wait for it to be over. Everything felt irksome and irritatingly mundane at the same time. There were moments in that overlong day, which were full of pain and grief, too, because whenever they could, whenever they had a moment free from the hawk-like gaze of Jane Cleary, the girls would recite their litany of the dead:

"That girl with the long, glossy hair, who smiled a lot."

"That boy with the leg that didn't work, the one who limped."

"The old fellow, who made toys out of sticks for the kids to play with."

"The old woman who used to laugh a lot and could see things that others couldn't."

That latter one was Granny.

The list was made more difficult, more of a work in progress, because the girls – though all, like Grace, notional

Christians – would not say the names of the dead, which resulted in a certain amount of confusion.

"That girl with the glossy hair… You mean Gwen? She's alive… I saw her this morning… she'd just a bit crook…"

And so on, lending a surreal quality to the grim task of remembering. Mrs Cleary, of course, made no reference to the events at Blood Creek.

By nightfall, it was deemed safe for the girls to go home. Things were quiet again, as if nothing had happened, which would suit the white fellows.

"But we won't forget," Vicky said, when Eliza shared this thought with her, "will we, Eliza? Memory is the only weapon that we have."

But when Vicky had gone home, Eliza wondered at her words. Cassie had told her that their dead – or at least, most of them – *had* been forgotten.

⁂

When the girls had all departed, Eliza was left alone with Jane. The Reverend Cleary was away again. Indeed, Eliza wondered how often he was actually home these days.

"Eliza, dear," Jane said, "let's go and sit and have a cup of tea."

Eliza made the tea and brought it into the parlour, that scruffy little room, which Jane had furnished in a close, but fake, imitation of a parlour in a London suburb, with overstuffed armchairs, ugly angular furniture, oriental rugs – moth-eaten and threadbare – and chintz curtains at the ill-fitting windows.

"I'm so glad you are here, my dear," Jane said. "I was very worried about you." Jane smiled. Her handsome face – all angles, the planes catching the lamplight – was framed by the curtains of blond hair that she wore tied into a coil at the back of her head. "And you know, dear Eliza, that it is all agreed."

Eliza wondered exactly what had been agreed.

"Your mother," Jane went on, "has decided that, in light of the unfortunate situation, you should come and be with me." Jane smiled. "You're to live with me from now on," she said. "Does that please you?"

Eliza didn't say anything, but Jane took her silence as assent and put her hand on Eliza's, where it rested on the arm of the chair.

"You'll have a new life, Eliza, with me."

Everybody wants me to have a new life, Eliza thought, *but nobody's asked me what I want.*

"And when I go back to England, Eliza, you'll come with me," Jane added.

They sat there in companiable silence, the afternoon turning to evening, ushering in the night. Eliza knew that she should be pleased. It was, after all, what she had once wanted, to spend her life with Jane, but things didn't seem so simple anymore.

Jane, apparently, sensed her doubts. "What's the matter, dear? Are you missing your mother?" she asked. "She wants the best for you, you know, and she's willing to make sacrifices for you to prosper."

"No, Jane, I'm not missing ma. It's just that I keep thinking about yesterday… what happened at the creek…"

It was hard to even say these words, let alone recall the events.

"Dear Eliza," Jane said, looking closely at her, "you must put it behind you, you know. Such things, I'm afraid, are inevitable. And though I don't condone the behaviour of the stockmen, I do know that there was great provocation."

"Provocation?" Eliza said. "What's a few head of cattle compared to what they did?"

"It wasn't only stock, Eliza. You know a shepherd was killed," Jane's tone was gentle, but would not entertain being gainsaid.

"The stockmen killed women and children," Eliza said – the simple truth.

"Come, Eliza," Jane said, "you're exaggerating. I hear that there was fighting, yes, and a number of men were killed, but such unfortunate and lamentable events will soon be a thing of the past." Jane smiled, with evident condescension. "It is inevitable that your mother's people will become part of our civilisation. Look at your mother and look at you. You, in particular, are a model for others, Eliza."

There was a saying that Jane had quoted to them from the Bible, about those with eyes who would not see and those with ears who would not hear. Foolish people, the Bible said, and Eliza decided that Jane, for all that she had formerly idolised her, was one of those. She made her decision in that moment.

※

"It's not far now, Eliza," Mr Lewis said. "We'll be there before nightfall."

Mr Lewis had been loath to take Eliza along with Gwen, but he had seen with his own eyes the way that Cal Armstrong had treated her in his store. And Gwen had told him that Eliza had been at what was already being called Blood Creek and witnessed the massacre, so he understood Eliza's need to get away.

"Have you told your mother about what you intend to do?" he'd asked Eliza.

"I'll send her a letter when I'm settled, Mr Lewis. I can't risk seeing her before I go, because of the boss," Eliza had answered.

Mr Lewis had eventually agreed, partly because – or so his wife told him – Eliza was related to them. She was family, part of that wider Kabiri kin, and family had to look out for each other.

It was common knowledge that Mr Lewis made a regular journey down the road to the coast to trade and to pick up supplies. When Gwen had told Eliza of his upcoming trip and added the fact that she would be going with her father, to what was deemed a safer place for a brown-skinned girl like her, who had a worrying and naïve tendency to flirt with any young male customers, Eliza was cheeky enough to ask to come along.

It suited Mr Lewis as well, because although Gwen was going to stay with family on the coast, the prospect of a 'level-headed girl' like Eliza accompanying her – Gwen was known to be rather flighty and unpredictable – to keep her in check, was an attractive one.

"Yes, not far," Mr Lewis repeated. "You girls have a rest, a bit of a snooze, and I'll wake you when we get there."

Though Gwen dozed off in the bed of the wagon, Eliza couldn't sleep. She was too excited about her new life; a life that *she* had chosen for herself, that no one else had. But as the sun went down, throwing the long shadow of the wagon on the road behind them, she cast her mind back to her friend, Cassie – more than a friend, more like a sister – and to what their life together might have been, if only they had been born in the same age.

CHAPTER FORTY-SEVEN

The way back to the house had never seemed so long and lonely. Eliza had been such a vivid, vital presence that her absence seemed to not only sap Cassie's energy, but to make the day less bright. But Cassie, though she was sad because she suspected that she would never see Eliza again, was not forlorn. Instead, she felt an oddly reassuring feeling – a certainty that she had done what she was meant to do. She had saved Eliza from the danger that had threatened her and given her another chance. It was that simple; the whys and wherefores of it were impossible to even begin to understand and were, thus, rendered irrelevant.

With the physical tiredness came an emotional one that was worse. She just wanted to lie down in her bed – where the scent of Eliza's body lingered – and sleep for days. She was glad Eve was out of the way – she'd gone to work – so she didn't have to provide answers that she would struggle to put together, but as she turned into the gravel driveway of the house, she saw Linda, looking out from her porch. She couldn't avoid her. They locked eyes.

"You look like you've seen a ghost, love. Everything alright?"

꙳

Linda made her a cup of tea and they sat in the kitchen.

"Where's your friend gone, then?" she asked.

"She had to go home."

"I thought she lived nearby," Linda said.

"No, a long way away," Cassie replied. Since she'd known Eliza, she had turned being vague into an art form.

"Lovely looking girl," Linda said, "but she'd got a fey quality about her... otherworldly, you could say."

Fuck, thought Cassie. *Linda, with her kaftans and incense, might come across as a superannuated hippie, but she's as sharp as a tack.*

"She reminded me of a girl I met when I was in America, before I came to Australia," Linda said. As Cassie listened, she felt herself becoming mesmerised by the woman's voice. "I'd hired a car – the pound, in those days, bought a lot of dollars – and I was touring the southern states. I was in Tennessee, south of Nashville, and I'd stopped near a creek, where there was a scrappy sort of picnic ground, to eat my lunch. I'd wandered away from the main picnic area and found a clearing just a little upstream to spread myself out on my blanket.

"It was a hot day and the water seemed inviting, so I took my sandals off and waded in. I was in the creek for a few minutes, feeling the tug of the water on my legs, surprised how strong the current was, when I was conscious that someone was there and I heard a voice.

"'Ma'am, you shouldn't be wading in that water, because of the moccasins.'

"The person who'd spoken was a young girl, perhaps twelve or thirteen years old, and she was watching me from the bank with a concerned look on her face, anxiously biting her lip.

"I told her I had taken my shoes off, but she grew even more agitated.

"'No, not that sort of moccasins, the water moccasins. Snakes!'

"Having the typical British overreaction to poisonous reptiles, I got out of the water as fast as I could.

"'I didn't mean to alarm you, ma'am,' the girl said, but I said it didn't matter and that I appreciated the warning.

"I sat back down on my blanket and felt that I should offer her something to thank her. I had a bar of chocolate – that American stuff, Hershey's, which I always found much sweeter than good old Cadbury's – but, as I held it up for her to take, she looked at it suspiciously, as if she'd never seen the like.

"At the time, this didn't surprise me as much as it might have, partly because the girl was dressed in a long dress – very Victorian-looking – and one of those poke bonnets. Her mode of dress would have been outlandish somewhere like London or Sydney, but in that part of Tennessee, there was a big Amish community, so it made sense. As did her wonder at the chocolate, because the Amish deliberately shun the modern world and all it involves.

"She eventually told me her name, Laura, and I told her mine. Though she was reluctant to stop calling me ma'am, I did finally manage to persuade her to call me Linda. I poured her a cup of tea from my flask and she took some biscuits, though she was disinclined to accept anything she regarded as charity. Then she went off, saying she would be back, and returned with two roasted ears of corn and a stoneware bottle containing what she called cider, but which was non-alcoholic apple juice.

"We spent most of the afternoon together, chatting. I told her I was from England and she asked if I'd ever met the queen. I was going to say I'd seen her on TV, but then realised that the Amish don't have TVs, so I just said I'd seen her in the distance.

"Laura was very shy and spent most of the afternoon with her head lowered, the bonnet shading her face, but she told me that her family were farmers – most the Amish are – and that her papa had cleared the forest and ploughed the land to sow corn. She said they kept a milk cow and pigs.

"I asked her if she went to school and she shook her head sadly, saying that there was no school nearby. I thought she meant that there was no suitable school the Amish would send their kids to, rather than that there were no schools.

"It was a strange, magical sort of afternoon. She disappeared again and brought me back a billy can of blueberries and then, a little later, said she had to go as she had chores. But just before she went, she told me – almost as if she was making a confession of some secret – that her brother was in the army and would have to fight in the war. And that she was worried for him.

"'Look,' she said and showed me the locket she wore around her neck. It was a cheap thing, not an expensive item of jewellery, but it opened up to show a picture – a black-and-white headshot – of a young man. He was in uniform but wore his hair long. The uniform was grey – a light grey against darker shades of grey – and had a row of shiny metal buttons, fastened up to the neck. The boy was wearing one of those military caps – a *kepi*, I think they call them – and was clutching an old-fashioned rifle. Though he was trying to keep his face deadpan, you could see the fear in his eyes.

"'Dressed up?' I said and she nodded.

"'That's his best uniform,' she said.

"'He's very handsome,' I added, because I thought I had to. She blushed, stowed the locket away and ran off."

Cassie had been silent while Linda talked, but now she was intrigued.

"I don't understand," she said.

"Neither did I, love," Linda said, smiling. "There are two possible explanations as far as I can see. Either the girl *was* Amish and the picture of the soldier – in civil war uniform – was just a story of hers, something she'd made up. Perhaps the locket was a family heirloom or her brother was one of those civil war reenactors, and the girl had got her wars confused. Or the other explanation is that Laura was, in fact, from the 1860s and we'd somehow – God knows how – met up through some strange, random quirk of time."

"What do you think, Linda?" Cassie asked.

"Well, love, I told you before that I believe time is cyclical, not linear, so I have no problem in accepting the fact that I met a girl from another century and spent the afternoon with her."

"But why did you decide to tell me?" Cassie asked.

"It's because, Cassie, you are the sort of girl I *can* tell, who won't think that I'm just a crazy old bat. And also, love, because I think Eliza is like Laura – someone out of another time who strayed into ours."

Cassie didn't know what to say, how to respond to Linda's revelation. It was the matter-of-fact way that she said it, more than anything else, which robbed her of words; the way that Linda could talk of such remarkable things as if they were ordinary, even mundane. But it was also something of a relief. Cassie wasn't the only one who'd met someone from the past.

"Although, you could actually just think I'm bonkers," Linda continued.

"Perhaps we both are, Linda," Cassie said. "Bonkers, that is. Or perhaps we're both eminently sane."

"Well, I wouldn't say 'eminently', love. 'Relatively' might be the better word," Linda said, laughing.

"But what does it all mean?" Cassie asked.

"I don't know, Cassie. I think we just have to accept that it happened and be thankful that it did. That I met Laura and you met Eliza. It's actually quite wonderful, you know."

Yes, she's right, Cassie thought. *It is quite wonderful.*

CHAPTER FORTY-EIGHT

Kate's residence was only a short walk away from the university. It was a bungalow on a quiet street of other bungalows, all with fenced-in yards, with a terrace at the back looking out on a scrubby lawn and some untended flower beds. Though the woman herself was so effortlessly stylish and cool, her house was surprisingly normal, almost bland in both décor and style. From what Cassie could see of the open-plan living room and dining room from the settee, the furniture was mainly of that generic Nordic flat-pack variety that had fast become a global fashion.

It was obvious to Cassie that though Kate inhabited the house, she didn't really live in it. Even though Kate had such strong local links, she was more of a nomadic scholar type than a homemaker and her attitude to domestic comfort was marked by an asceticism that was almost nun-like. She would have probably been quite content to dwell in a convent cell, except for the fact that she seemed to have a penchant for electronic gadgets, which included the rather expensive coffee maker that sat on the side of one of the kitchen worktops. She was fiddling with it at that moment, going through the rather long-winded process that had to be followed to produce a cup of coffee.

"I don't always bother with this machine," Kate was saying. "It often seems like a hell of a fuss to produce a cup of coffee, though, I have to admit, the stuff it produces is remarkably good."

Cassie smiled and nodded. She was just glad to have been invited to Kate's inner sanctum, a place hardly any of Kate's colleagues or students had ever visited. Eve had been intrigued when Cassie had told her about the invitation and, it also had to be said, rather jealous, though she'd tried to do her best to hide the fact. Even though Cassie had only been a part of the campus community for such a short time, she was well aware that Kate was a rather distant and formidable figure to many of her colleagues. So, the rather unlikely and incongruous connection that had grown up between Cassie and Kate had puzzled Eve, all the more so because Cassie was as vague as ever about what they did or what they talked about. And it wasn't that Cassie was being deliberately evasive, rather it was that she wouldn't have adequately been able to explain what had led to their mutual interest – and particularly Cassie's – in the massacre at Blood Creek.

"I usually use a coffee plunger in the mornings," Kate was saying. "It's much quicker and easier when I'm in a hurry."

Cassie imagined that Kate was always in something of a hurry. She was that sort of person – one of those high-achievers, always with so much to do, unlike Cassie.

"I don't know where we left things, Cassie," Kate continued, as she brought the coffee over. "I told you about the missionaries, didn't I?"

"You just mentioned their names – the Clearys."

Kate looked at Cassie with a certain appreciation. "Well remembered, Cassie," she said. "Yes, the Clearys. And John was able to find – he's a hell of a researcher, I should add – a digitised copy of part of the diary of Jane Cleary, the wife."

Cassie, doing her best to appear interested, but not too interested, felt her heart beating fast, her breath growing shallow, as she heard the familiar name – a tenuous connection with Eliza and what might have happened to her.

"Diaries like this one tend to get lost in attics, bookshops or generally abandoned, but it just so happened that the missionary society the Clearys worked for kept an archive and Mrs Cleary's diary ended up in it after her death. Her husband's diary didn't – such are the vagaries of historiographic survival. It was lost somewhere. And fortuitously a PhD student, researching the history of Christian missions in Queensland, scanned a number of documents into a computer, including Mrs Cleary's diary."

Kate had opened up the screen of the laptop on the table before them, clicked on an icon and opened up a file. It was a photographic facsimile of a handwritten journal and not the easiest of documents to read.

"It's generally a very domestic account, particularly concerned with the missionary school that Mrs Cleary ran – her one-woman attempt to civilise the local indigenous girls…"

But Cassie was only half listening. Most of her attention was focused on that document before her on the screen, as she looked for one familiar name and found it. The date was partially obscured, but the year was clear: 1872.

Peter is away again. I can't in all conscience complain, as I know he is about the Lord's work, but I must admit to experiencing feelings of loneliness and more, almost a sense of desolation and loss. I am left to the rough ministrations of Betty, who means well, but is, at heart, a simple, crude creature. There are few white women within a day's ride of the mission and these few are not the sort whose society I would seek. I would remain as alone as a castaway on a coral island if it wasn't for my dear Eliza, who has come to stay with me and comfort me. She is such a dear girl that I am loath to be parted from her. Last night she helped me bathe and evinced a gentility and delicacy unmatched among her people.

As she read the words, Cassie was surprised to feel, again, that prickle of jealousy.

"There's the briefest reference to the massacre, Cassie," Kate was saying. "Let me find it."

Once found, Cassie read Jane Cleary's words:

Word reached me today of an unpleasant incident at the Creek, so I kept the girls, my dear charges, at the mission at the end of the afternoon for their safety. Peter and I had been aware for a while that tensions were building between the local Aborigines and the stockmen from Montrose Station and it was only a matter of time before things came to a head. I heard that some of the local black fellows were killed in the skirmish and that others have fled. I must admit that I have thought little of these poor souls, as my mind has been consumed by worry. The reason for this anxiety is that Eliza, my Eliza, is missing...

"That's about it," Kate said. "She just refers to an unpleasant incident at the creek, then calls it a skirmish. Either she's in denial or she just doesn't know the extent of it."

Kate reached over and switched the laptop off. Cassie had wanted to read on, find any other references to Eliza, but to do so would have elicited too many questions from Kate – questions that she didn't want to answer.

"I've been thinking about what happened to you, Cassie. Why you saw what you did." Kate's expression was serious as she looked at Cassie and something else as well: curious, almost. Or even admiring. "Are you familiar with the idea of liminal spaces, Cassie?"

Cassie said that she wasn't. She didn't really know what Kate was talking about.

"A liminal space, as I understand it, is a transitional space, between two other areas or zones. It can be a physical space, like a corridor between rooms, or a beach between ocean and land. It can also be emotional, metaphorical, even, but I'll spare you all the detailed philosophy." Kate frowned, as if hesitant about what she was going to say. Cassie was equally uncertain. "What I'm trying to get at, Cassie... suggest, I suppose, or theorise... is that there are liminal spaces in regard to time..."

"Non-linear time," Cassie said. "Cyclical time, you mean."

Kate looked at her with surprise. "Exactly, Cassie," she said. "I think that there exists the possibility of straying into these transitional spaces and witnessing, or even experiencing, things that happened in the past or will happen in the future." Kate smiled. "Sounds a little crazy, doesn't it?" she said.

"No, not really," Cassie replied, thinking that Linda, for all that she was so different from Kate, would have wholeheartedly agreed with her.

"If I said the same thing to one of the elders of my people," Kate continued, "they'd just nod their heads and say that they already knew all about it. It's contemporary western science that would have a problem with it, because there's no empirical proof."

"So, you think that's what happened to me?" Cassie asked.

"Yes, I do, Cassie," Kate said. "I can't explain it, but I don't believe in spiritualism… well, not as it's usually practised… so, while the explanation is not strictly scientific, it makes sense to me." Kate looked closely at Cassie, scrutinising her face. "You don't seem surprised."

"No, it makes sense to me, too."

Cassie couldn't help thinking that Kate suspected she had more to tell her, but she didn't pursue the matter and instead got up to make more coffee.

"There was something else I wanted to ask you, Cassie," Kate said, when she came back with the two cups. "I wanted to co-author a paper with John about the Blood Creek massacre, about the historical facts and the cultural background to it."

"I'm glad," Cassie said, "because then, at least, it will be remembered."

Sometimes remembering was all you could do, Cassie thought. And in that act of remembrance was the beginning of acknowledgment.

"Well, considering that you kicked all this off, so to

speak, I wanted to get your permission to proceed," Kate said, looking a little embarrassed, not being used to having to get other people's say-so before proceeding.

"Yes, of course," Cassie said.

"We'll credit you, Cassie. Be sure of that."

⋙

Later, when Cassie was leaving, Kate asked the question that Cassie had difficulty answering, "So, what's on the cards, Cassie? What are you going to do with yourself?"

She hadn't really thought much about it, but suddenly she knew.

"I think I'm going to go back to England for a while," she answered.

"Climate doesn't suit you?" Kate asked, smiling.

"No, that's not it," Cassie said. "In fact, the place has grown on me, but a friend of mine said that you have to go back to face things, your fears, things that you've tried to run away from. So, that's what I'm going to do."

"Good luck with that, Cassie," Kate said and to Cassie's surprise – as Kate wasn't a touchy-feely person – she hugged her.

CHAPTER FORTY-NINE

Cassie sat in her usual place on Blood Creek, where the rock ledge jutted out into the water, and where Eliza and so many other girls like her had once laughed and swam and lived out their lives, before they were driven away. Before white men had come to wipe them off the face of the land and to erase their history, as if it had never happened.

She felt close to Eliza, sitting there on that rock, even closer because of the knowledge she had of Eliza's fate. Because, before she had left Kate, she had asked the woman to send her a copy of Jane Cleary's diary, which she had pored over the night before, staying up late until she found the entry she wanted:

March 5th 1872. I have the saddest of news to relate today and my heart feels fit to burst, because my darling Eliza has run away from me. Peter has no sympathy for me. He tells me that it is my own fault for investing so much in a shiftless girl, who will revert with ease to her savage state, now that she is out of my orbit.

There is a rumour – and I have no firm news, because the local blacks will tell me nothing – that she has gone to the coast with the Lewis girl, Gwen. Mr Lewis is not back yet, so I cannot question him and, anyway, Peter forbids me to make enquiries, as he says that the girl was too much of a pet to me and played me for a fool. I do not know what to do, I am distraught, but I will seek solace in prayer…

So, Eliza had got way, Cassie thought, and even if her future was uncertain, at least it was *her* future, and not one that Jane Cleary had devised for her.

She did have some sympathy for the missionary, despite the jealousy that she had felt about her interest in her friend, as they had both, in their separate ways, lost Eliza.

But as Cassie thought this, she realised that it wasn't really true, because Eliza would always be with her, she knew – not physically there, but a constant presence, a bright star in the firmament that she could find and fix on, whenever she was lost on this earth.

She'd known Eliza for only the briefest of times, but, as Eliza had said, you never know how long you get to have with somebody. It was as true of Eliza as it was of Carys, her lost love. But, at least, she'd had that time with Carys and with Eliza. What more could you ask for from life?

She got up, her hand feeling the warmth of the rock as she did so, and walked away from Blood Creek.